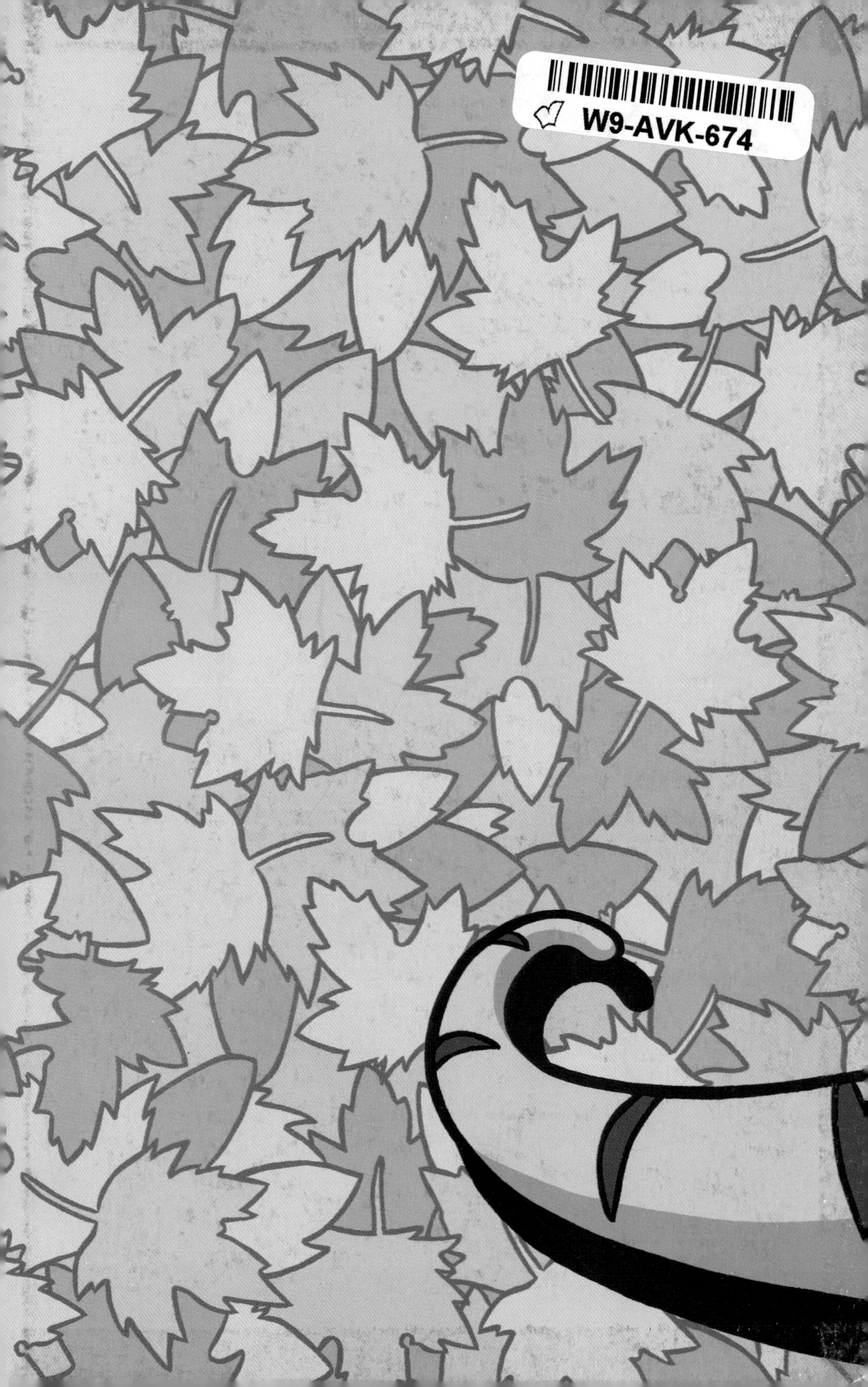

JELLABY

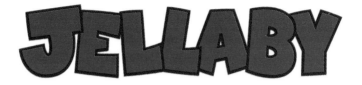

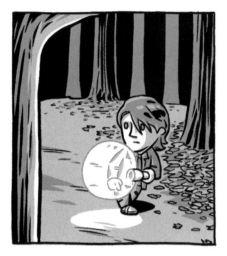

JELLABY

by
KEAN SOO

HYPERION BOOKS
FOR CHILDREN
New York

ACKNOWLEDGMENTS:

SPECIAL THANKS TO CALISTA BRILL, ROBERTA PRESSEL, JUDY HANSEN, HOPE LARSON, DAVID & NICOLAS SEIGNERET, BEN HU, JASON TURNER, CLIO CHIANG, KAZU KIBUISHI, AND OF COURSE, ALL MY FRIENDS AND FAMILY FOR THEIR LOVE AND SUPPORT

AND A VERY SPECIAL THANK-YOU TO THE CANADA COUNCIL FOR THE ARTS FOR THEIR SUPPORT OF THIS WORK

For information address Hyperion Books for Children,
114 Fifth Avenue, New York, New York, 10011-5690.

Printed in Singapore

First Edition
1 3 5 7 9 10 8 6 4 2

Library of Congress Cataloging-in-Publication Data on file.

Hardcover edition:
ISBN-13: 978-1-4231-0337-0
ISBN-10: 1-4231-0337-8

Paperback edition:
ISBN-13: 978-1-4231-0303-5
ISBN-10: 1-4231-0303-3

Visit www.hyperionbooksforchildren.com

CHAPTER ONE

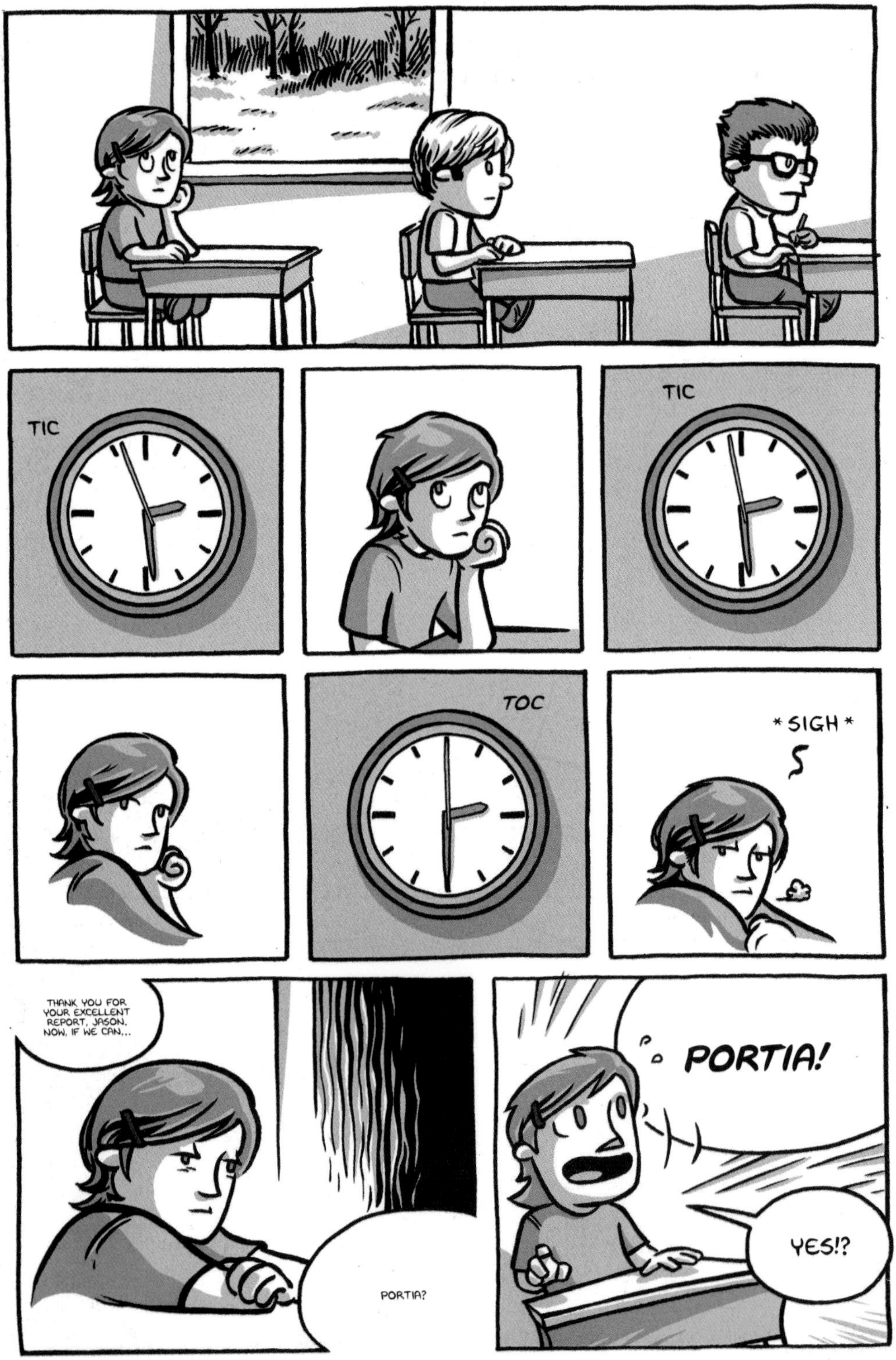

TIC
TIC
TOC
* SIGH *
THANK YOU FOR YOUR EXCELLENT REPORT, JASON. NOW, IF WE CAN...
PORTIA?
PORTIA!
YES!?

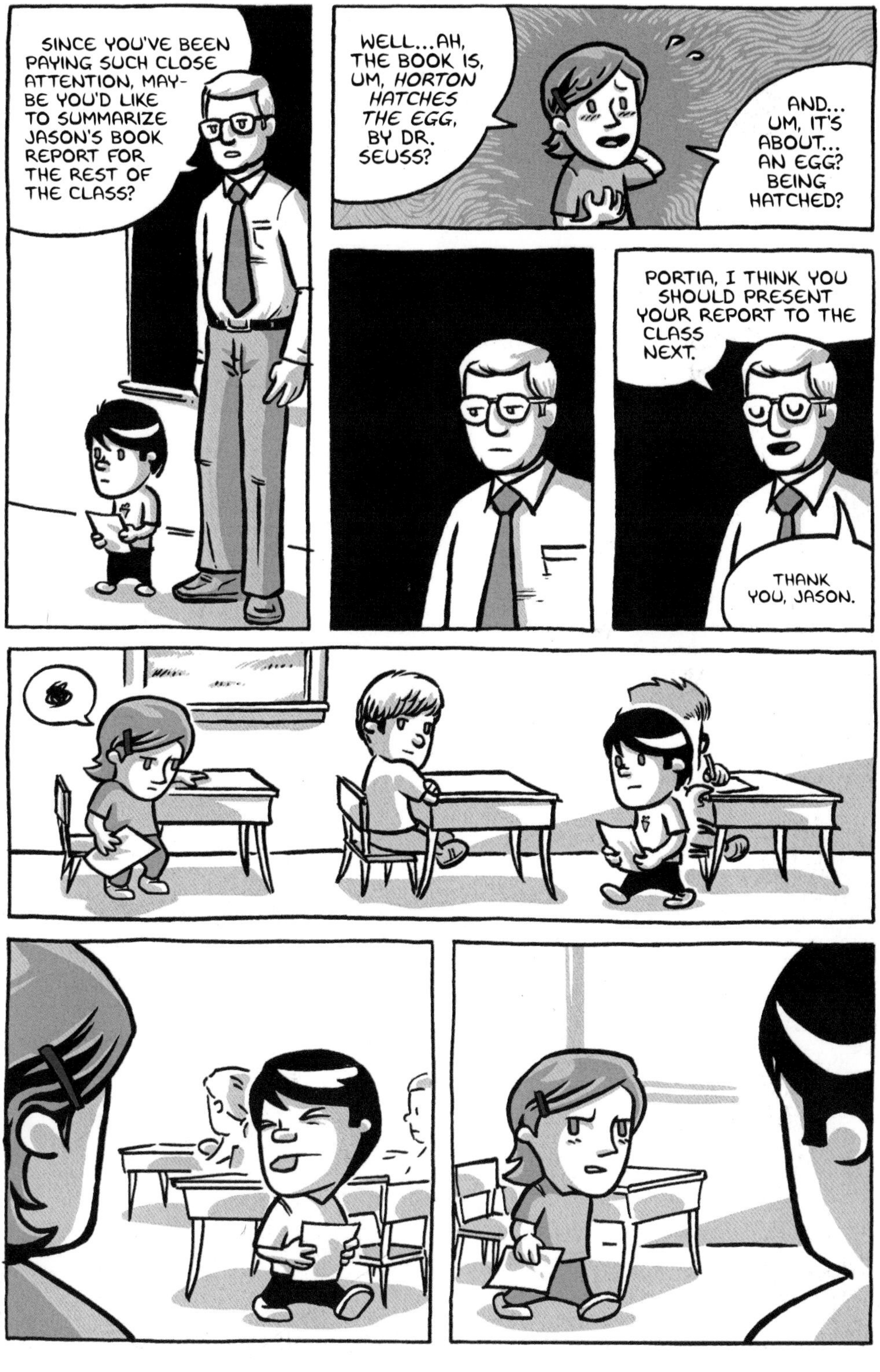
SINCE YOU'VE BEEN PAYING SUCH CLOSE ATTENTION, MAY-BE YOU'D LIKE TO SUMMARIZE JASON'S BOOK REPORT FOR THE REST OF THE CLASS?
WELL...AH, THE BOOK IS, UM, *HORTON HATCHES THE EGG,* BY DR. SEUSS?
AND... UM, IT'S ABOUT... AN EGG? BEING HATCHED?
PORTIA, I THINK YOU SHOULD PRESENT YOUR REPORT TO THE CLASS NEXT.
THANK YOU, JASON.

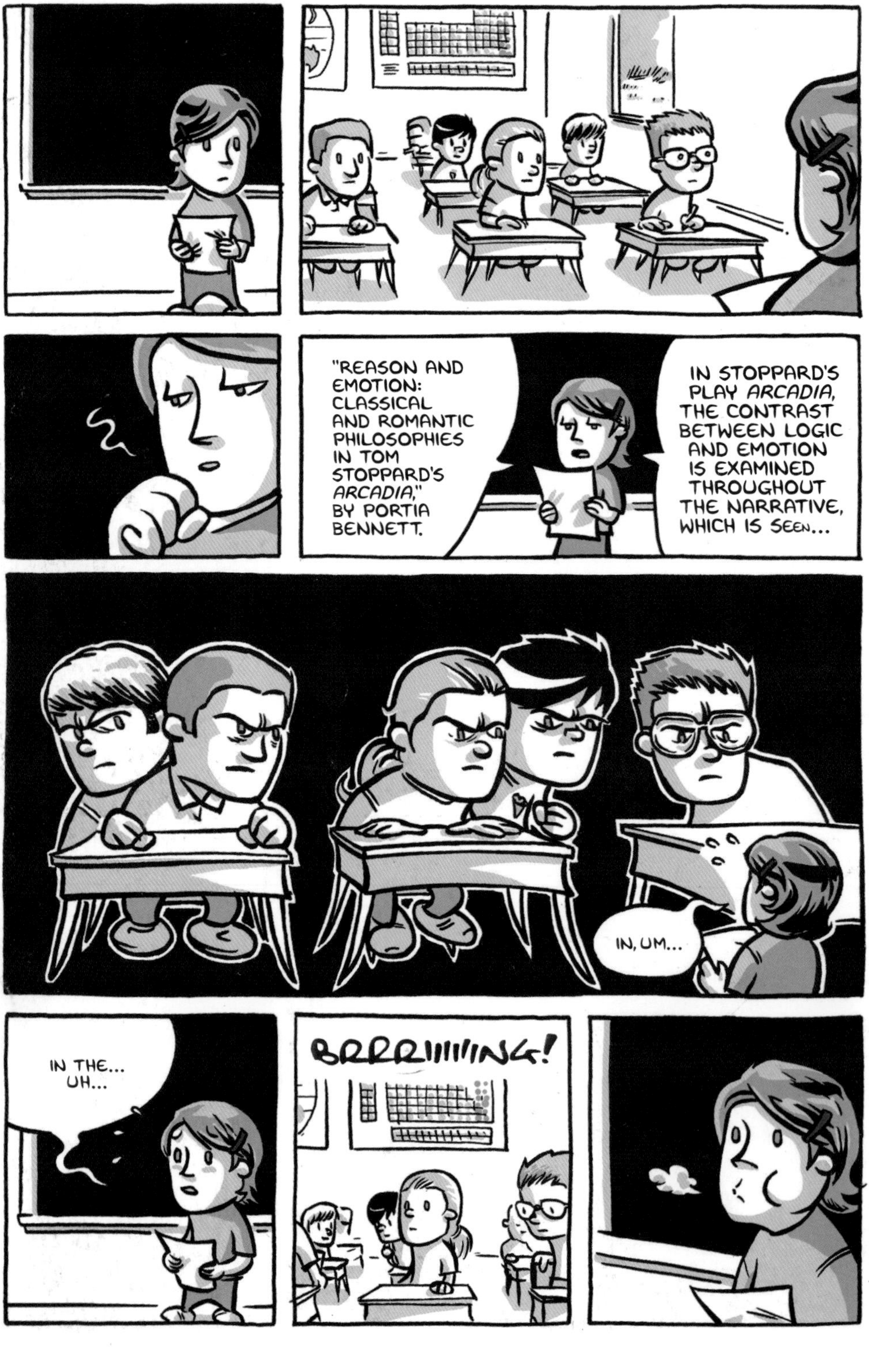

"REASON AND EMOTION: CLASSICAL AND ROMANTIC PHILOSOPHIES IN TOM STOPPARD'S *ARCADIA*," BY PORTIA BENNETT.
IN STOPPARD'S PLAY *ARCADIA*, THE CONTRAST BETWEEN LOGIC AND EMOTION IS EXAMINED THROUGHOUT THE NARRATIVE, WHICH IS SEEN...
IN, UM...
IN THE... UH...
BRRRIIIIING!

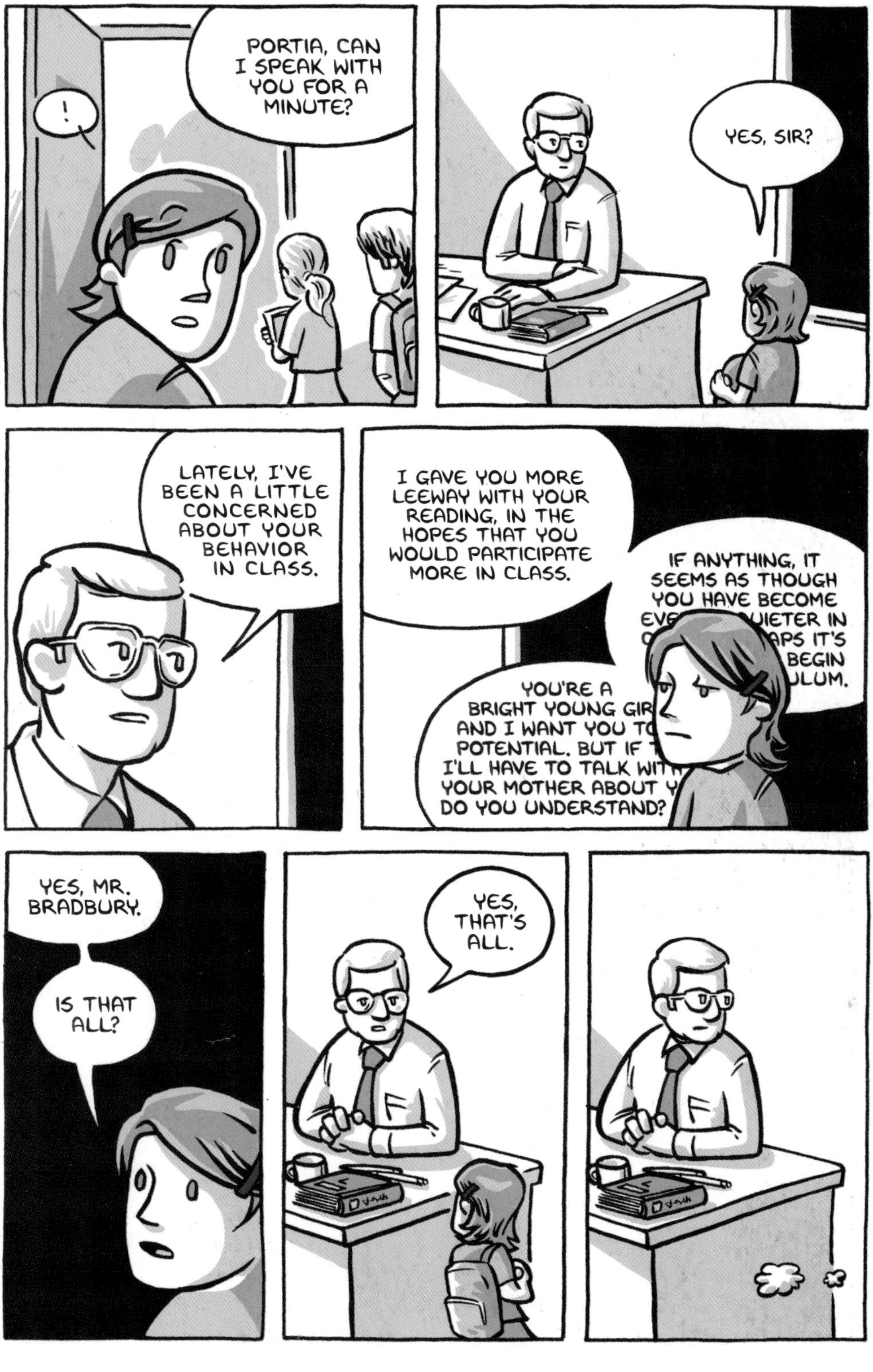
!
PORTIA, CAN I SPEAK WITH YOU FOR A MINUTE?
YES, SIR?
LATELY, I'VE BEEN A LITTLE CONCERNED ABOUT YOUR BEHAVIOR IN CLASS.
I GAVE YOU MORE LEEWAY WITH YOUR READING, IN THE HOPES THAT YOU WOULD PARTICIPATE MORE IN CLASS.
IF ANYTHING, IT SEEMS AS THOUGH YOU HAVE BECOME
YOU'RE A BRIGHT YOUNG GIR
AND I WANT YOU TO
POTENTIAL. BUT IF
I'LL HAVE TO TALK WIT
YOUR MOTHER ABOUT
DO YOU UNDERSTAND?
YES, MR. BRADBURY.
IS THAT ALL?
YES, THAT'S ALL.

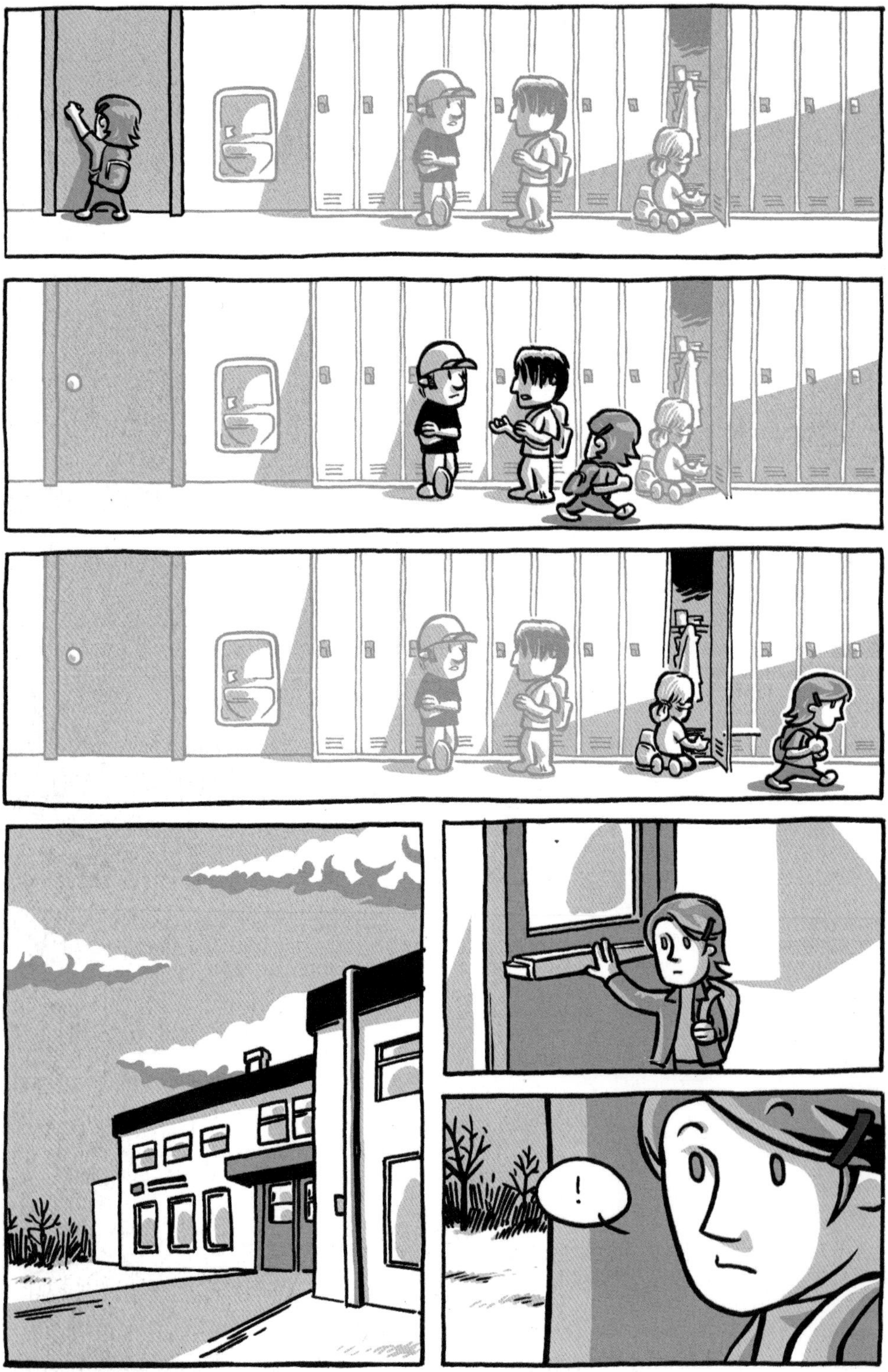
!

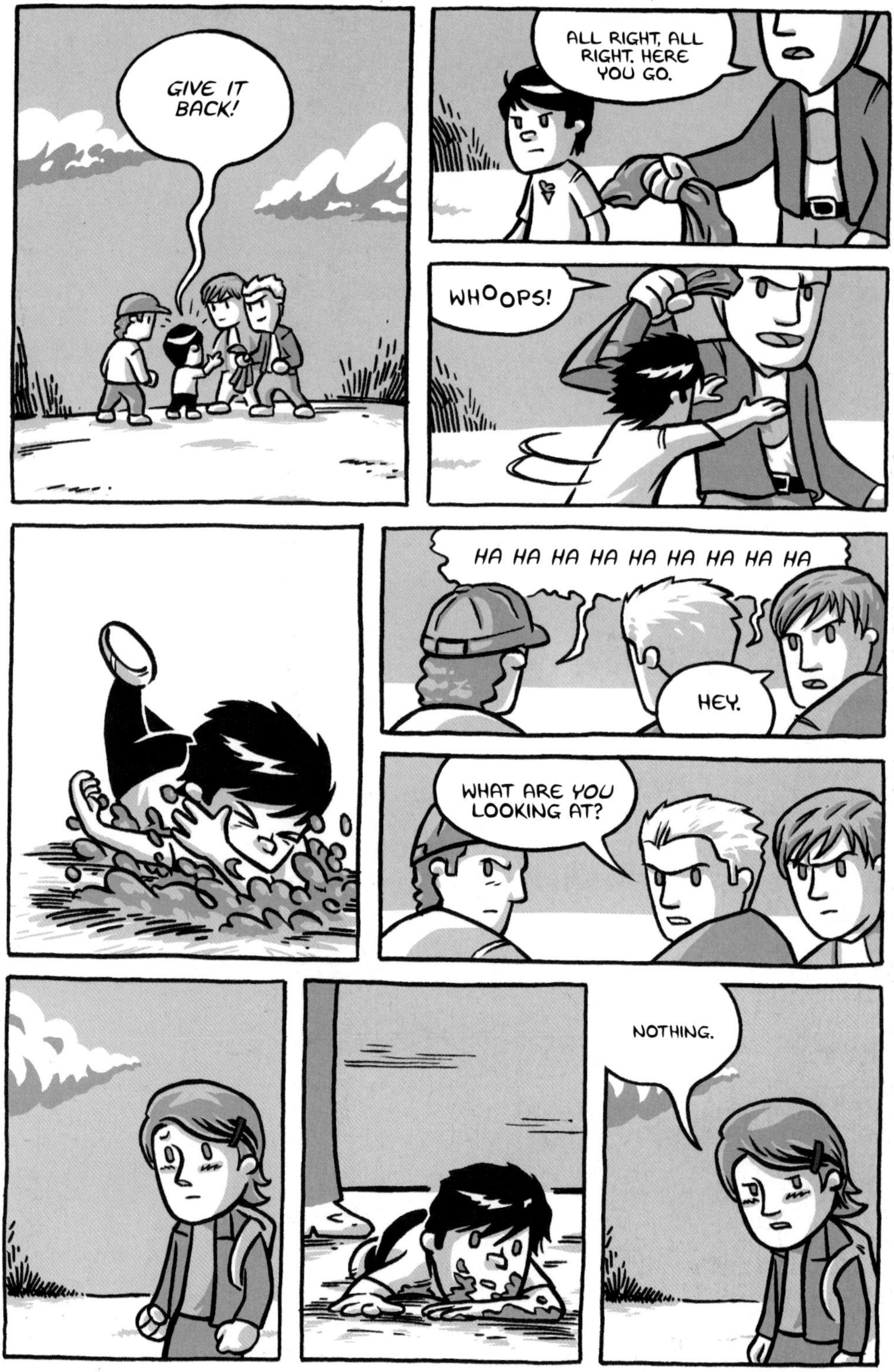
GIVE IT BACK!
ALL RIGHT, ALL RIGHT. HERE YOU GO.
WHOOPS!
HA HA HA HA HA HA HA HA HA
HEY.
WHAT ARE YOU LOOKING AT?
NOTHING.

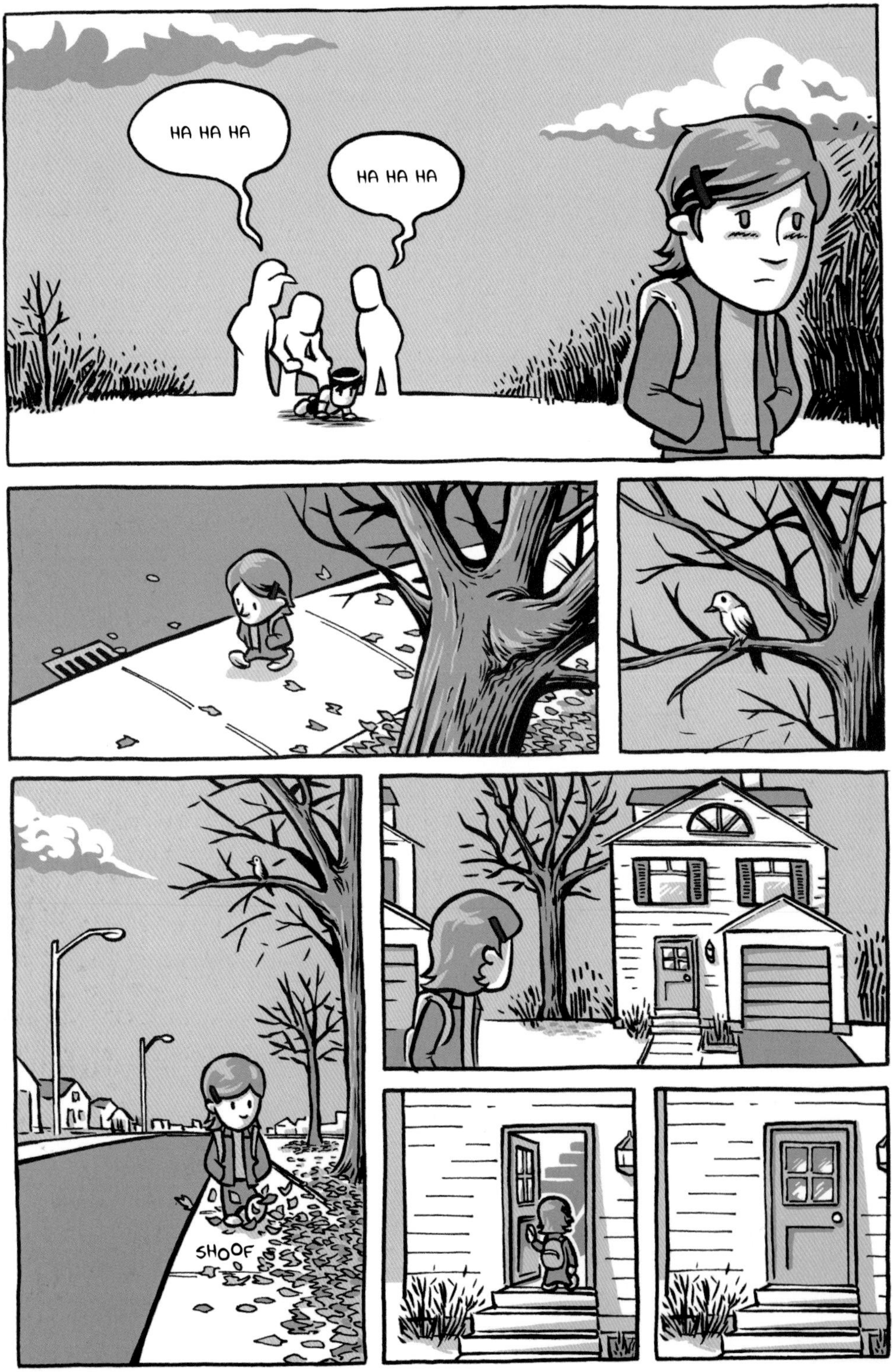
HA HA HA
HA HA HA
SHOOF

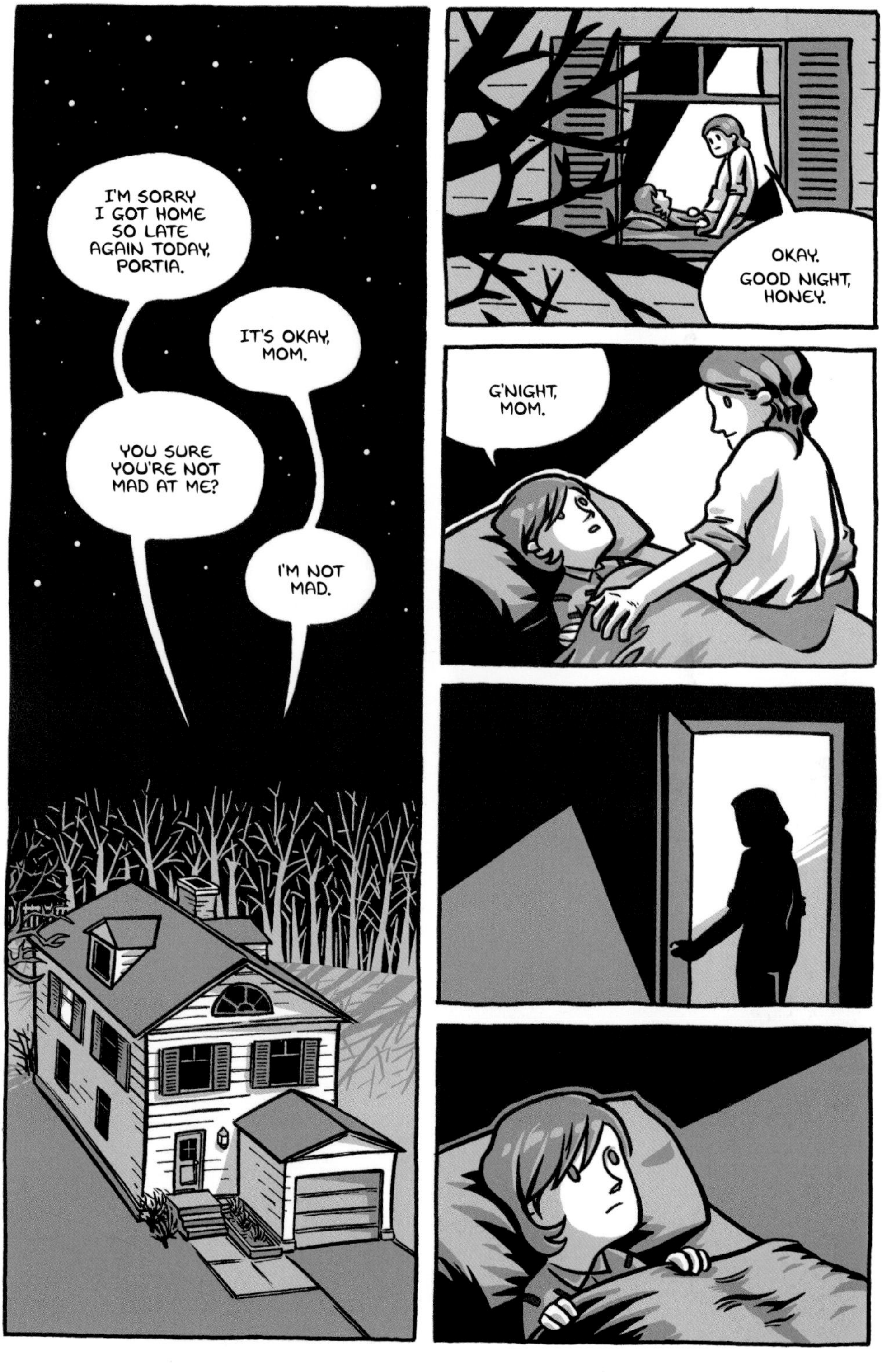
I'M SORRY I GOT HOME SO LATE AGAIN TODAY, PORTIA.
IT'S OKAY, MOM.
YOU SURE YOU'RE NOT MAD AT ME?
I'M NOT MAD.
OKAY. GOOD NIGHT, HONEY.
G'NIGHT, MOM.

SSSSSSSSSSSSSSSSHSSHSSHHHHHHHHH

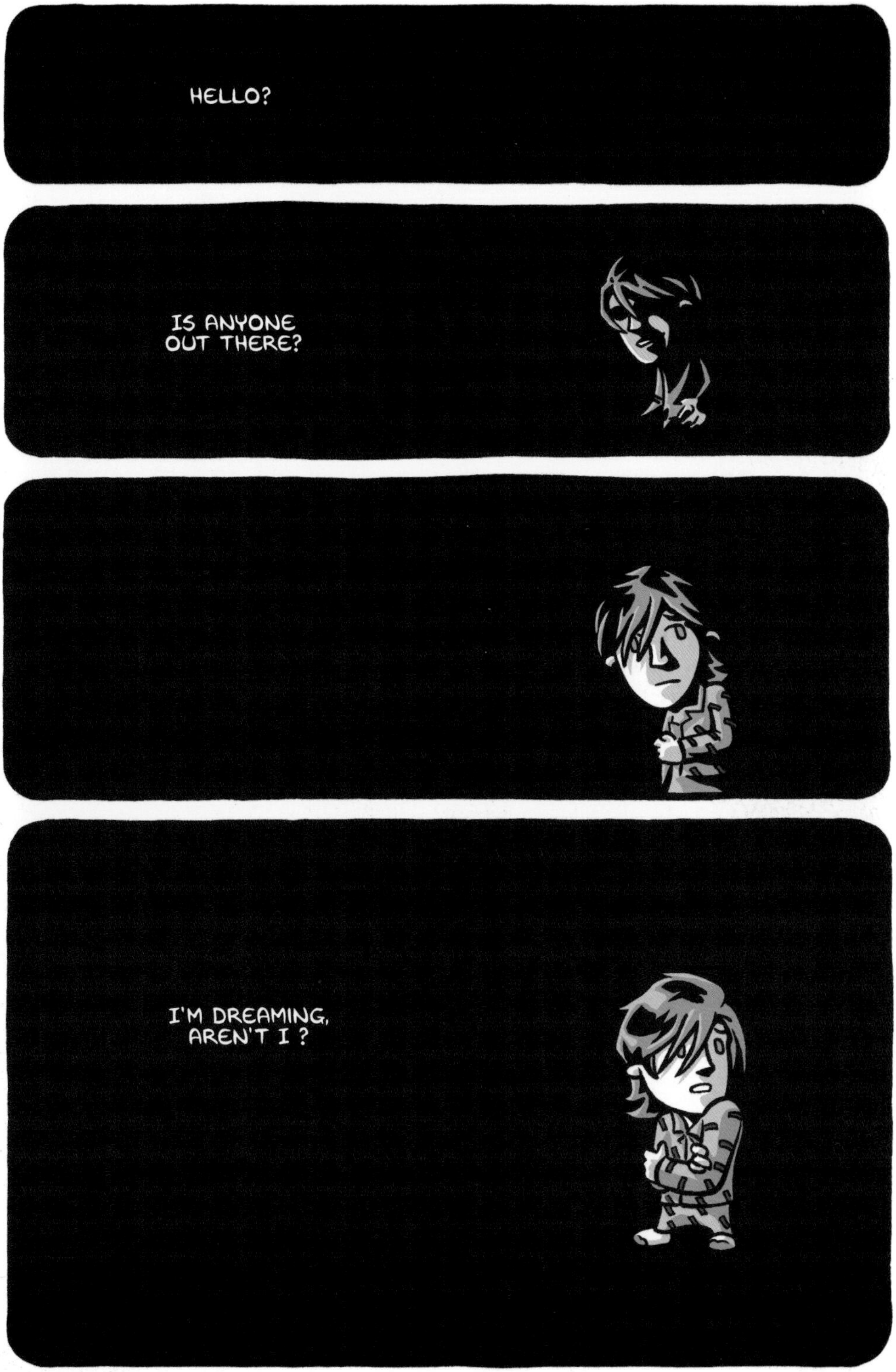
HELLO?
IS ANYONE OUT THERE?
I'M DREAMING, AREN'T I ?

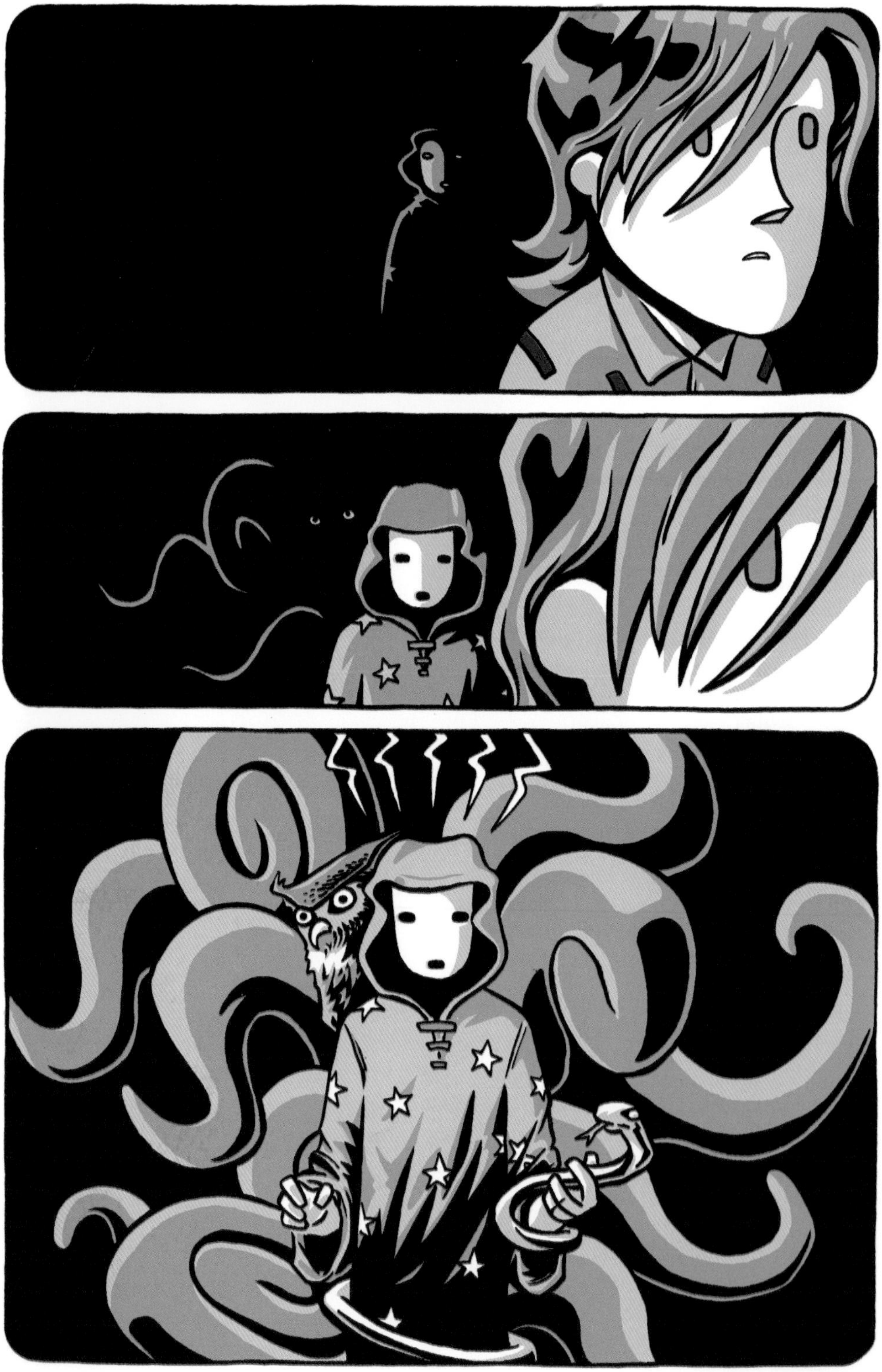

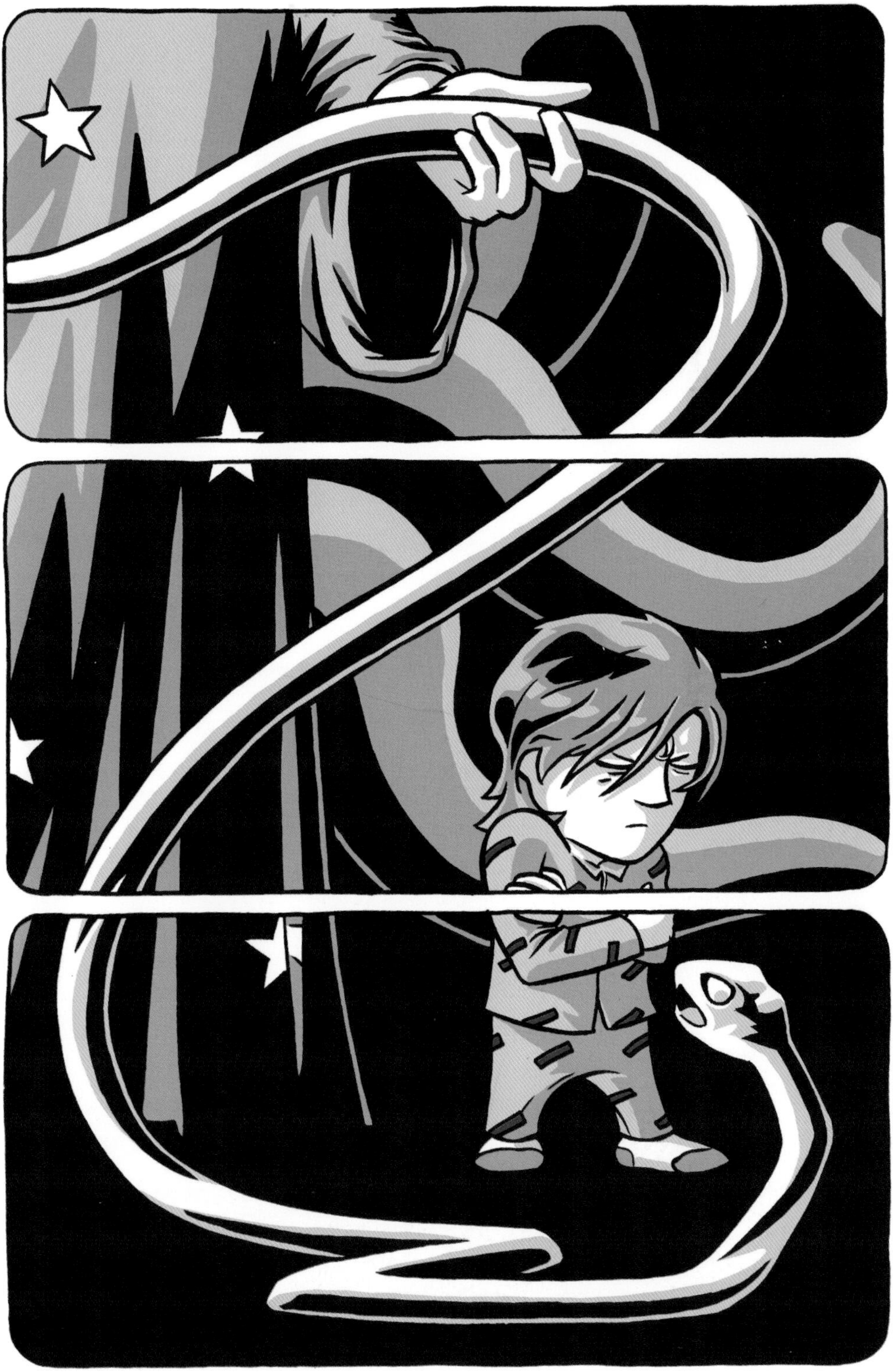

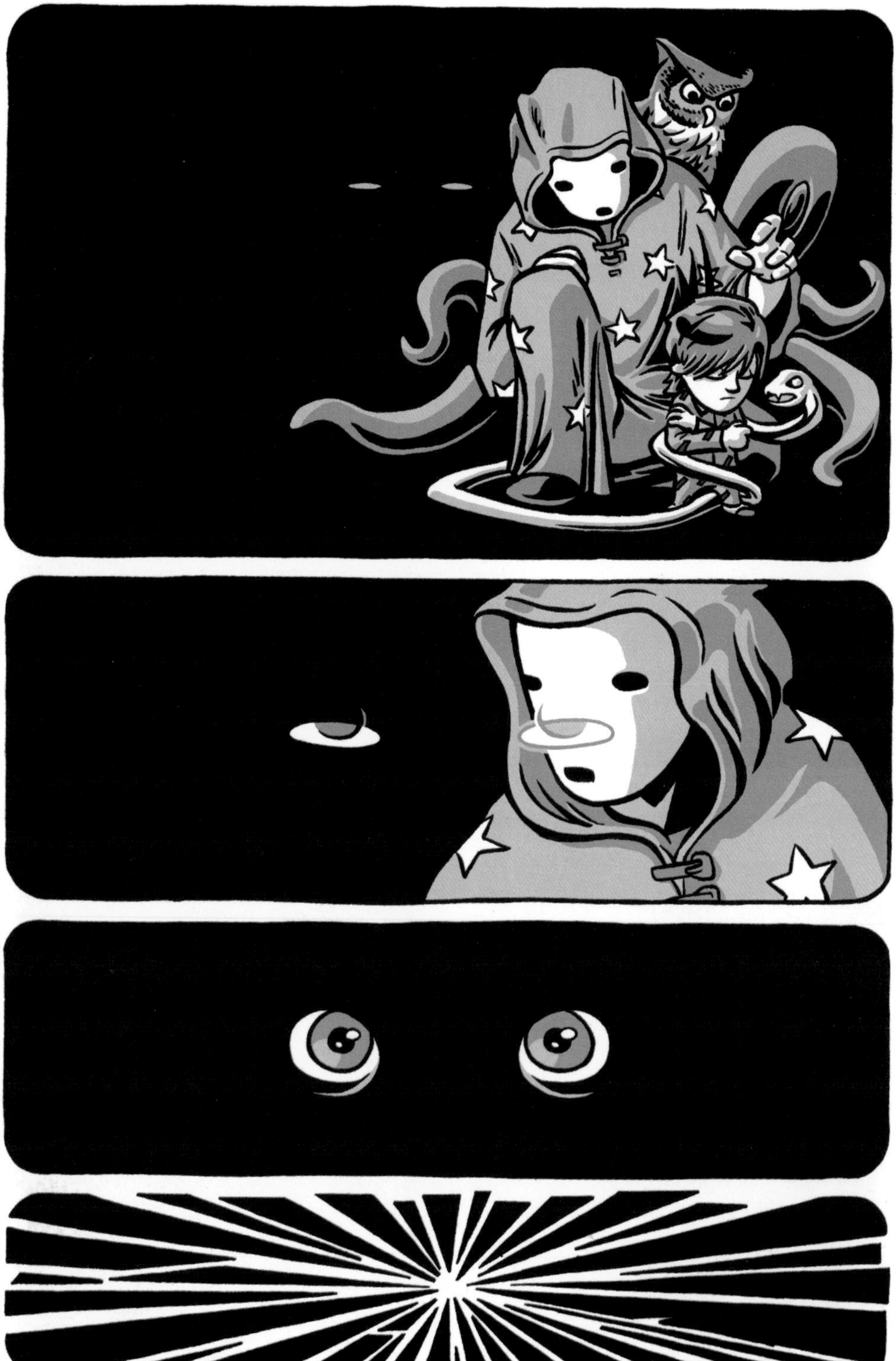

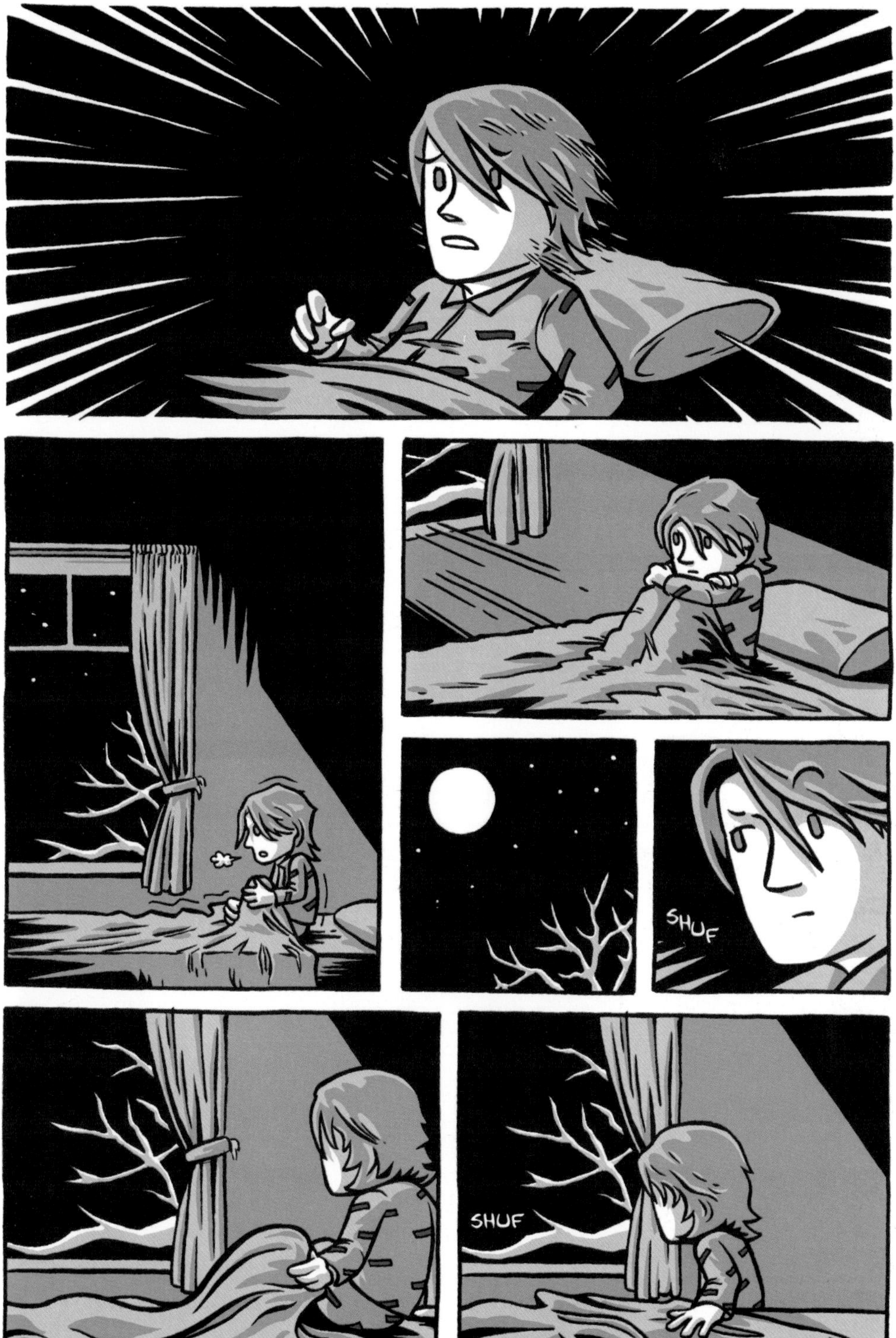
SHUF
SHUF

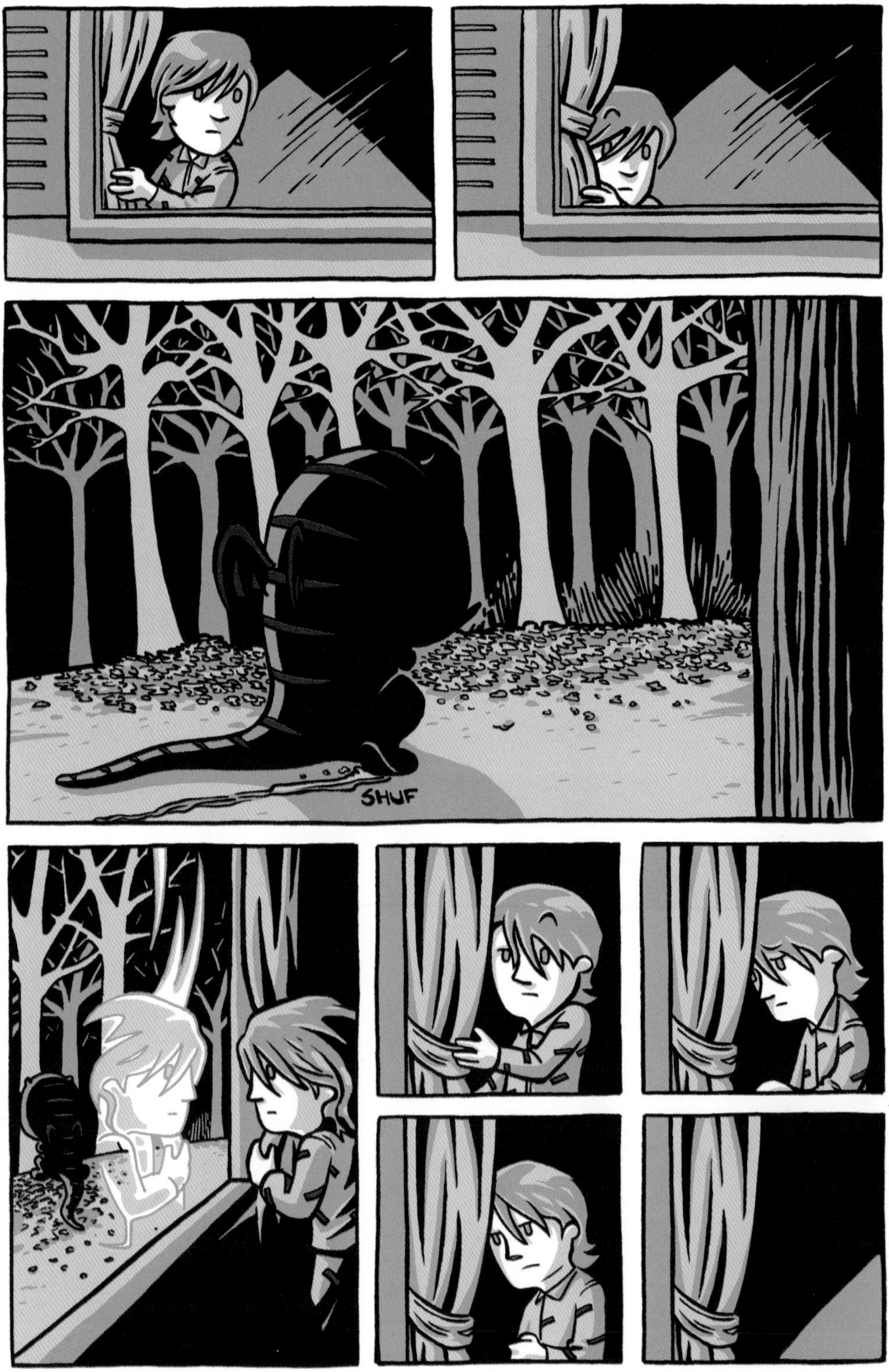
SHUF

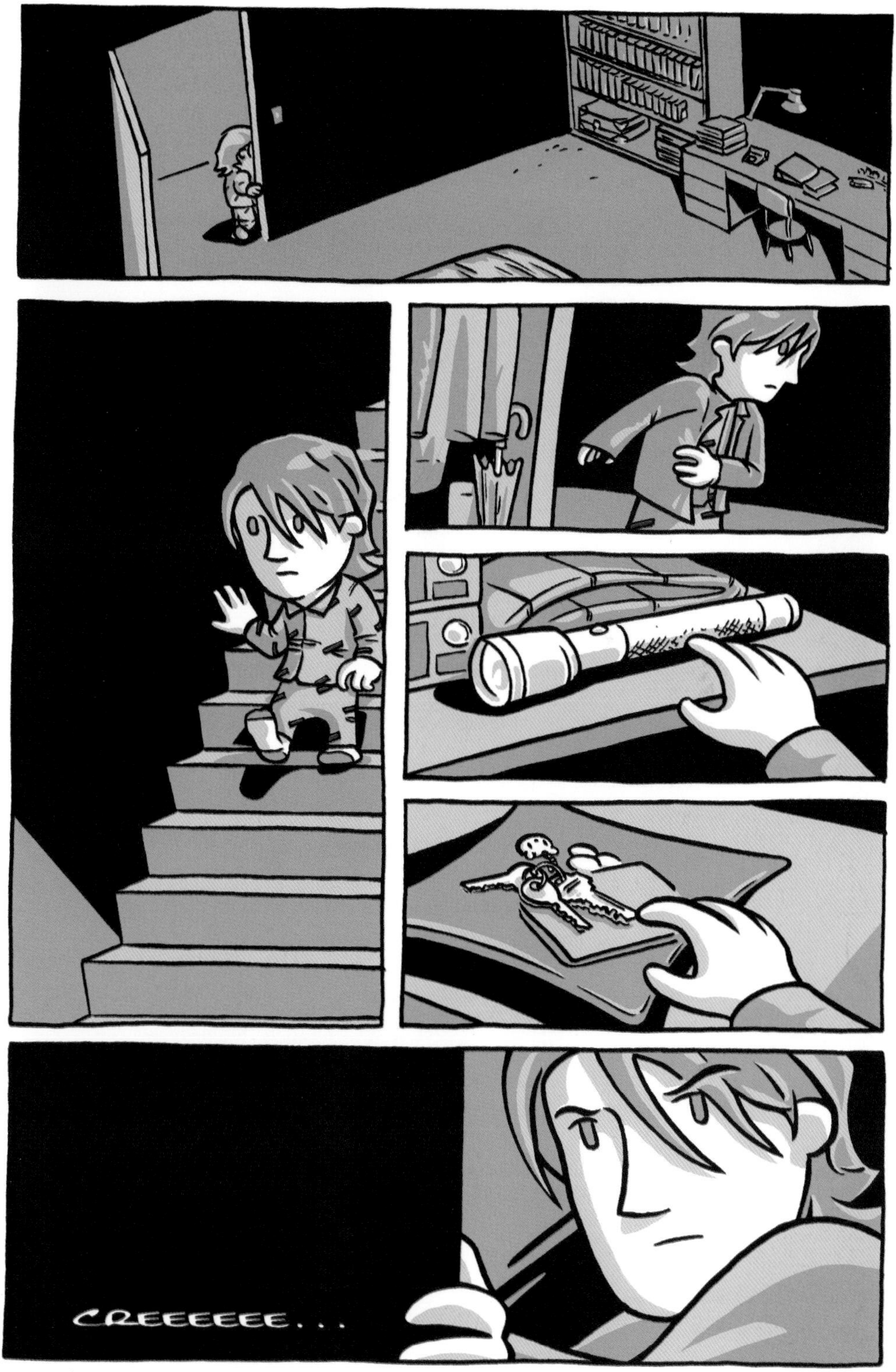
CREEEEEEE...

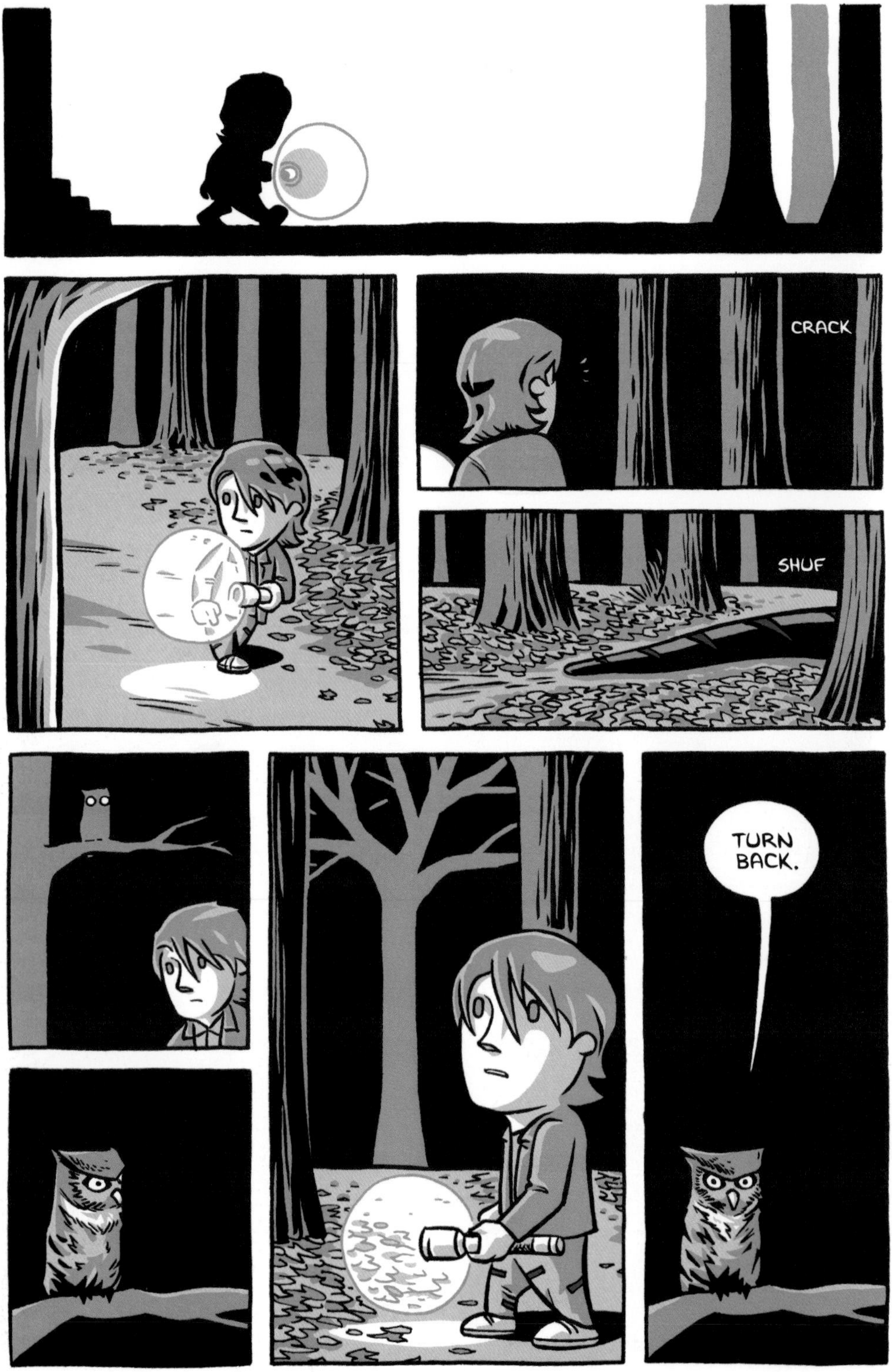
CRACK
SHUF
TURN BACK.

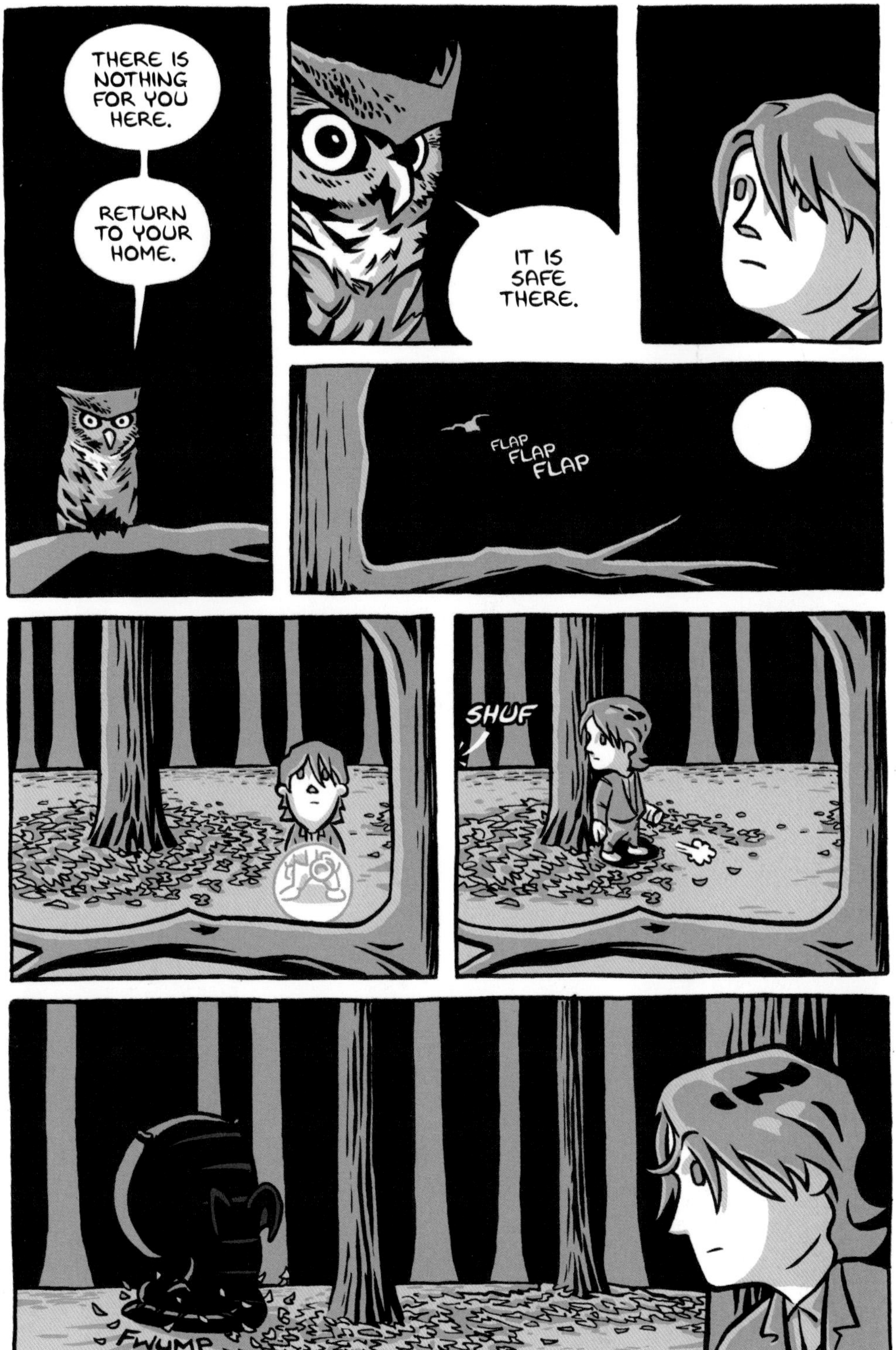
THERE IS NOTHING FOR YOU HERE.
RETURN TO YOUR HOME.
IT IS SAFE THERE.
FLAP FLAP FLAP
SHUF
FWUMP

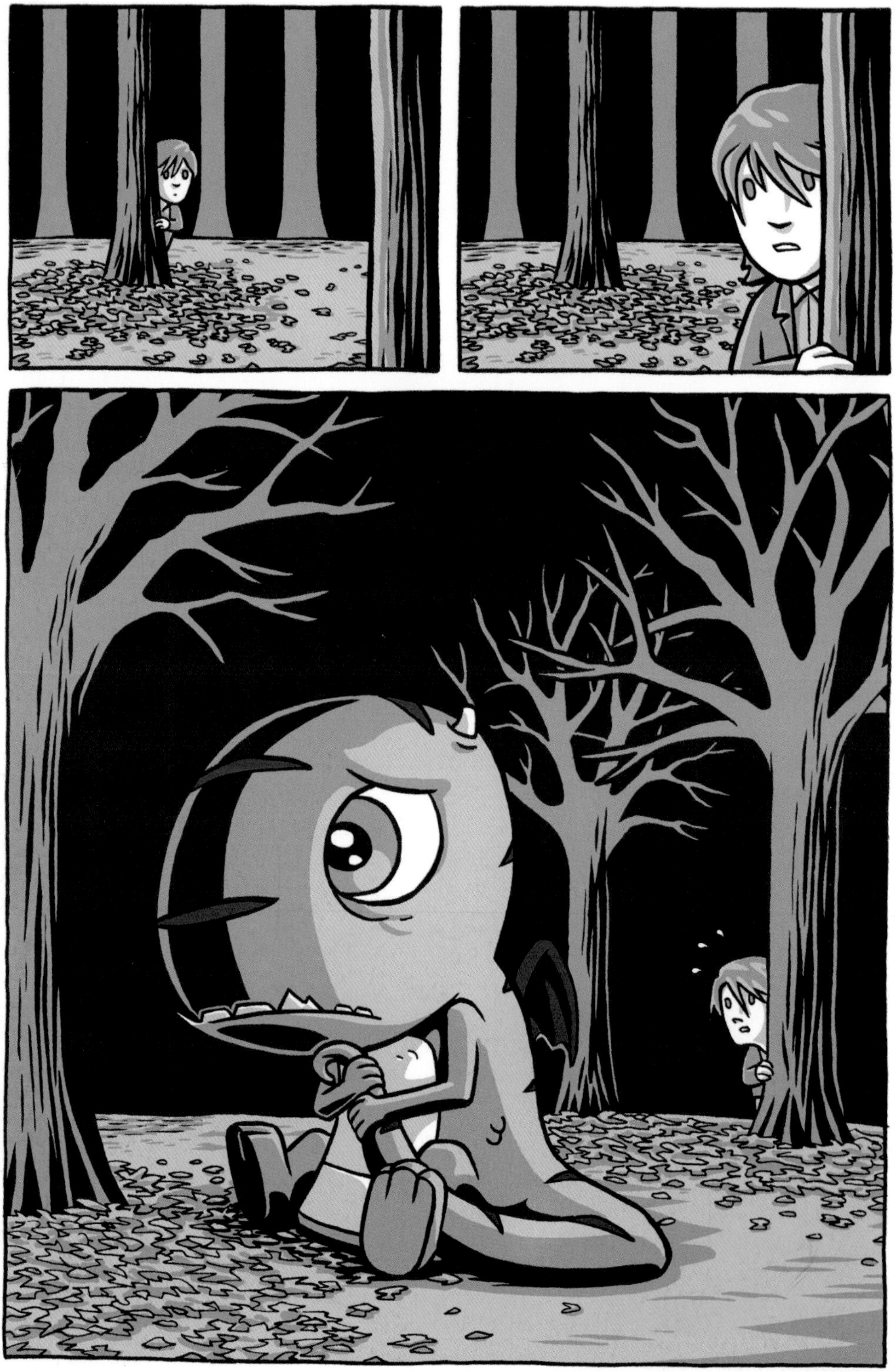

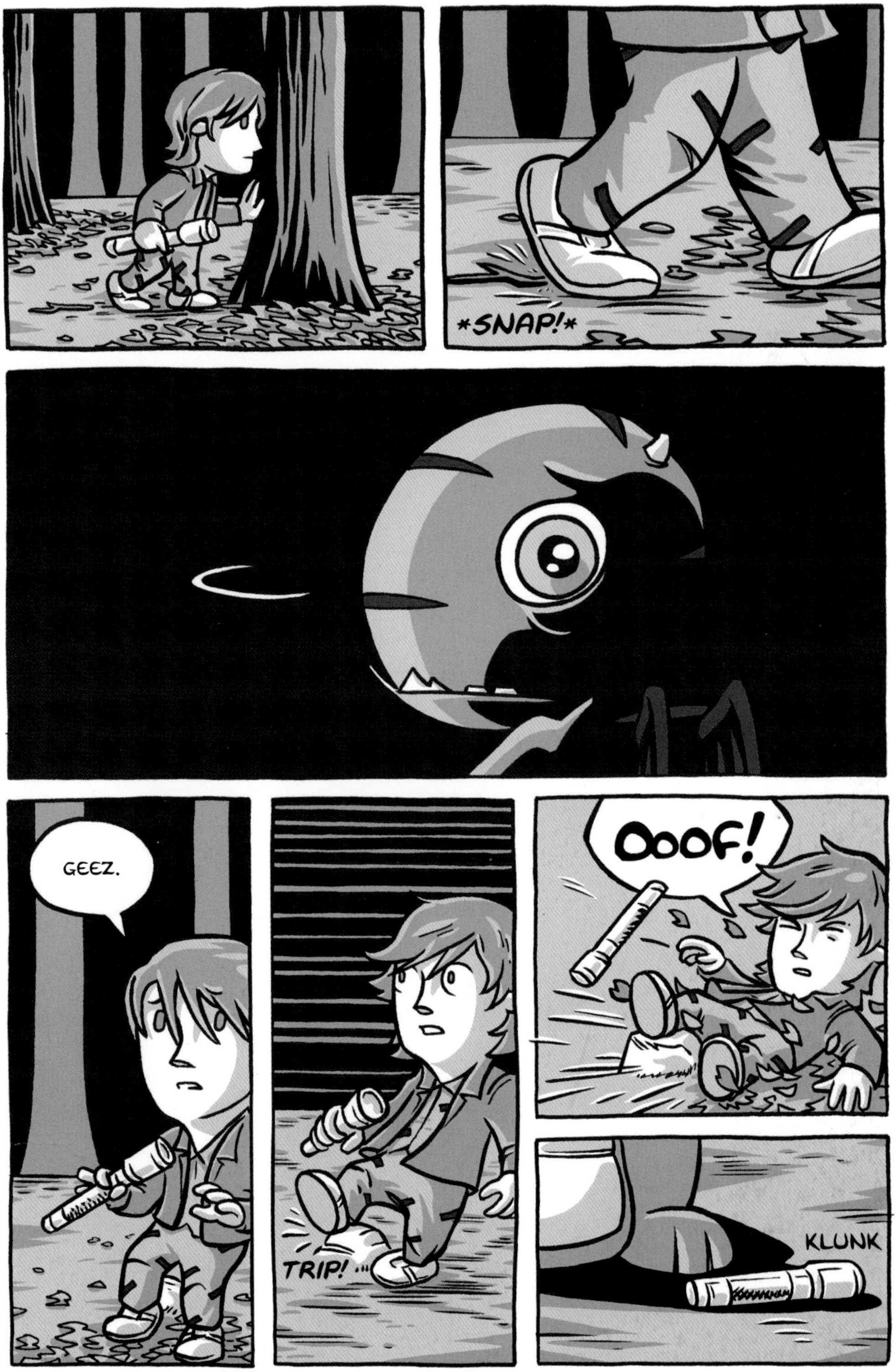
SNAP!
GEEZ.
TRIP!
OOOF!
KLUNK

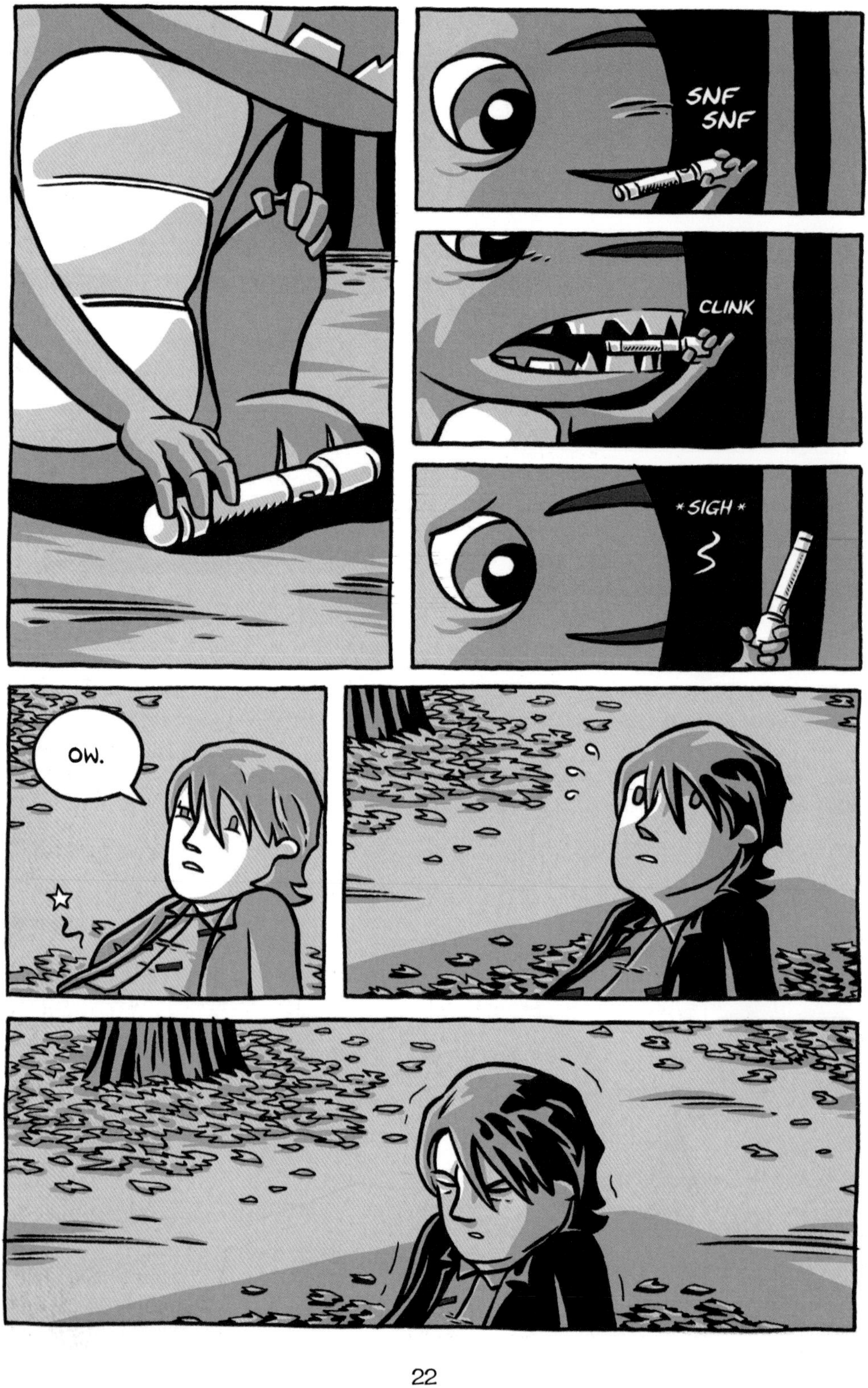
SNF
SNF
CLINK
SIGH
OW.

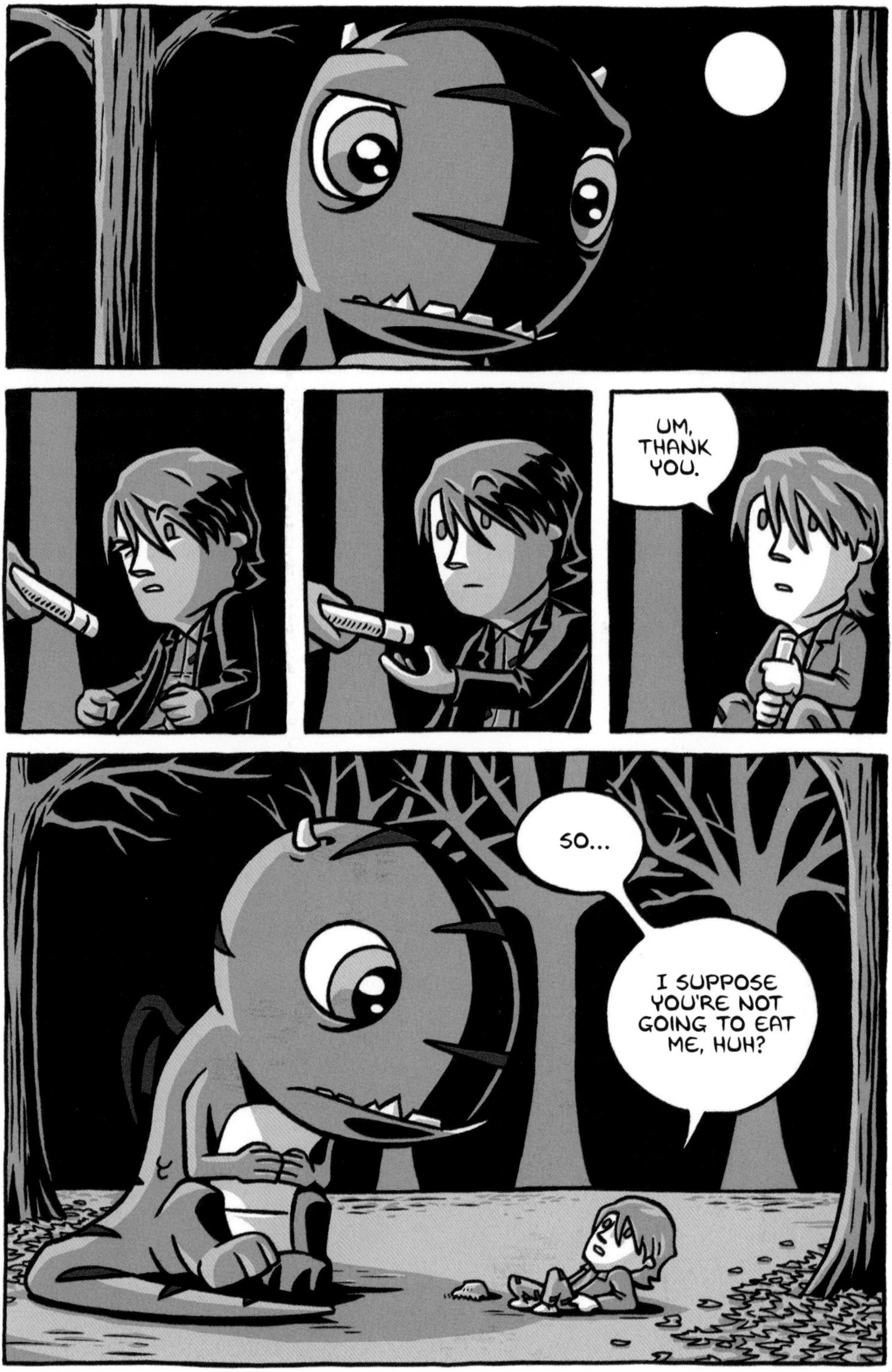
UM, THANK YOU.
SO...
I SUPPOSE YOU'RE NOT GOING TO EAT ME, HUH?

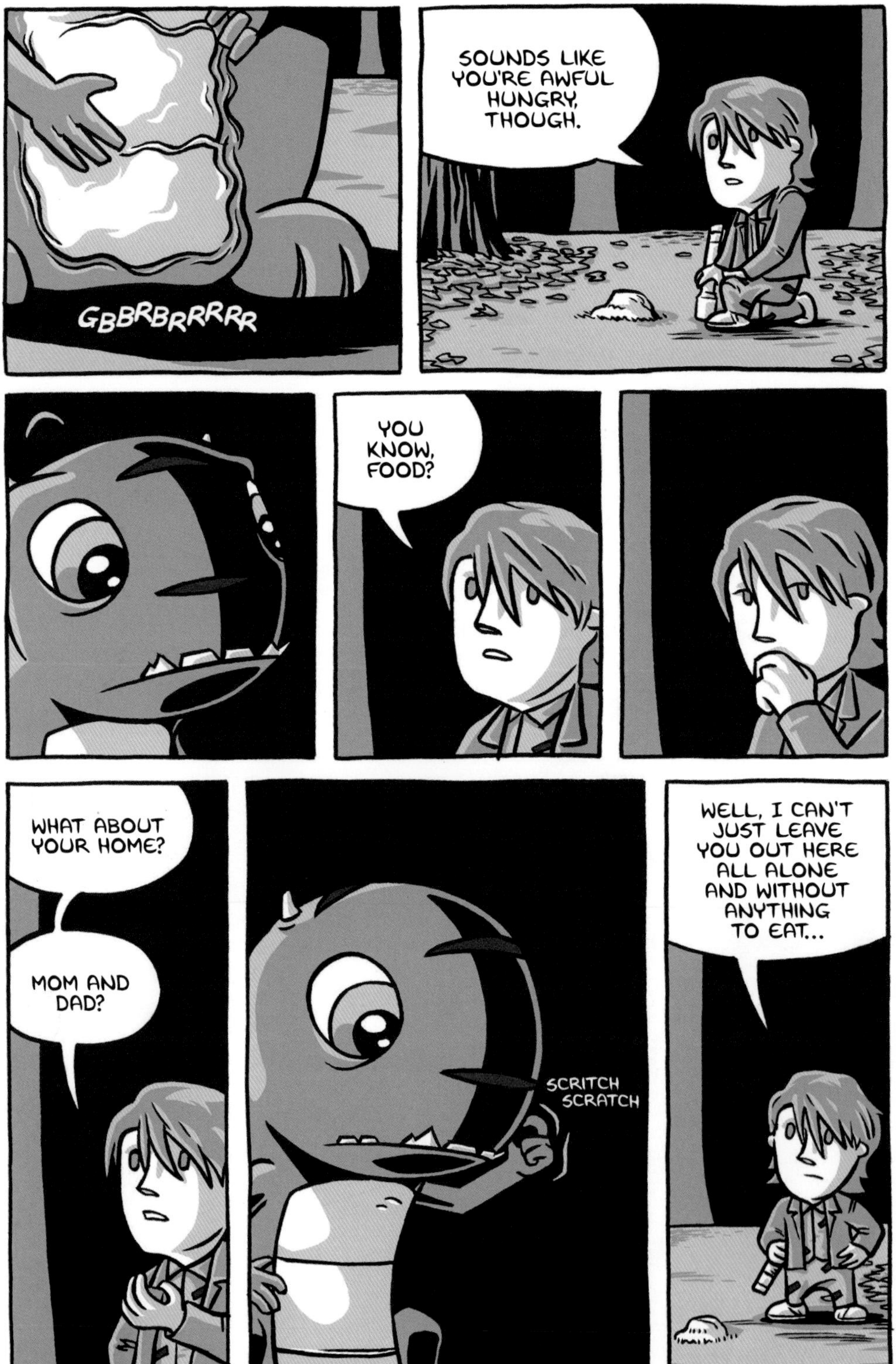
GBBRBRRRRR
SOUNDS LIKE YOU'RE AWFUL HUNGRY, THOUGH.
YOU KNOW, FOOD?
WHAT ABOUT YOUR HOME?
MOM AND DAD?
SCRITCH SCRATCH
WELL, I CAN'T JUST LEAVE YOU OUT HERE ALL ALONE AND WITHOUT ANYTHING TO EAT...

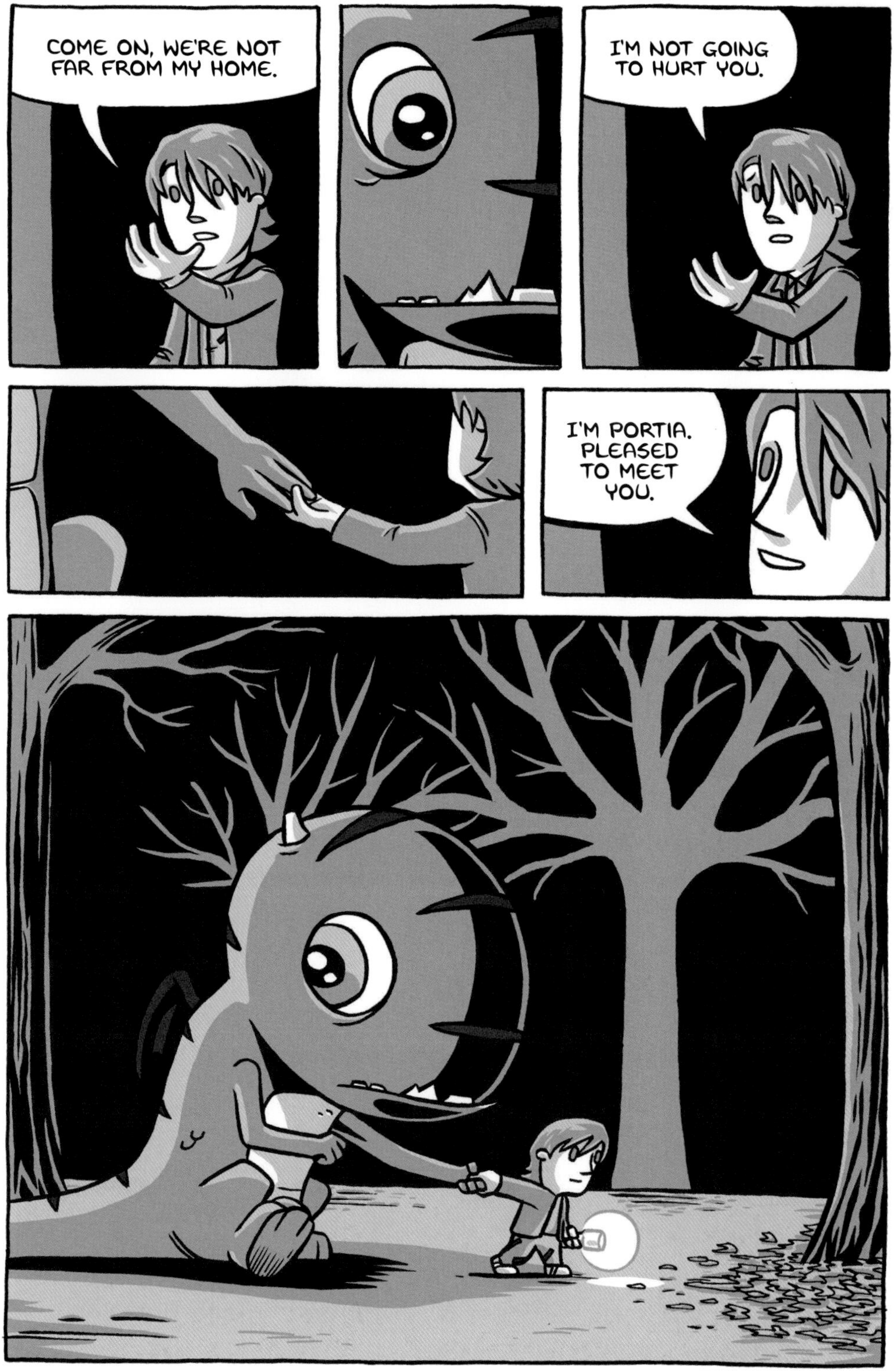
COME ON, WE'RE NOT FAR FROM MY HOME.
I'M NOT GOING TO HURT YOU.
I'M PORTIA. PLEASED TO MEET YOU.

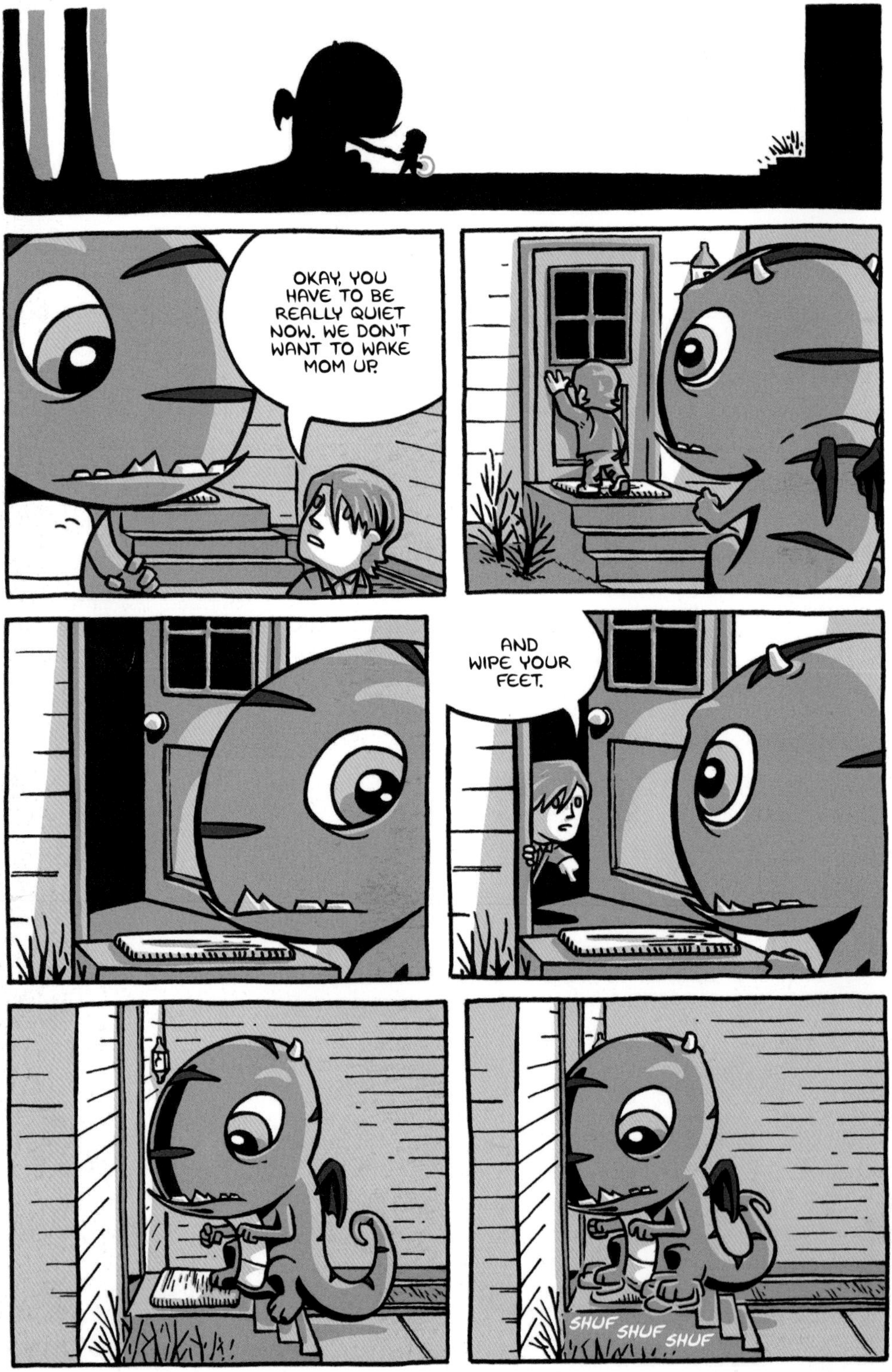
OKAY, YOU HAVE TO BE REALLY QUIET NOW. WE DON'T WANT TO WAKE MOM UP.
AND WIPE YOUR FEET.
SHUF SHUF SHUF

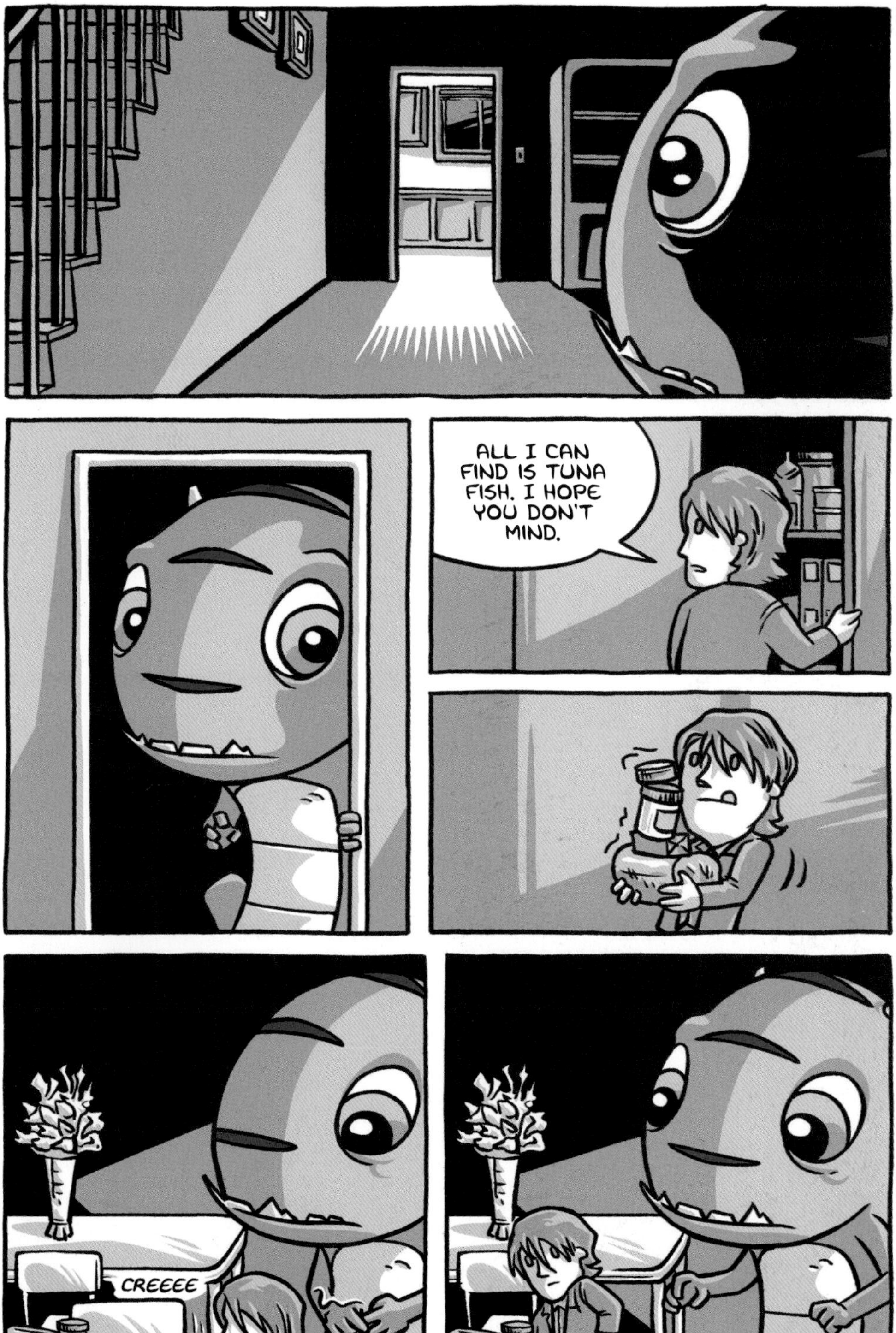
ALL I CAN FIND IS TUNA FISH. I HOPE YOU DON'T MIND.
CREEEE

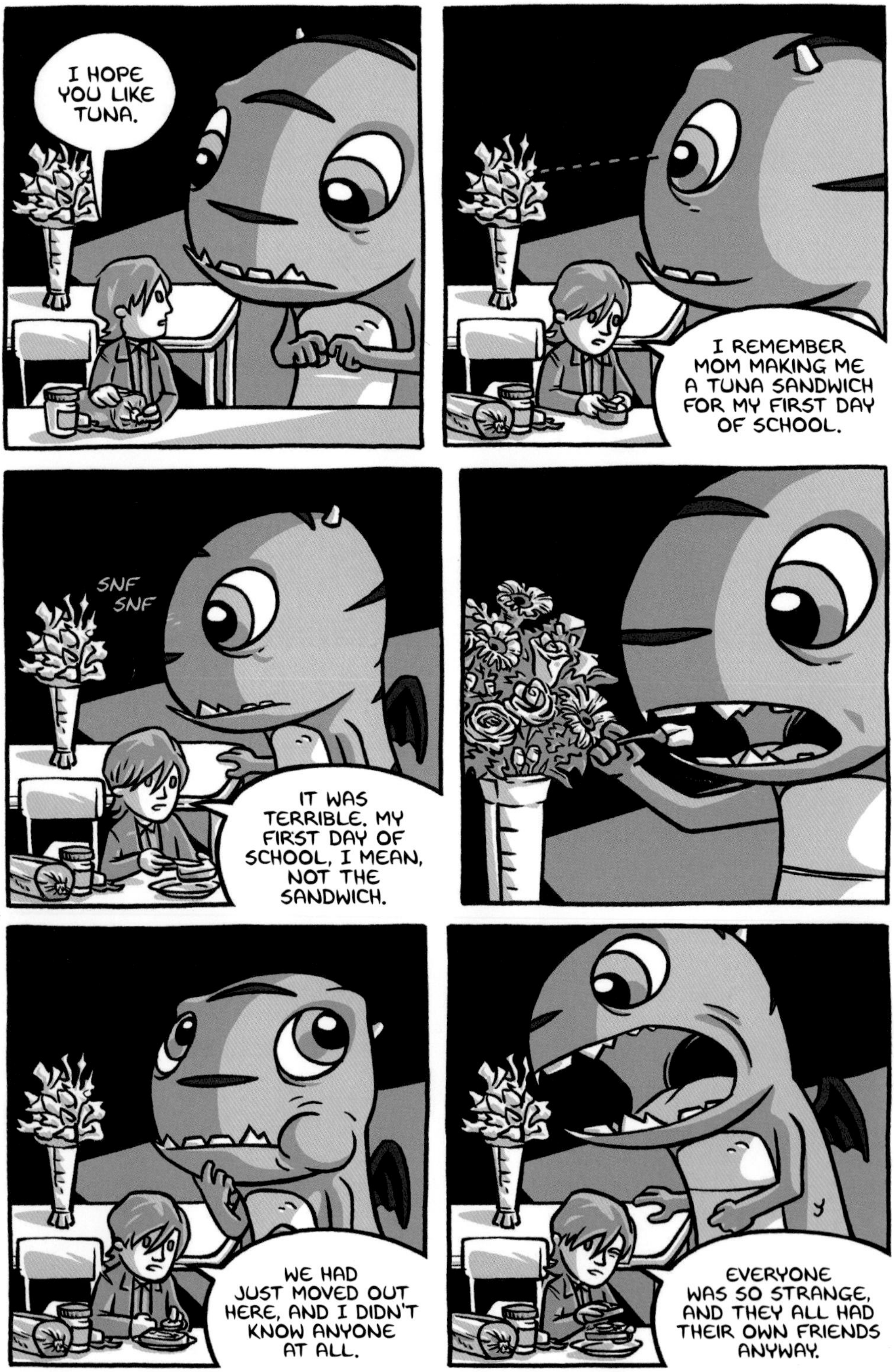
I HOPE YOU LIKE TUNA.
I REMEMBER MOM MAKING ME A TUNA SANDWICH FOR MY FIRST DAY OF SCHOOL.
SNF SNF
IT WAS TERRIBLE. MY FIRST DAY OF SCHOOL, I MEAN, NOT THE SANDWICH.
WE HAD JUST MOVED OUT HERE, AND I DIDN'T KNOW ANYONE AT ALL.
EVERYONE WAS SO STRANGE, AND THEY ALL HAD THEIR OWN FRIENDS ANYWAY.

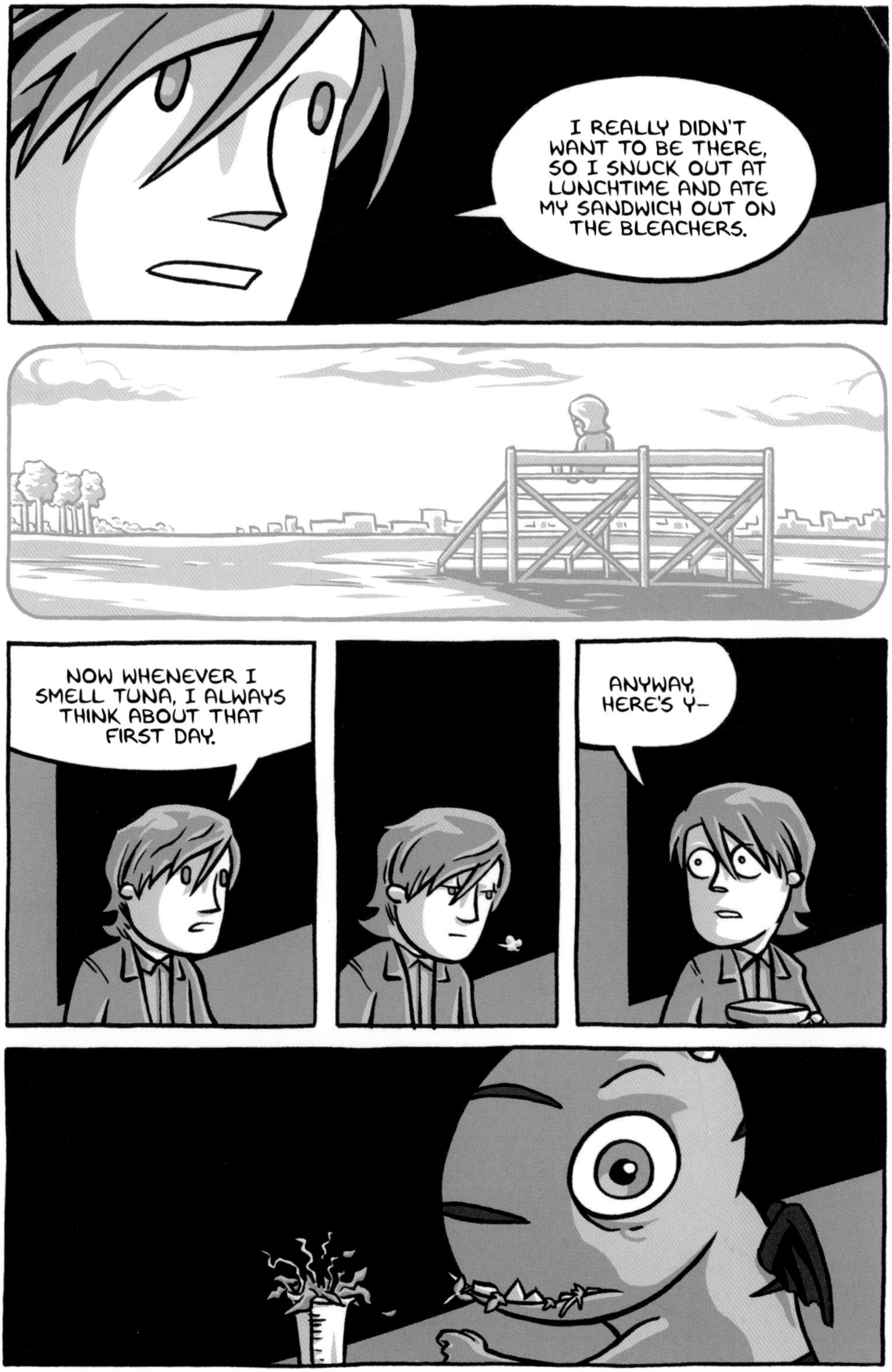
I REALLY DIDN'T WANT TO BE THERE, SO I SNUCK OUT AT LUNCHTIME AND ATE MY SANDWICH OUT ON THE BLEACHERS.
NOW WHENEVER I SMELL TUNA, I ALWAYS THINK ABOUT THAT FIRST DAY.
ANYWAY, HERE'S Y—

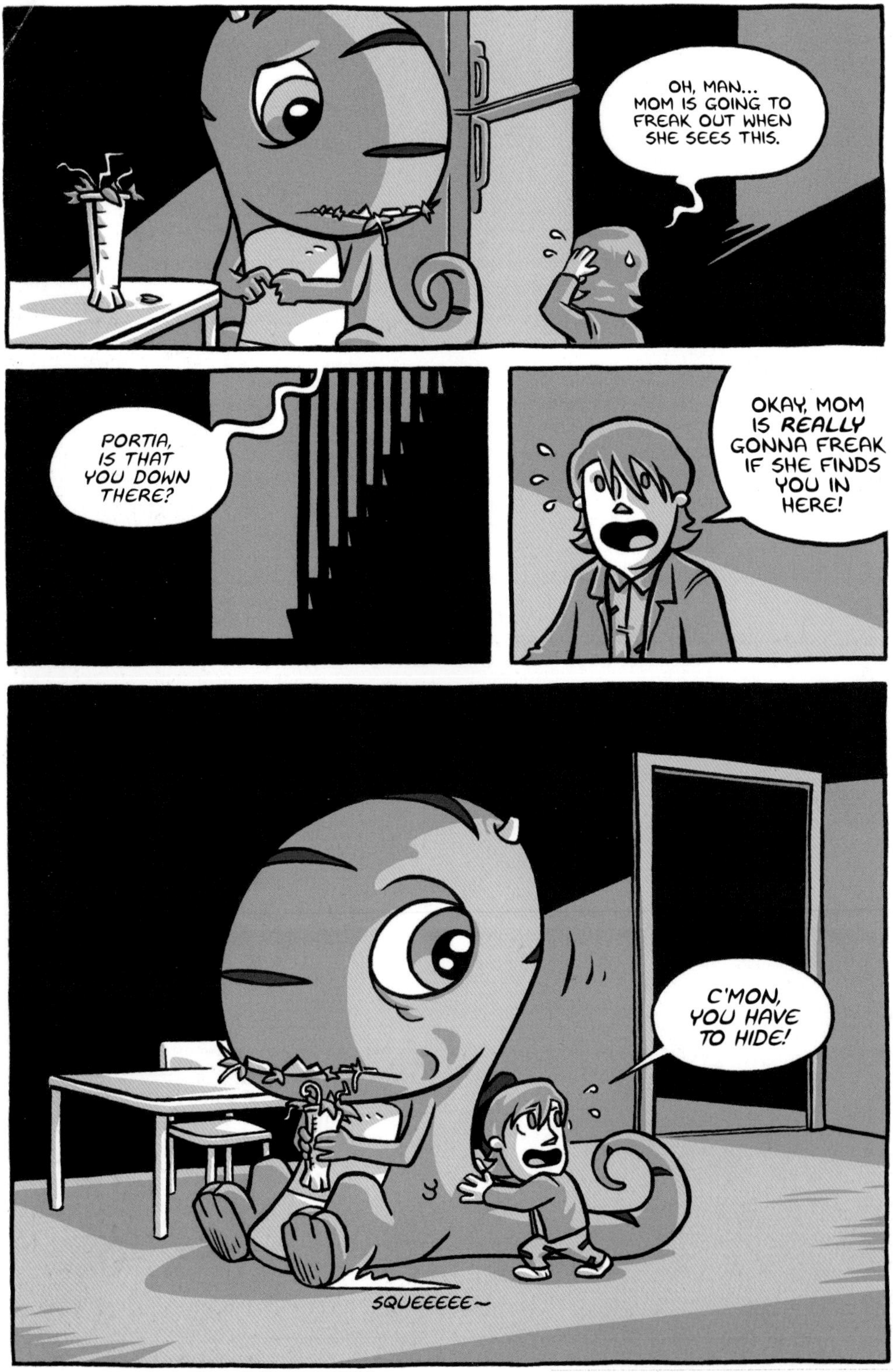
OH, MAN... MOM IS GOING TO FREAK OUT WHEN SHE SEES THIS.
PORTIA, IS THAT YOU DOWN THERE?
OKAY, MOM IS REALLY GONNA FREAK IF SHE FINDS YOU IN HERE!
C'MON, YOU HAVE TO HIDE!
SQUEEEEEE~

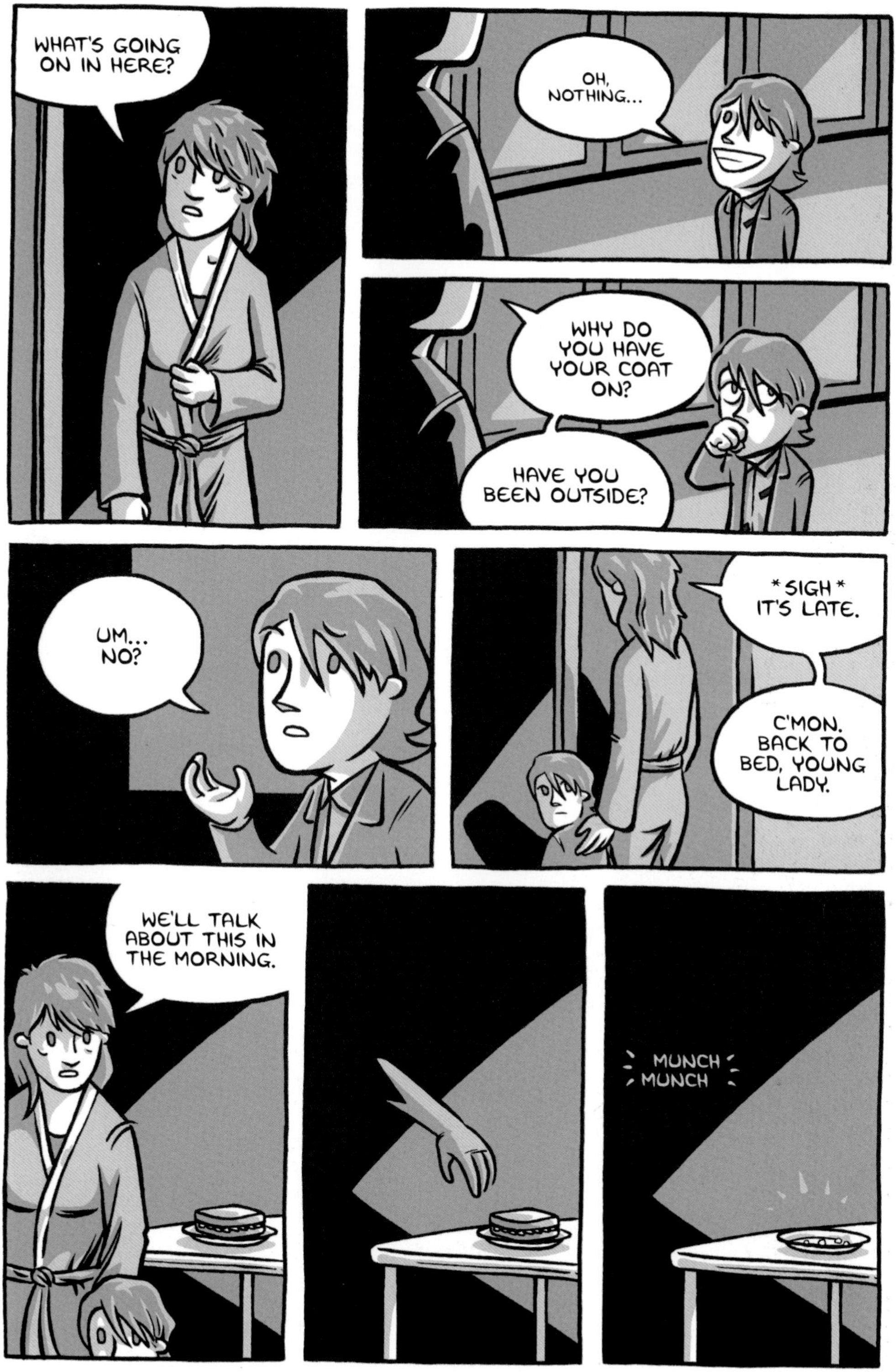
WHAT'S GOING ON IN HERE?
OH, NOTHING...
WHY DO YOU HAVE YOUR COAT ON?
HAVE YOU BEEN OUTSIDE?
UM... NO?
SIGH IT'S LATE.
C'MON. BACK TO BED, YOUNG LADY.
WE'LL TALK ABOUT THIS IN THE MORNING.
MUNCH MUNCH

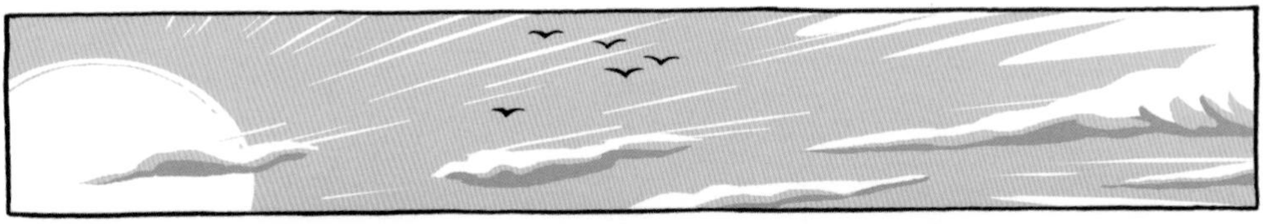

CHAPTER TWO

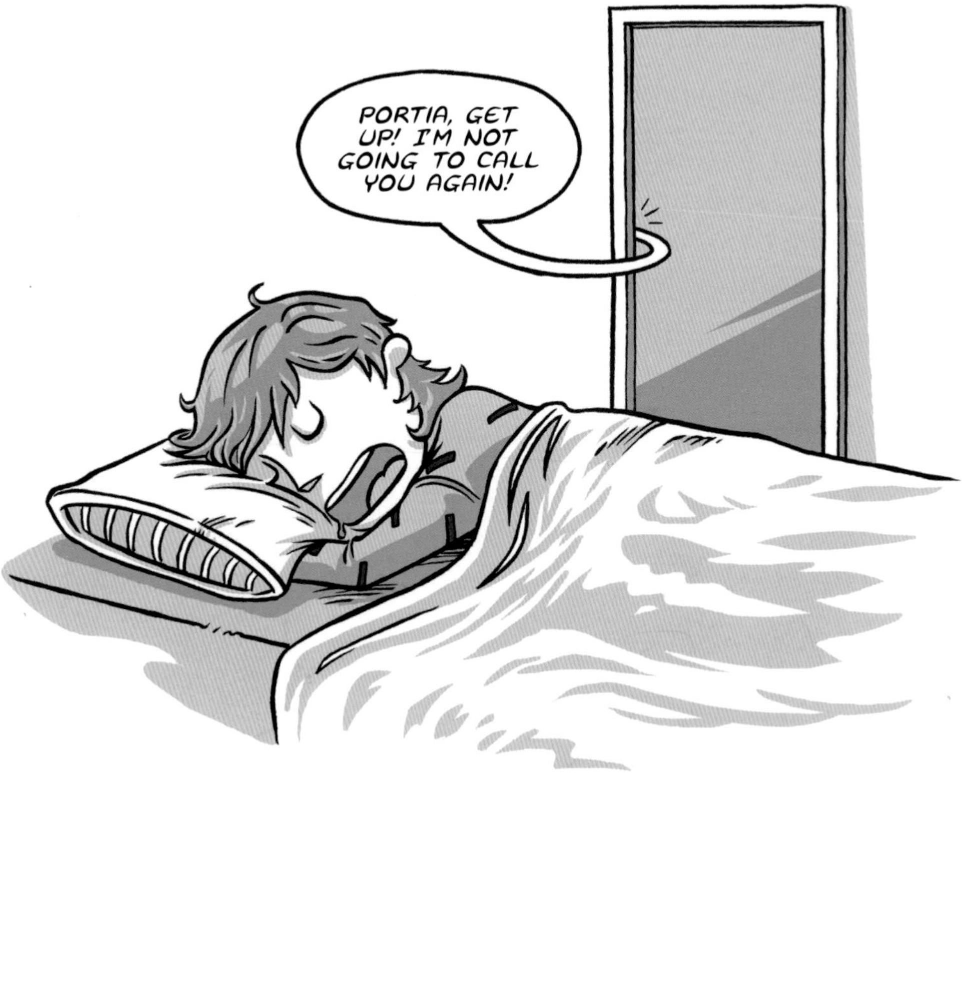
PORTIA, GET UP! I'M NOT GOING TO CALL YOU AGAIN!

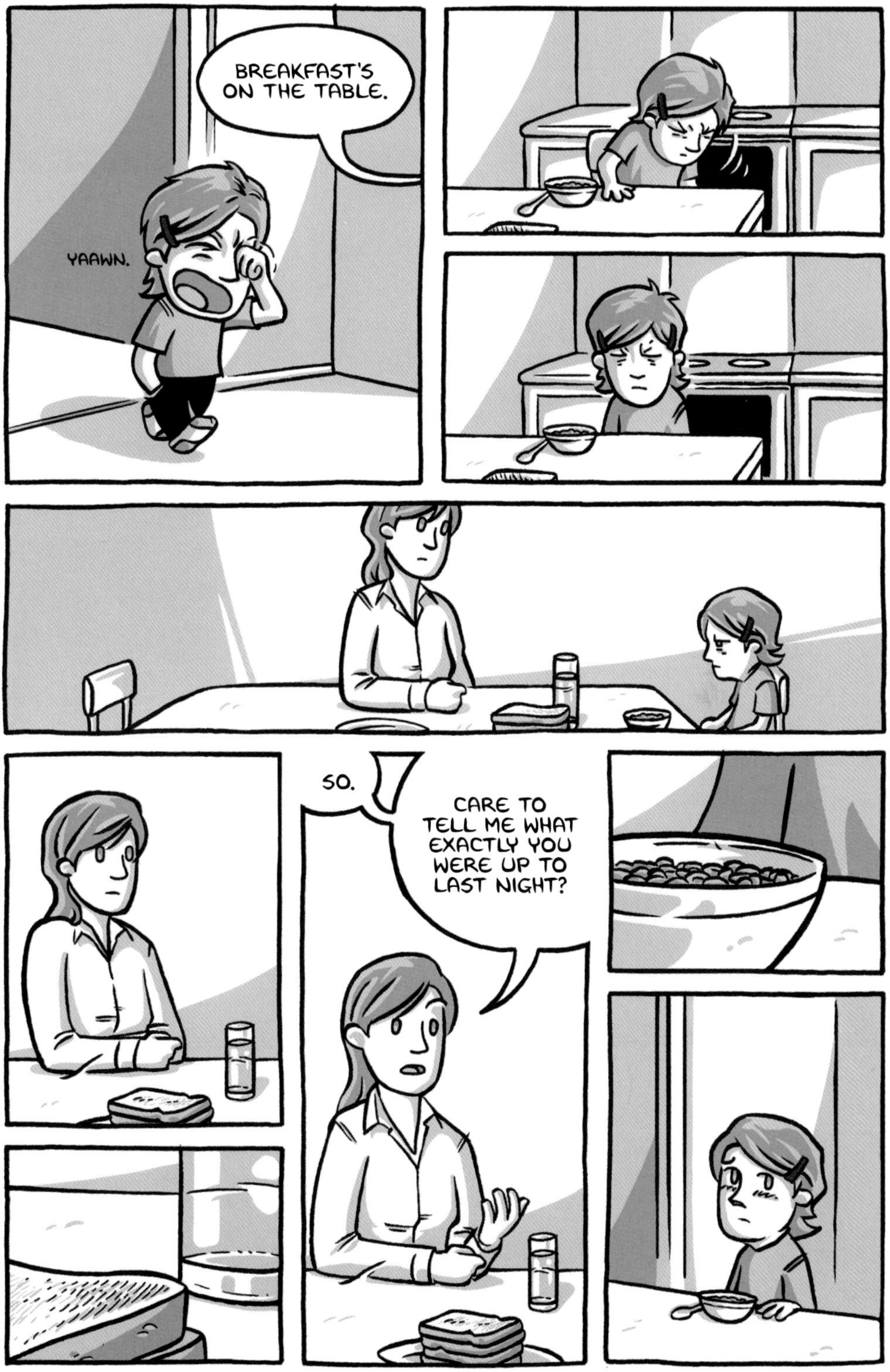
BREAKFAST'S ON THE TABLE.
YAAWN.
SO.
CARE TO TELL ME WHAT EXACTLY YOU WERE UP TO LAST NIGHT?

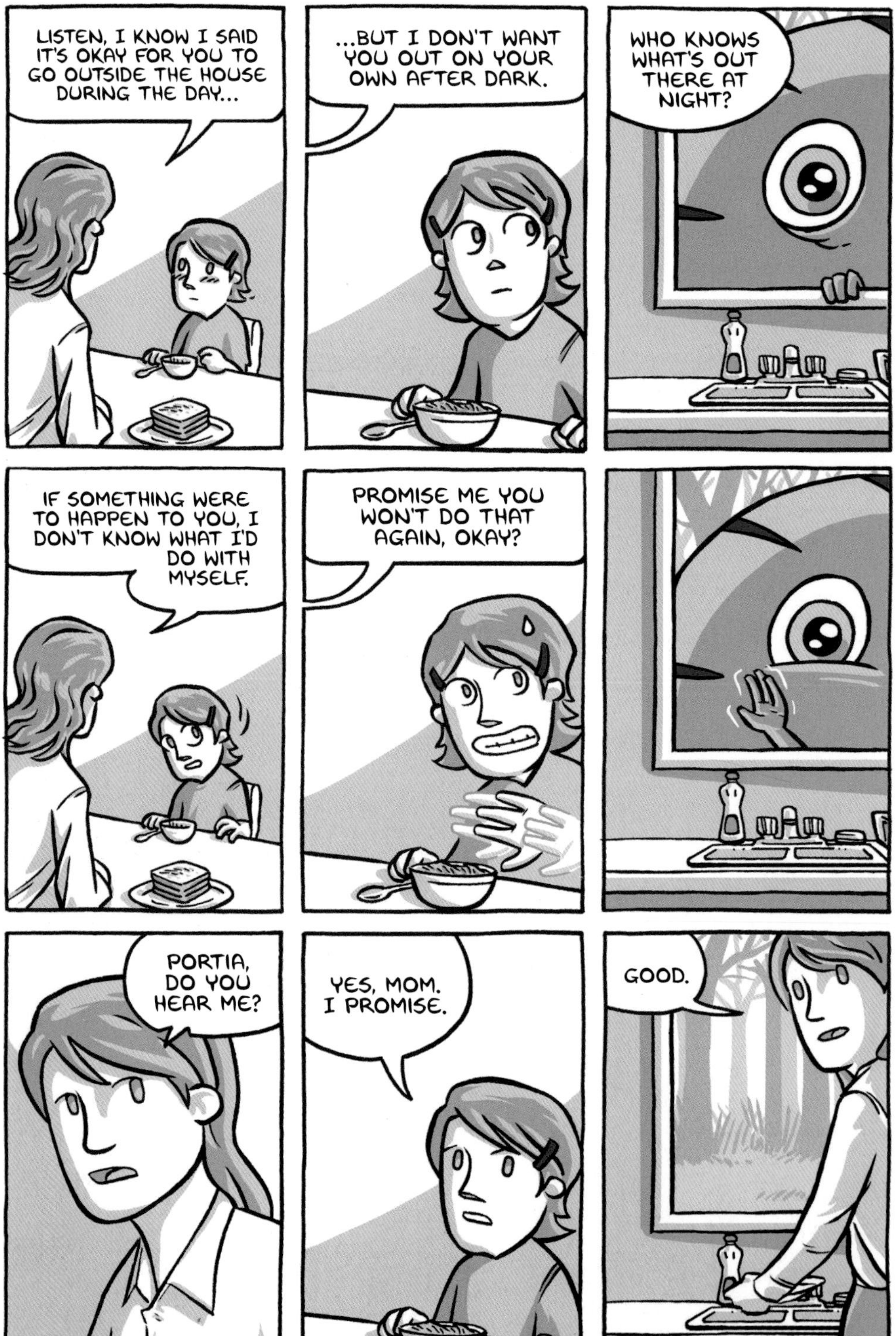
LISTEN, I KNOW I SAID IT'S OKAY FOR YOU TO GO OUTSIDE THE HOUSE DURING THE DAY...
...BUT I DON'T WANT YOU OUT ON YOUR OWN AFTER DARK.
WHO KNOWS WHAT'S OUT THERE AT NIGHT?
IF SOMETHING WERE TO HAPPEN TO YOU, I DON'T KNOW WHAT I'D DO WITH MYSELF.
PROMISE ME YOU WON'T DO THAT AGAIN, OKAY?
PORTIA, DO YOU HEAR ME?
YES, MOM. I PROMISE.
GOOD.

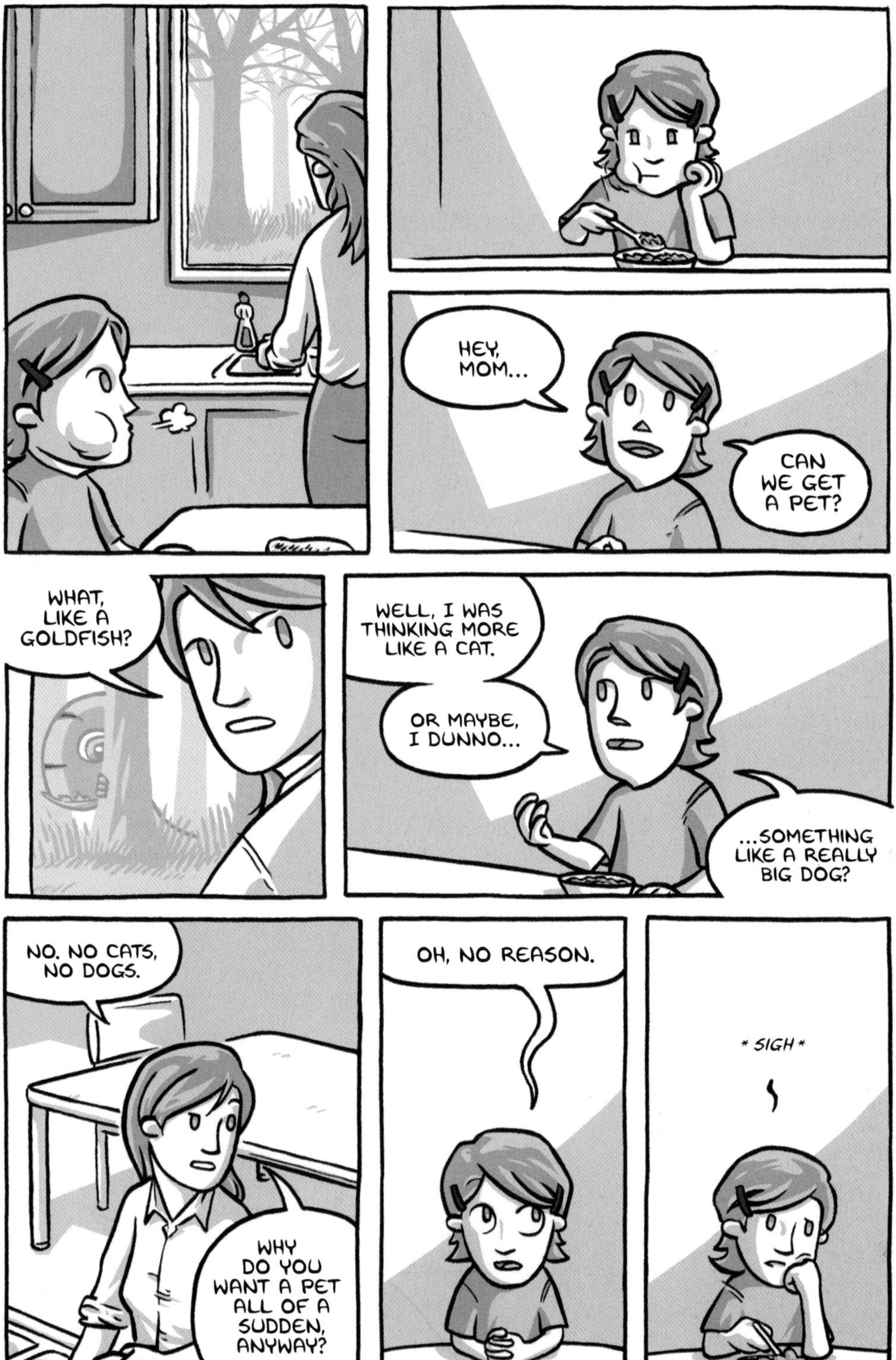
HEY, MOM...
CAN WE GET A PET?
WHAT, LIKE A GOLDFISH?
WELL, I WAS THINKING MORE LIKE A CAT.
OR MAYBE, I DUNNO...
...SOMETHING LIKE A REALLY BIG DOG?
NO. NO CATS, NO DOGS.
WHY DO YOU WANT A PET ALL OF A SUDDEN, ANYWAY?
OH, NO REASON.
* SIGH *

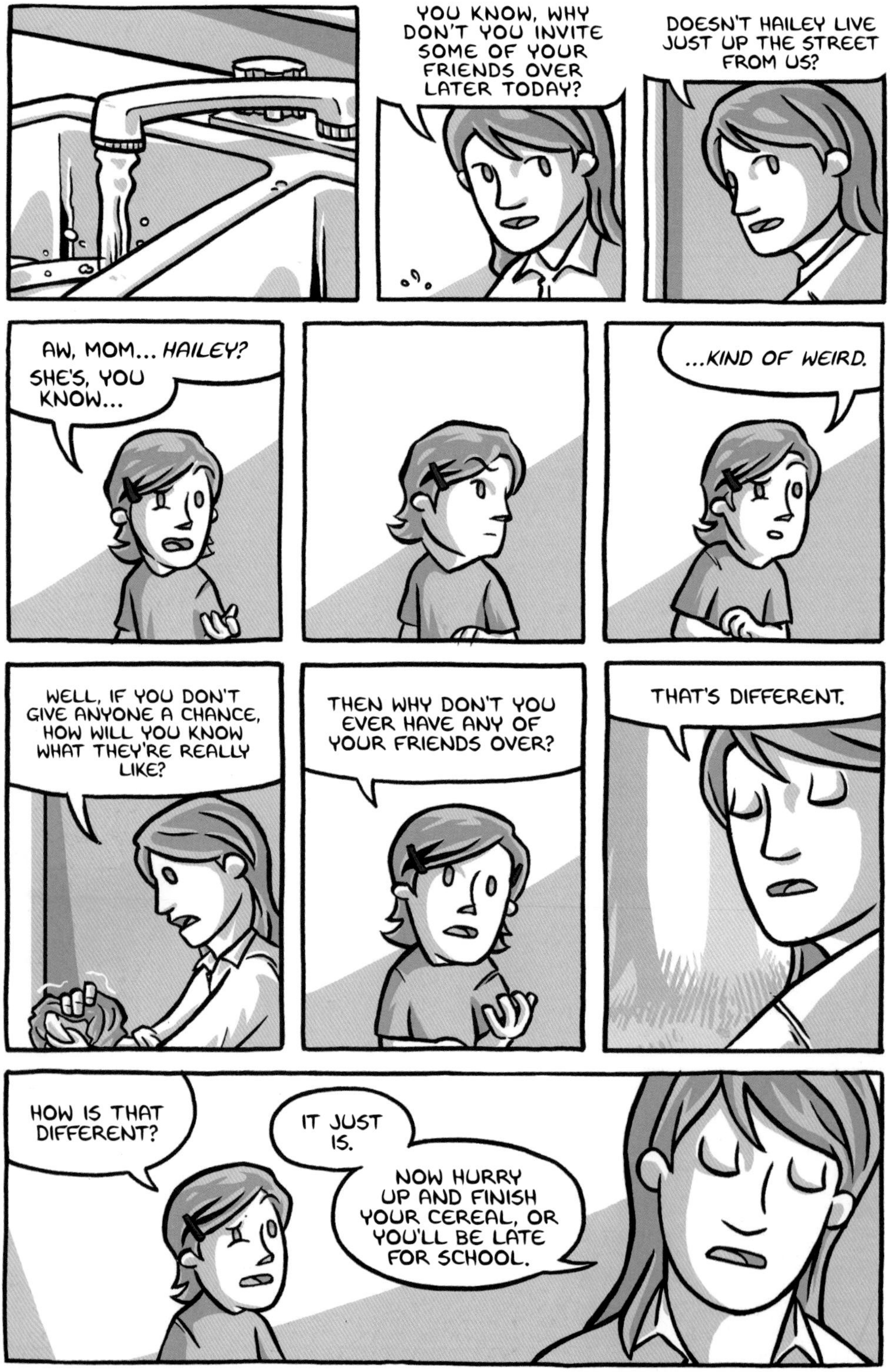
YOU KNOW, WHY DON'T YOU INVITE SOME OF YOUR FRIENDS OVER LATER TODAY?
DOESN'T HAILEY LIVE JUST UP THE STREET FROM US?
AW, MOM... *HAILEY?*
SHE'S, YOU KNOW...
...*KIND OF WEIRD.*
WELL, IF YOU DON'T GIVE ANYONE A CHANCE, HOW WILL YOU KNOW WHAT THEY'RE REALLY LIKE?
THEN WHY DON'T YOU EVER HAVE ANY OF YOUR FRIENDS OVER?
THAT'S DIFFERENT.
HOW IS THAT DIFFERENT?
IT JUST IS.
NOW HURRY UP AND FINISH YOUR CEREAL, OR YOU'LL BE LATE FOR SCHOOL.

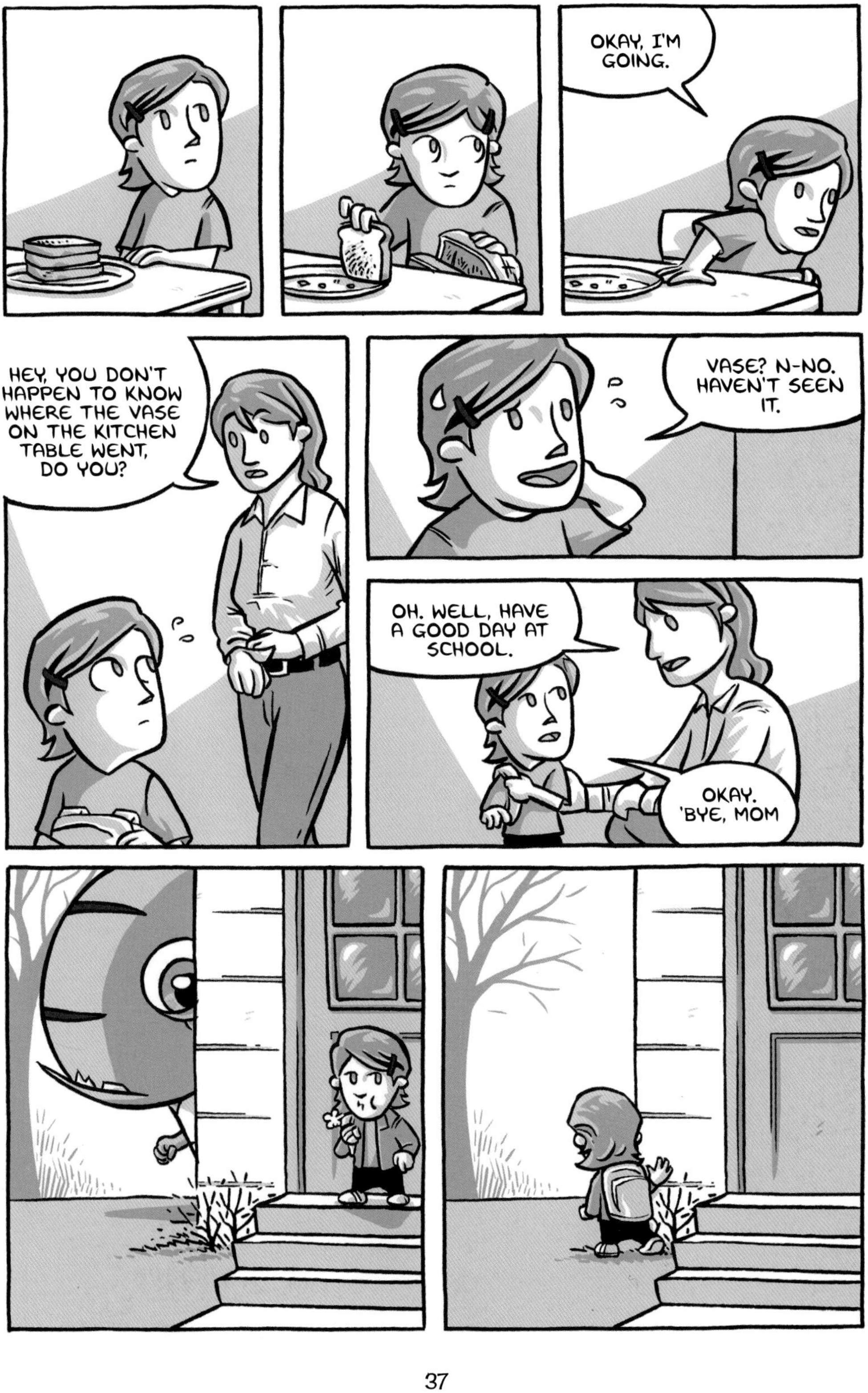
OKAY, I'M GOING.
HEY, YOU DON'T HAPPEN TO KNOW WHERE THE VASE ON THE KITCHEN TABLE WENT, DO YOU?
VASE? N-NO. HAVEN'T SEEN IT.
OH. WELL, HAVE A GOOD DAY AT SCHOOL.
OKAY. 'BYE, MOM

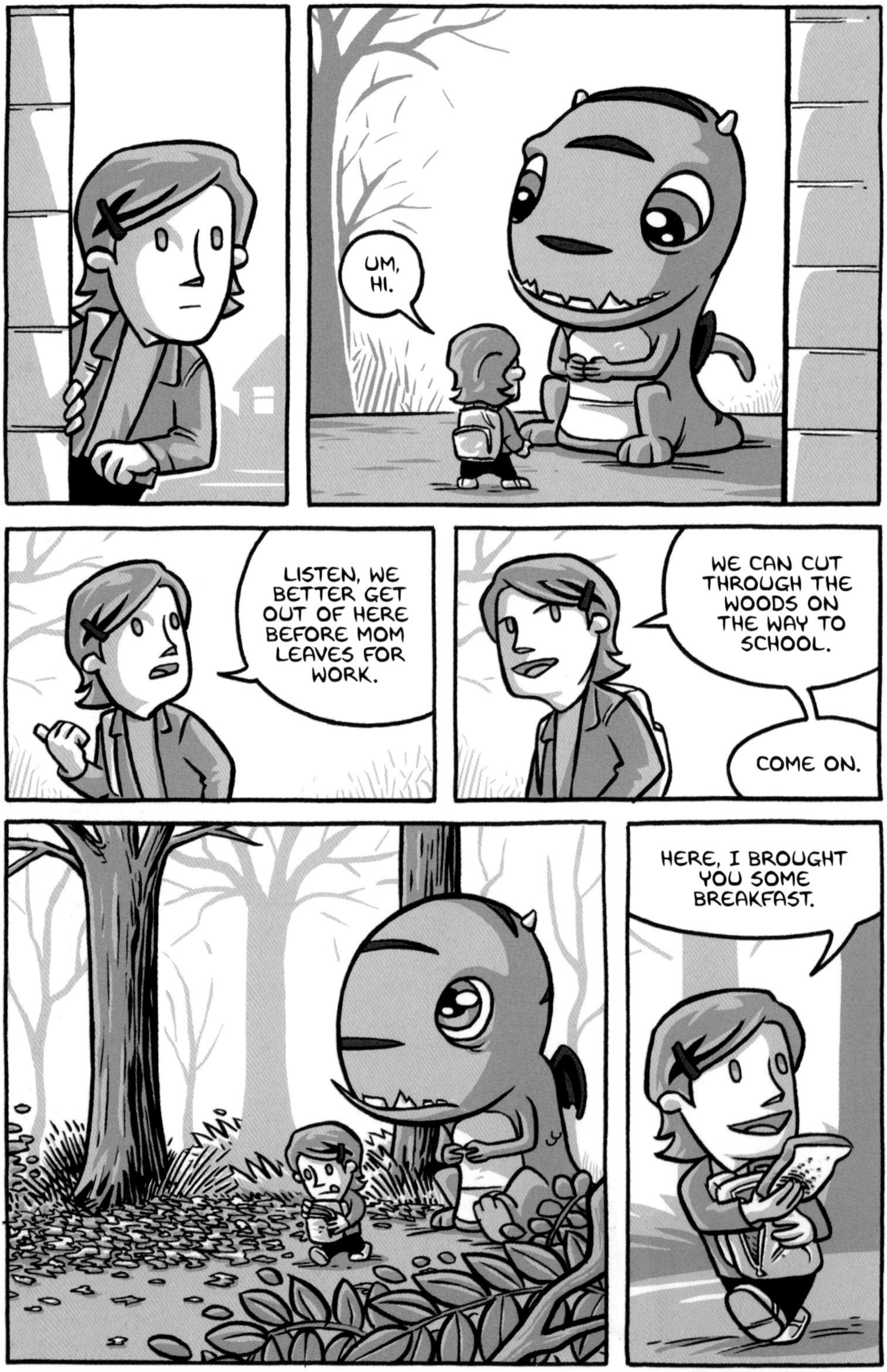
UM, HI.
LISTEN, WE BETTER GET OUT OF HERE BEFORE MOM LEAVES FOR WORK.
WE CAN CUT THROUGH THE WOODS ON THE WAY TO SCHOOL.
COME ON.
HERE, I BROUGHT YOU SOME BREAKFAST.

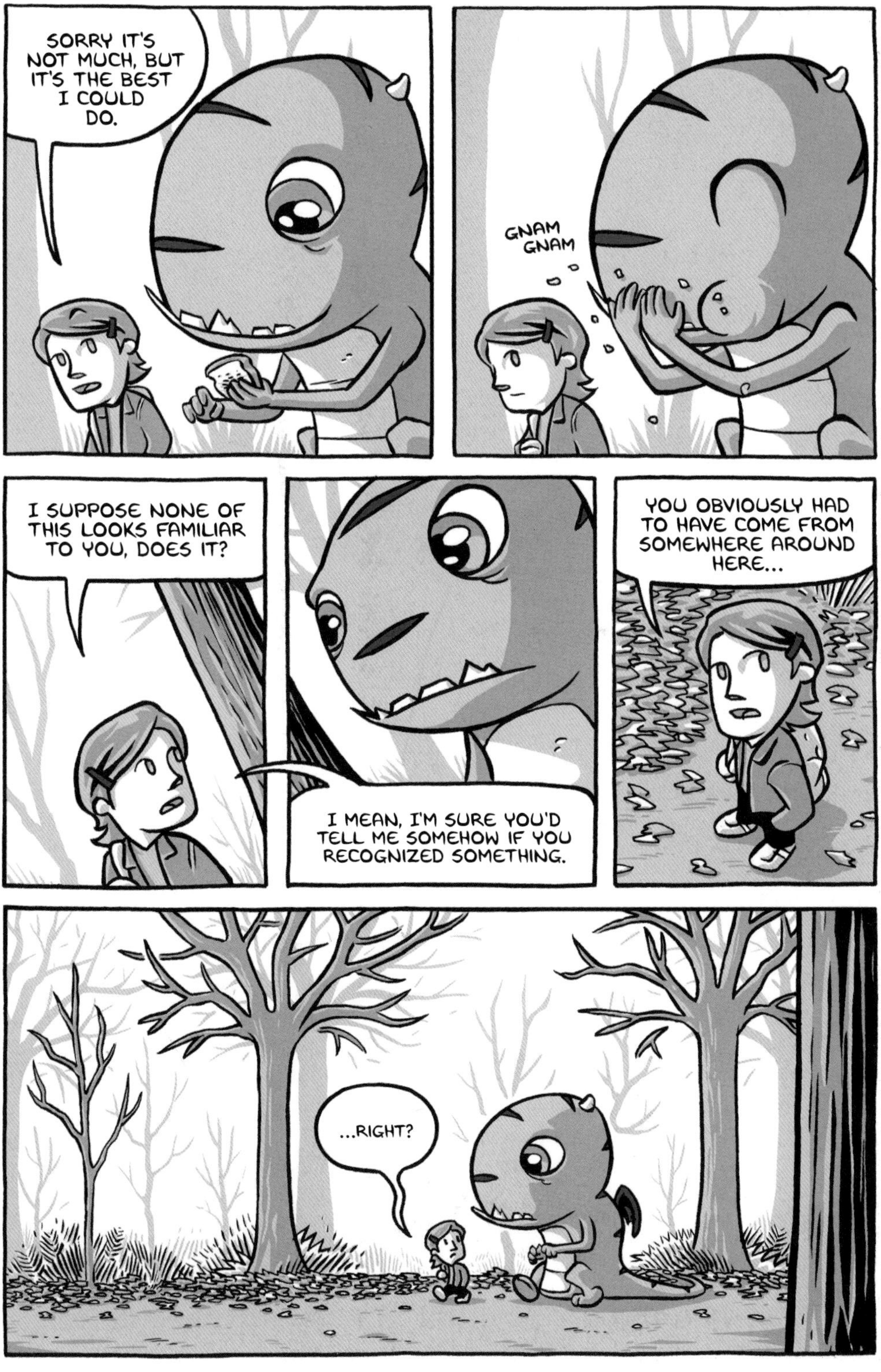
SORRY IT'S NOT MUCH, BUT IT'S THE BEST I COULD DO.
GNAM GNAM
I SUPPOSE NONE OF THIS LOOKS FAMILIAR TO YOU, DOES IT?
I MEAN, I'M SURE YOU'D TELL ME SOMEHOW IF YOU RECOGNIZED SOMETHING.
YOU OBVIOUSLY HAD TO HAVE COME FROM SOMEWHERE AROUND HERE...
...RIGHT?

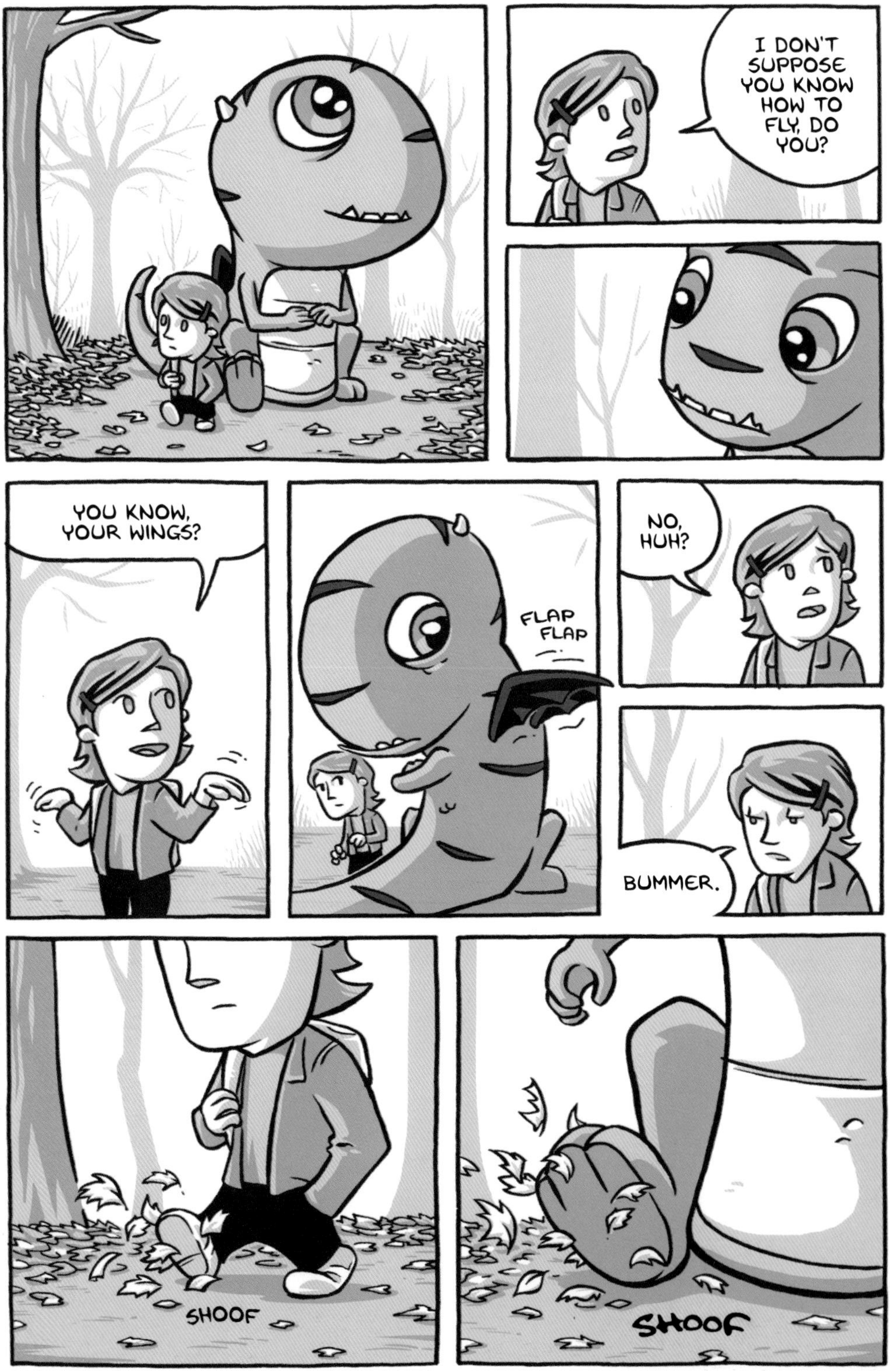
I DON'T SUPPOSE YOU KNOW HOW TO FLY, DO YOU?
YOU KNOW, YOUR WINGS?
FLAP FLAP
NO, HUH?
BUMMER.
SHOOF
SHOOF

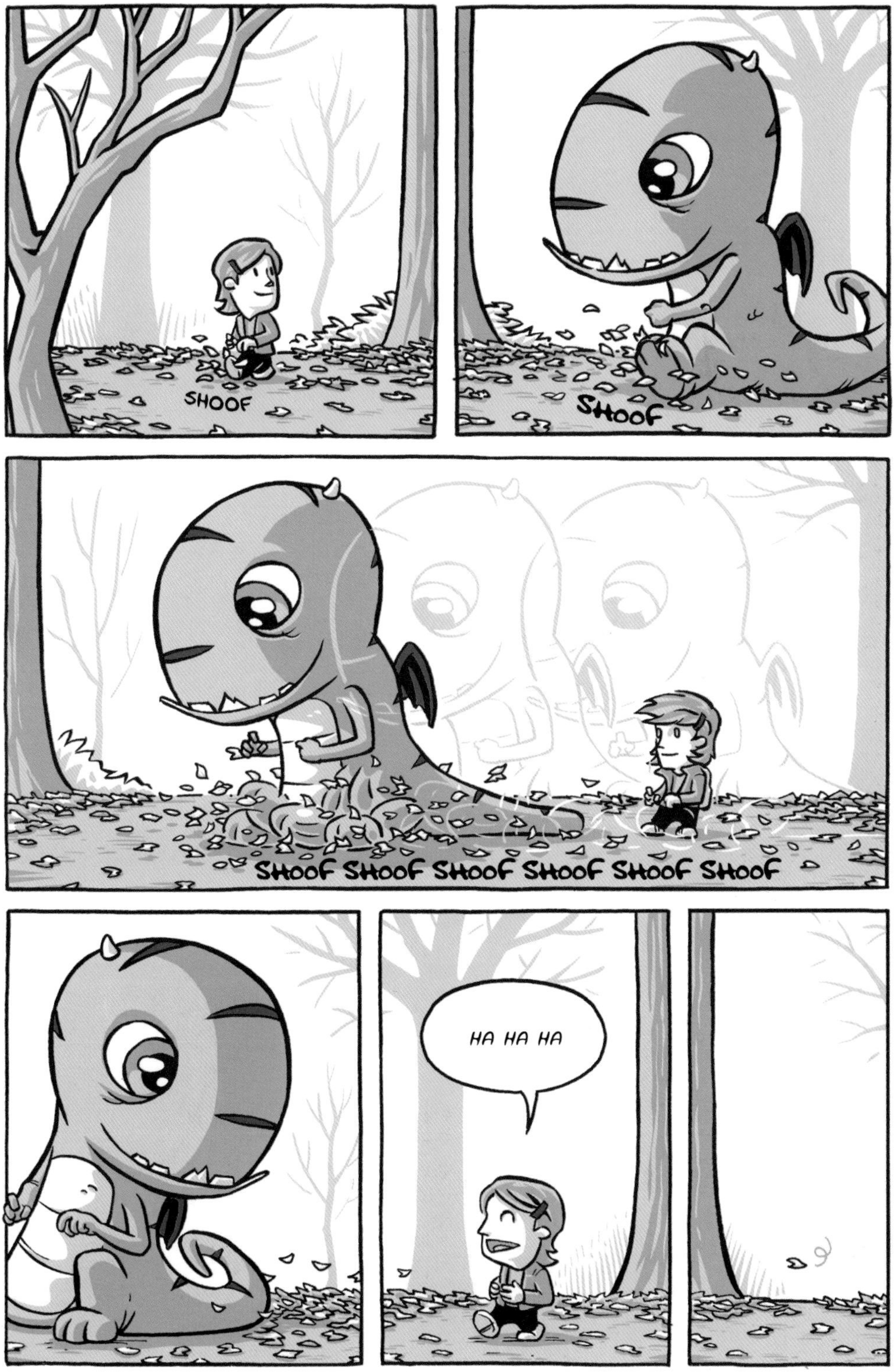
SHOOF
SHOOF
SHOOF SHOOF SHOOF SHOOF SHOOF SHOOF
HA HA HA

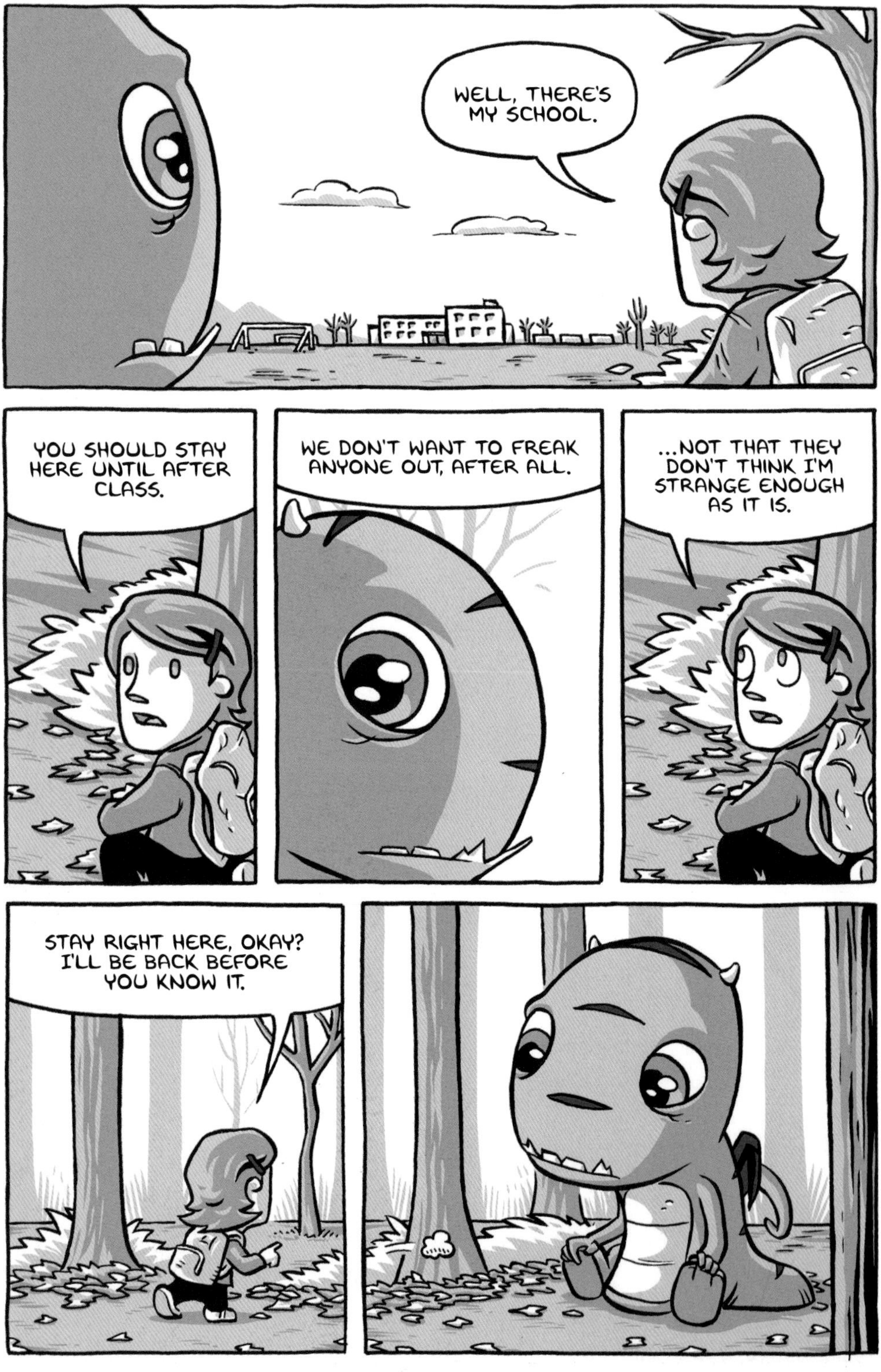
WELL, THERE'S MY SCHOOL.
YOU SHOULD STAY HERE UNTIL AFTER CLASS.
WE DON'T WANT TO FREAK ANYONE OUT, AFTER ALL.
...NOT THAT THEY DON'T THINK I'M STRANGE ENOUGH AS IT IS.
STAY RIGHT HERE, OKAY? I'LL BE BACK BEFORE YOU KNOW IT.

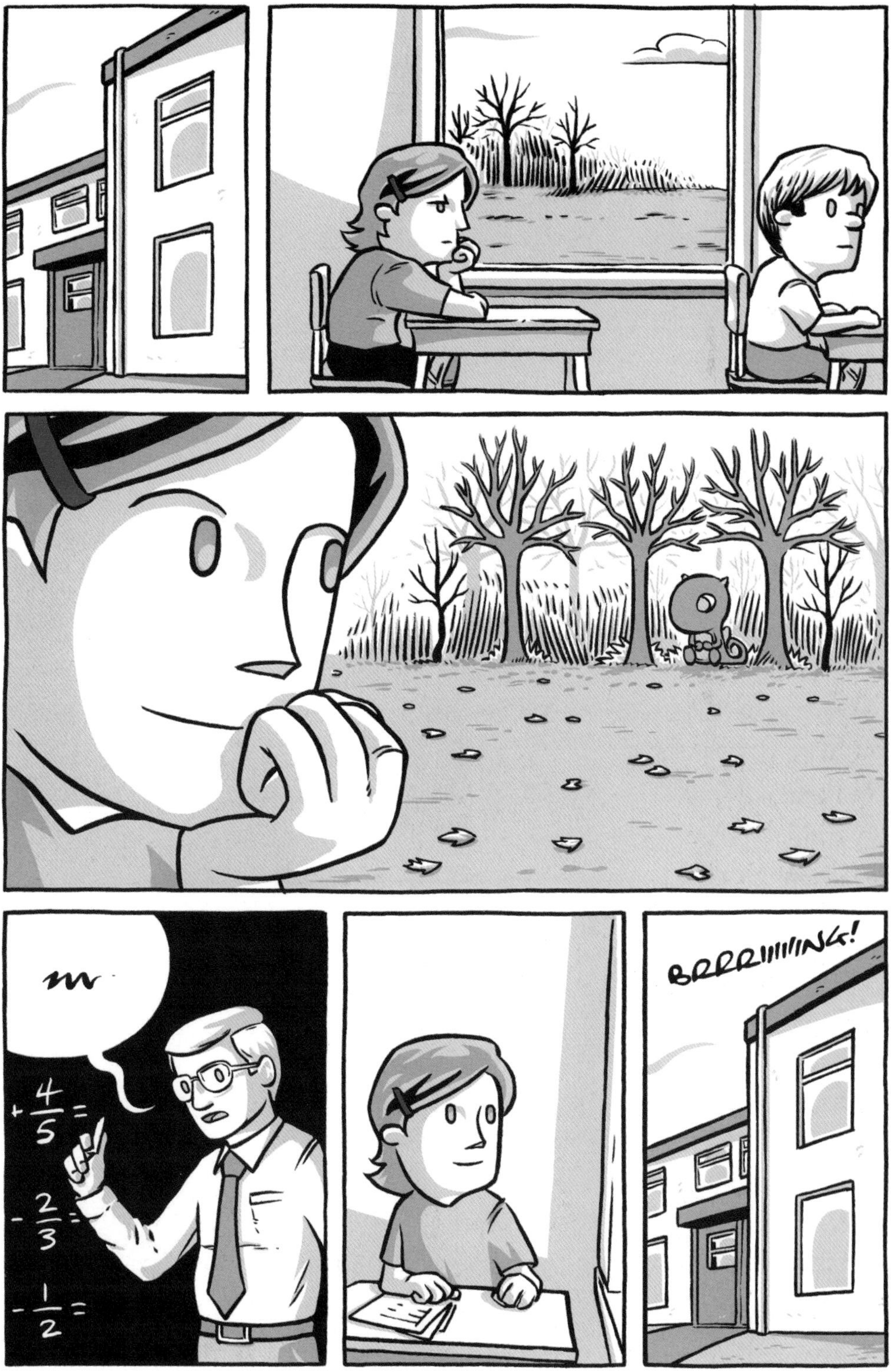
+ 4/5 =
- 2/3 =
- 1/2 =
BRRRIIIIING!

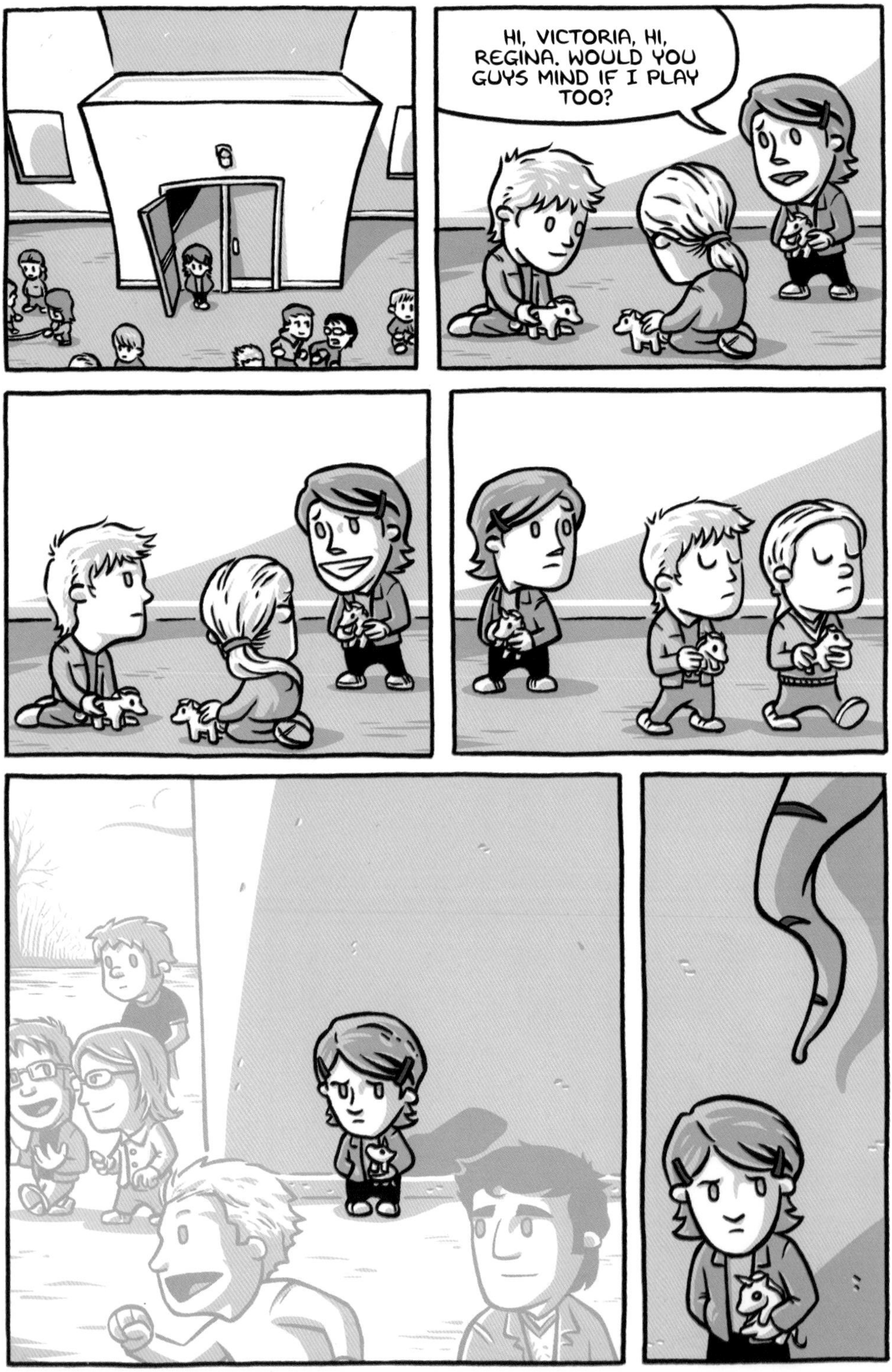
HI, VICTORIA, HI, REGINA. WOULD YOU GUYS MIND IF I PLAY TOO?

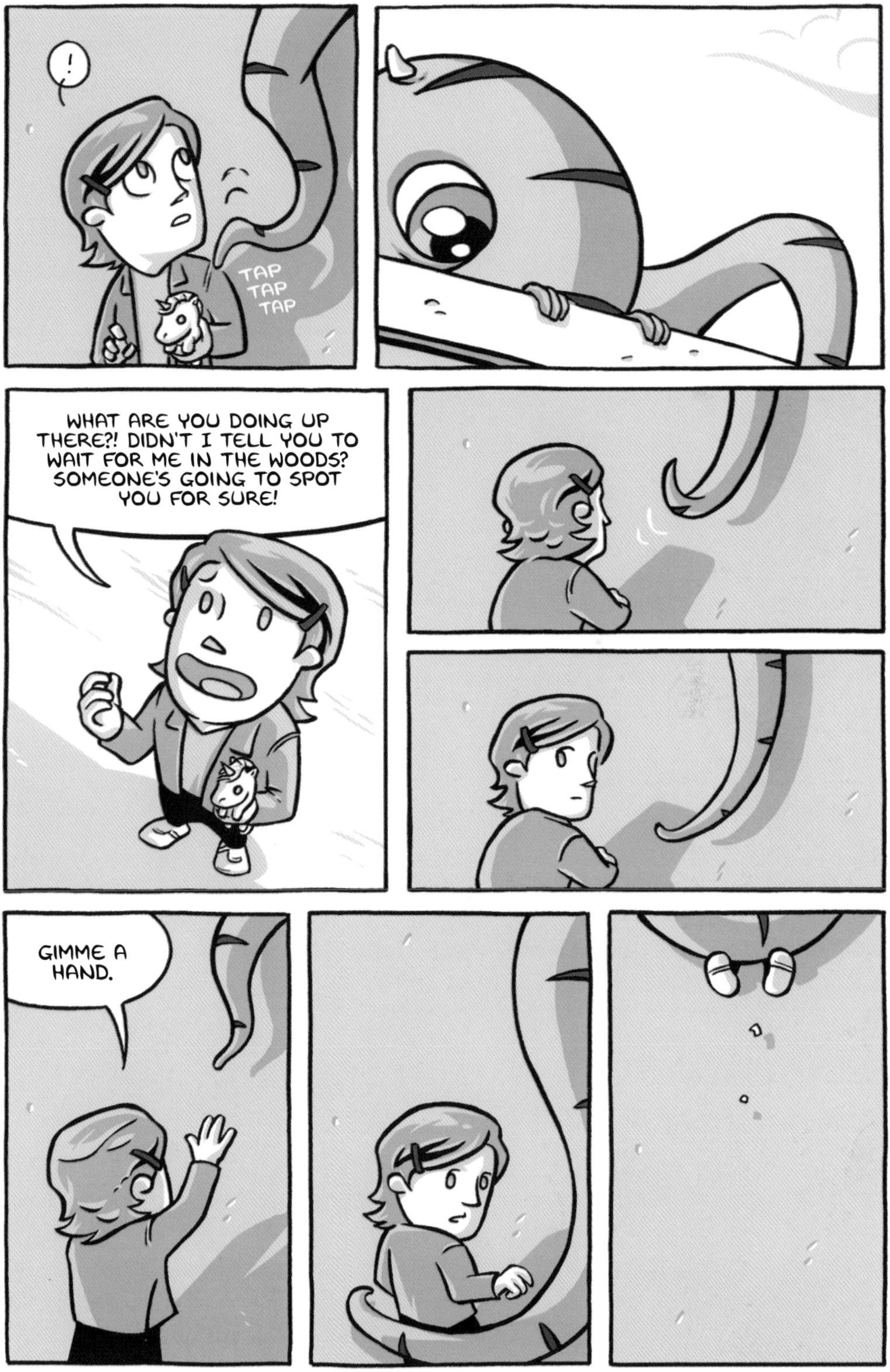
!
TAP TAP TAP
WHAT ARE YOU DOING UP THERE?! DIDN'T I TELL YOU TO WAIT FOR ME IN THE WOODS? SOMEONE'S GOING TO SPOT YOU FOR SURE!
GIMME A HAND.

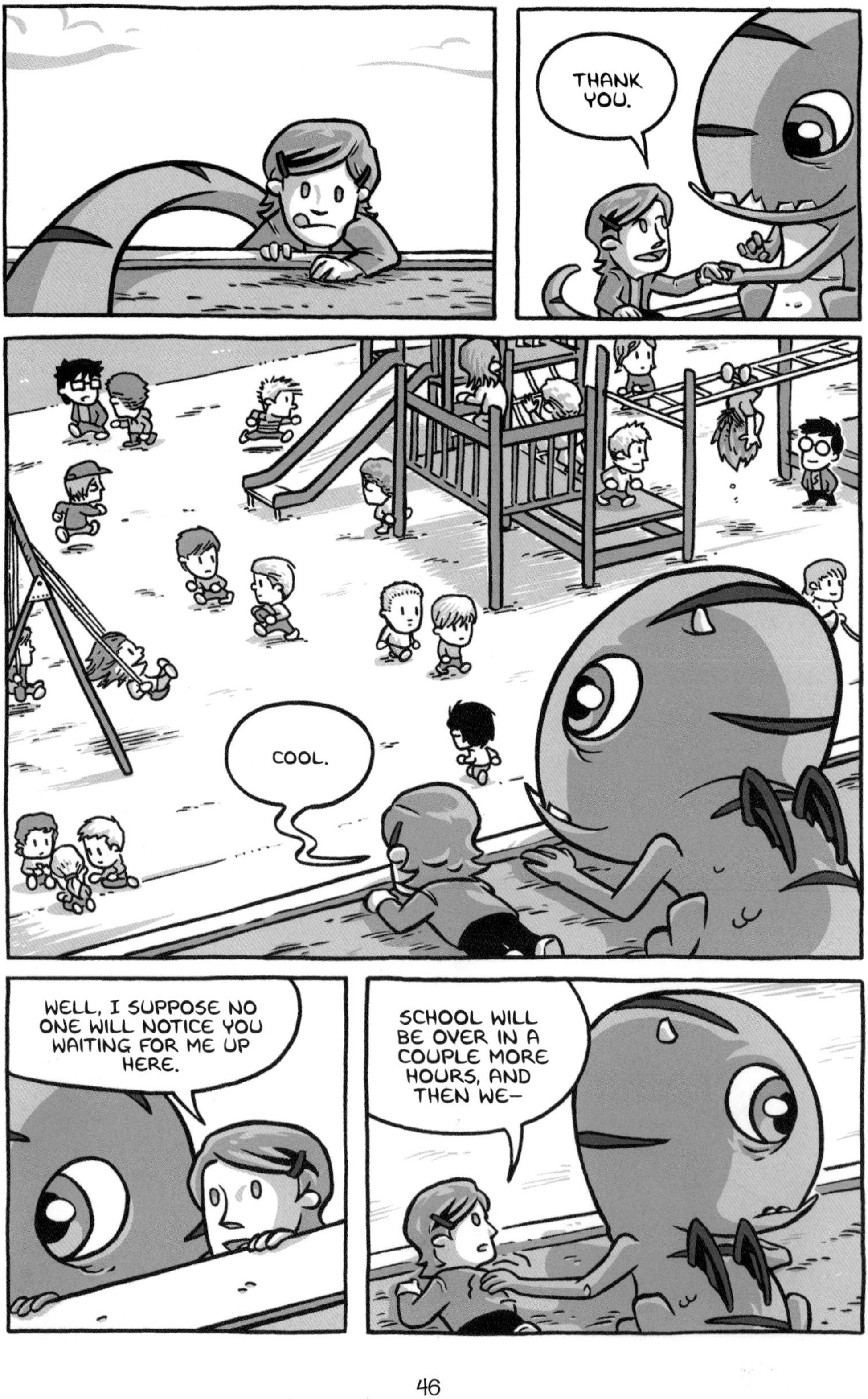
THANK YOU.
COOL.
WELL, I SUPPOSE NO ONE WILL NOTICE YOU WAITING FOR ME UP HERE.
SCHOOL WILL BE OVER IN A COUPLE MORE HOURS, AND THEN WE–

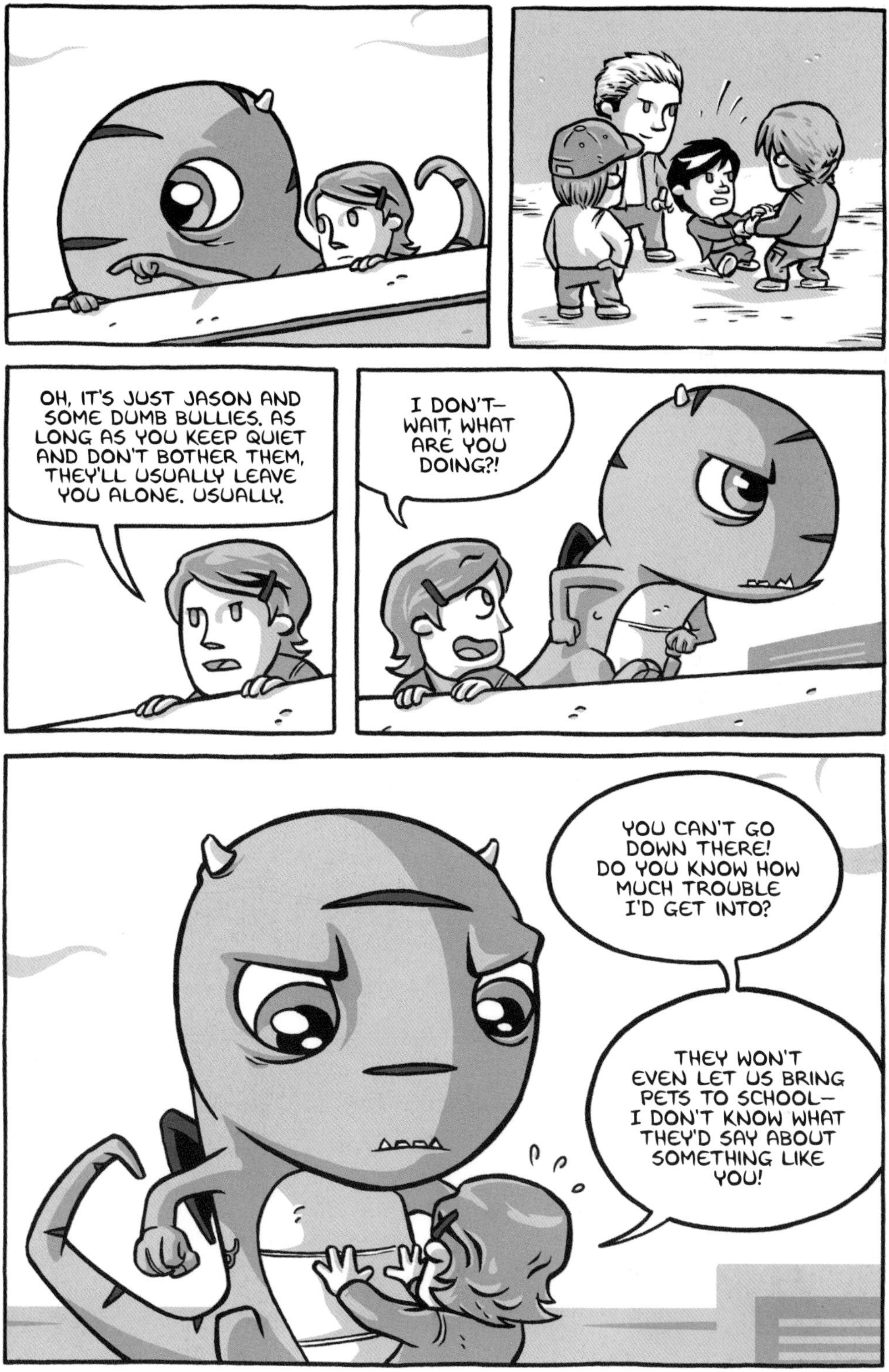
OH, IT'S JUST JASON AND SOME DUMB BULLIES. AS LONG AS YOU KEEP QUIET AND DON'T BOTHER THEM, THEY'LL USUALLY LEAVE YOU ALONE. USUALLY.
I DON'T— WAIT, WHAT ARE YOU DOING?!
YOU CAN'T GO DOWN THERE! DO YOU KNOW HOW MUCH TROUBLE I'D GET INTO?
THEY WON'T EVEN LET US BRING PETS TO SCHOOL— I DON'T KNOW WHAT THEY'D SAY ABOUT SOMETHING LIKE YOU!

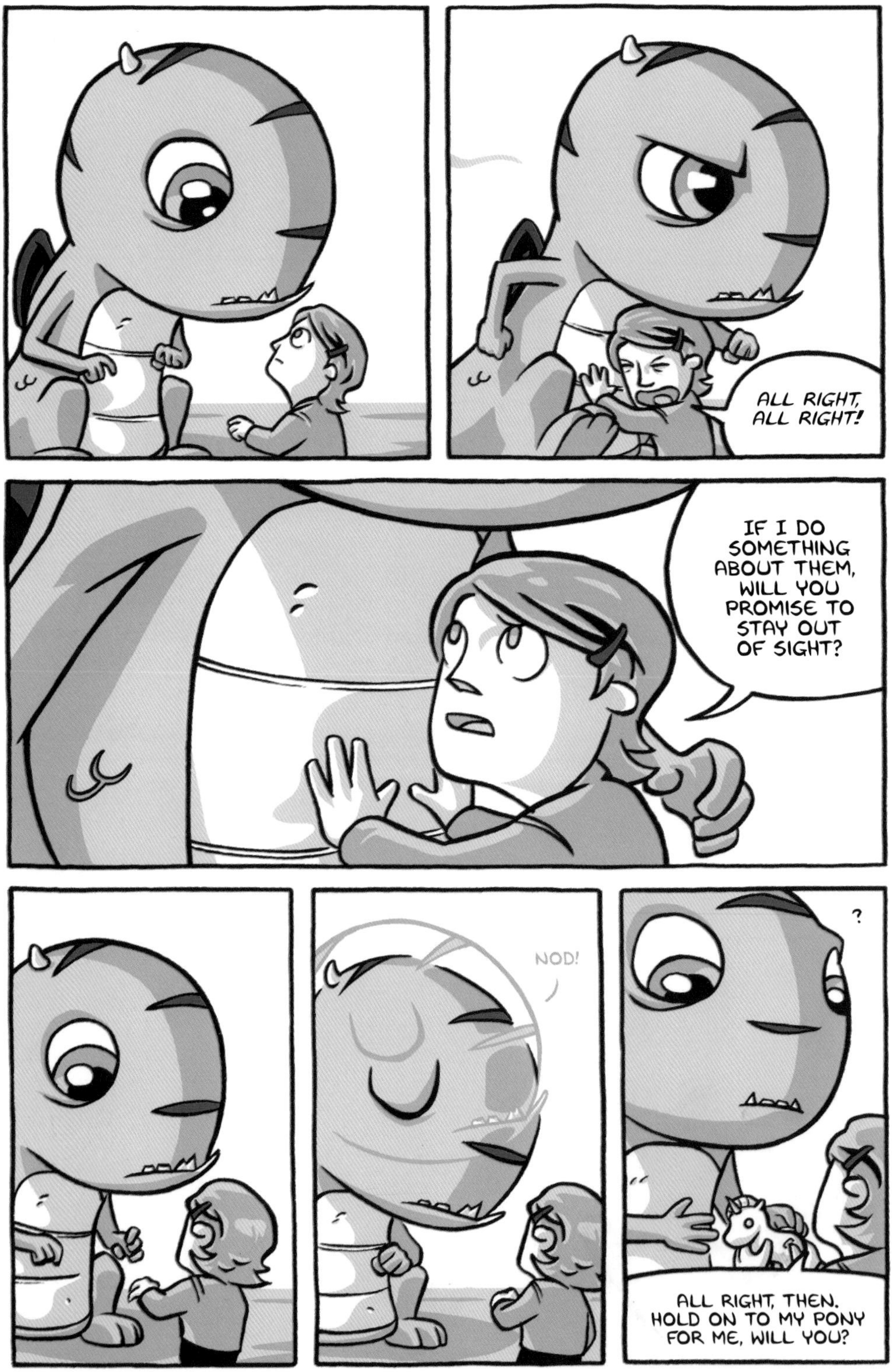
ALL RIGHT, ALL RIGHT!
IF I DO SOMETHING ABOUT THEM, WILL YOU PROMISE TO STAY OUT OF SIGHT?
NOD!
?
ALL RIGHT, THEN. HOLD ON TO MY PONY FOR ME, WILL YOU?

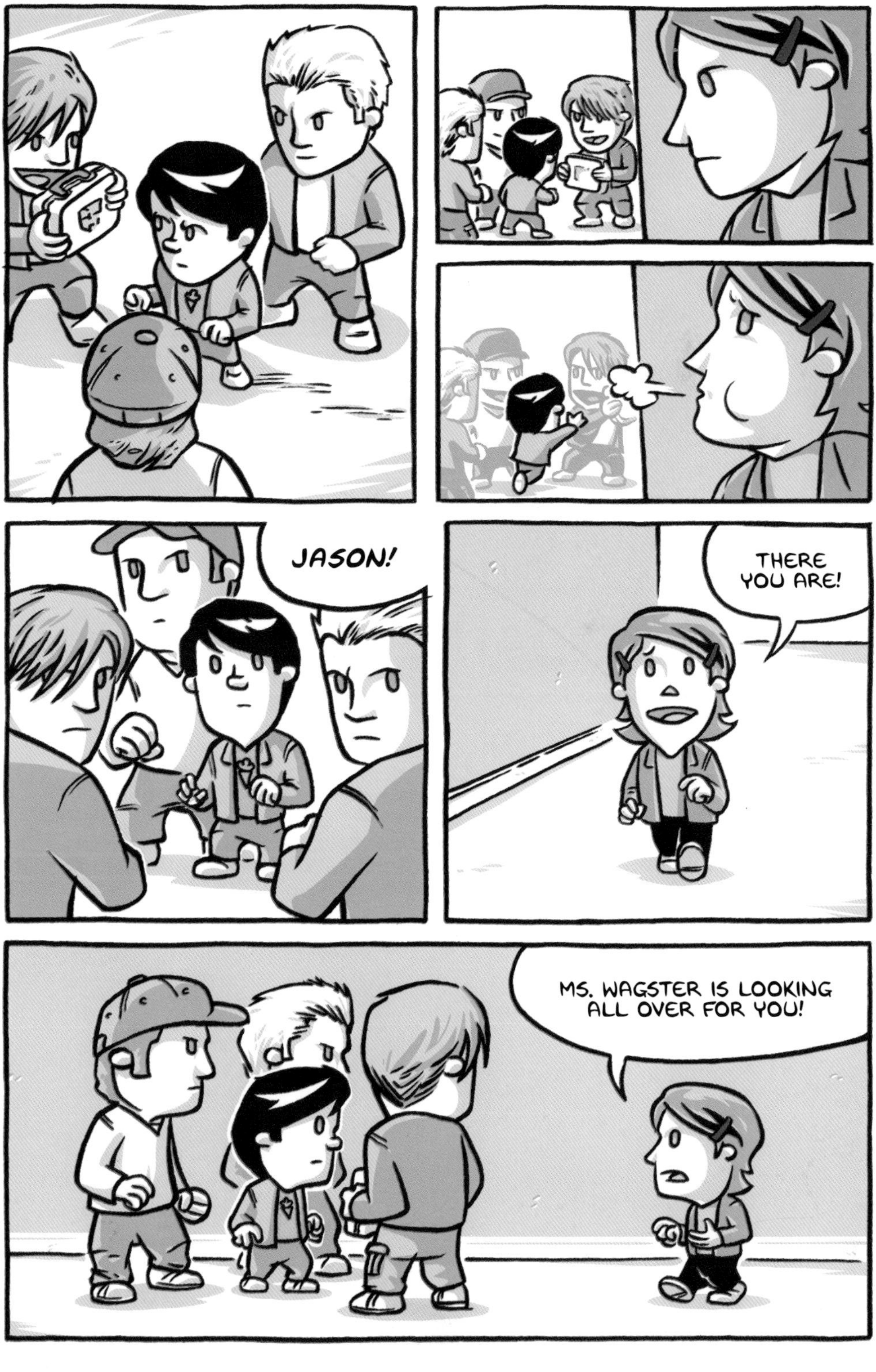
JASON!
THERE YOU ARE!
MS. WAGSTER IS LOOKING ALL OVER FOR YOU!

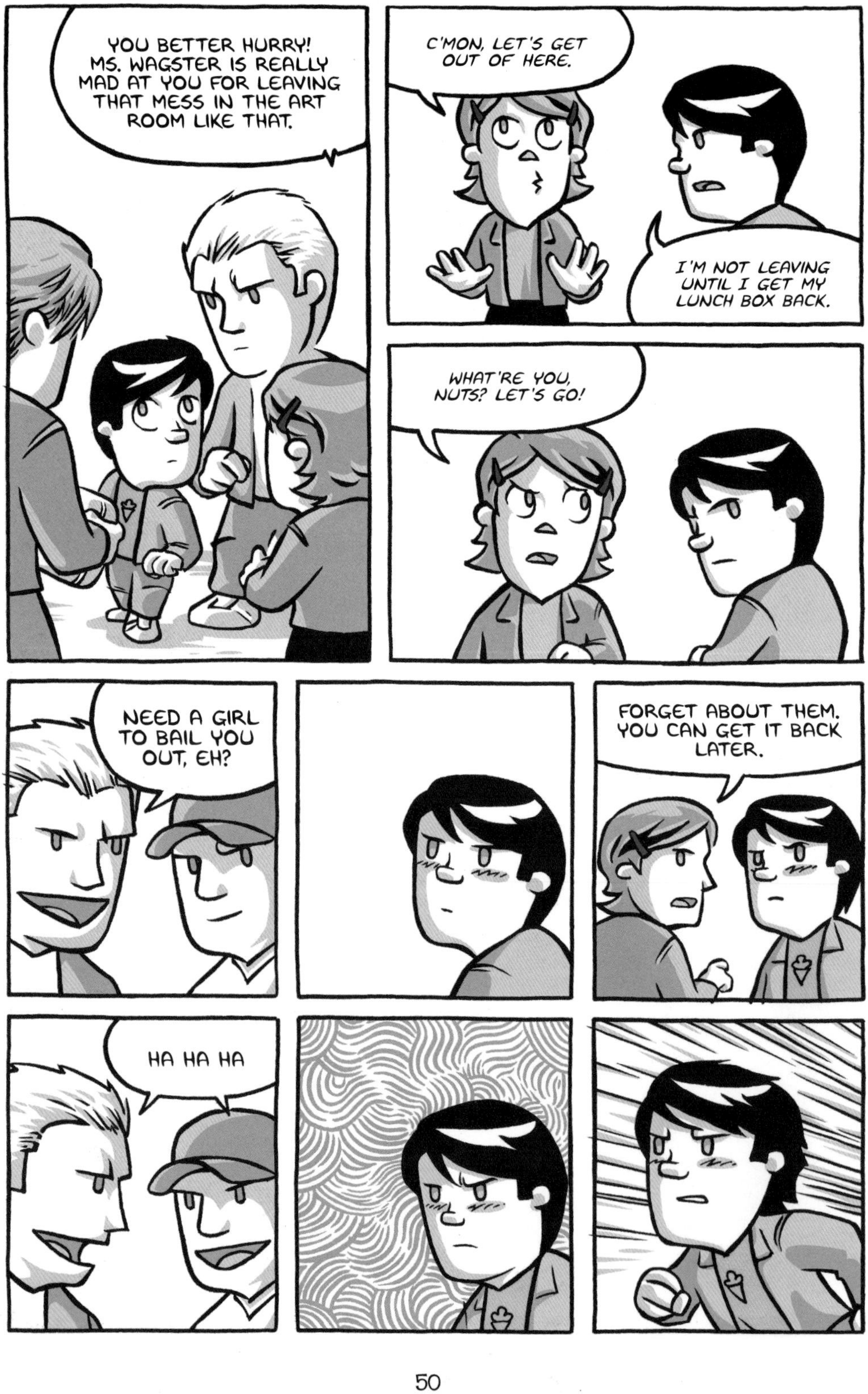
YOU BETTER HURRY! MS. WAGSTER IS REALLY MAD AT YOU FOR LEAVING THAT MESS IN THE ART ROOM LIKE THAT.
C'MON, LET'S GET OUT OF HERE.
I'M NOT LEAVING UNTIL I GET MY LUNCH BOX BACK.
WHAT'RE YOU, NUTS? LET'S GO!
NEED A GIRL TO BAIL YOU OUT, EH?
FORGET ABOUT THEM. YOU CAN GET IT BACK LATER.
HA HA HA

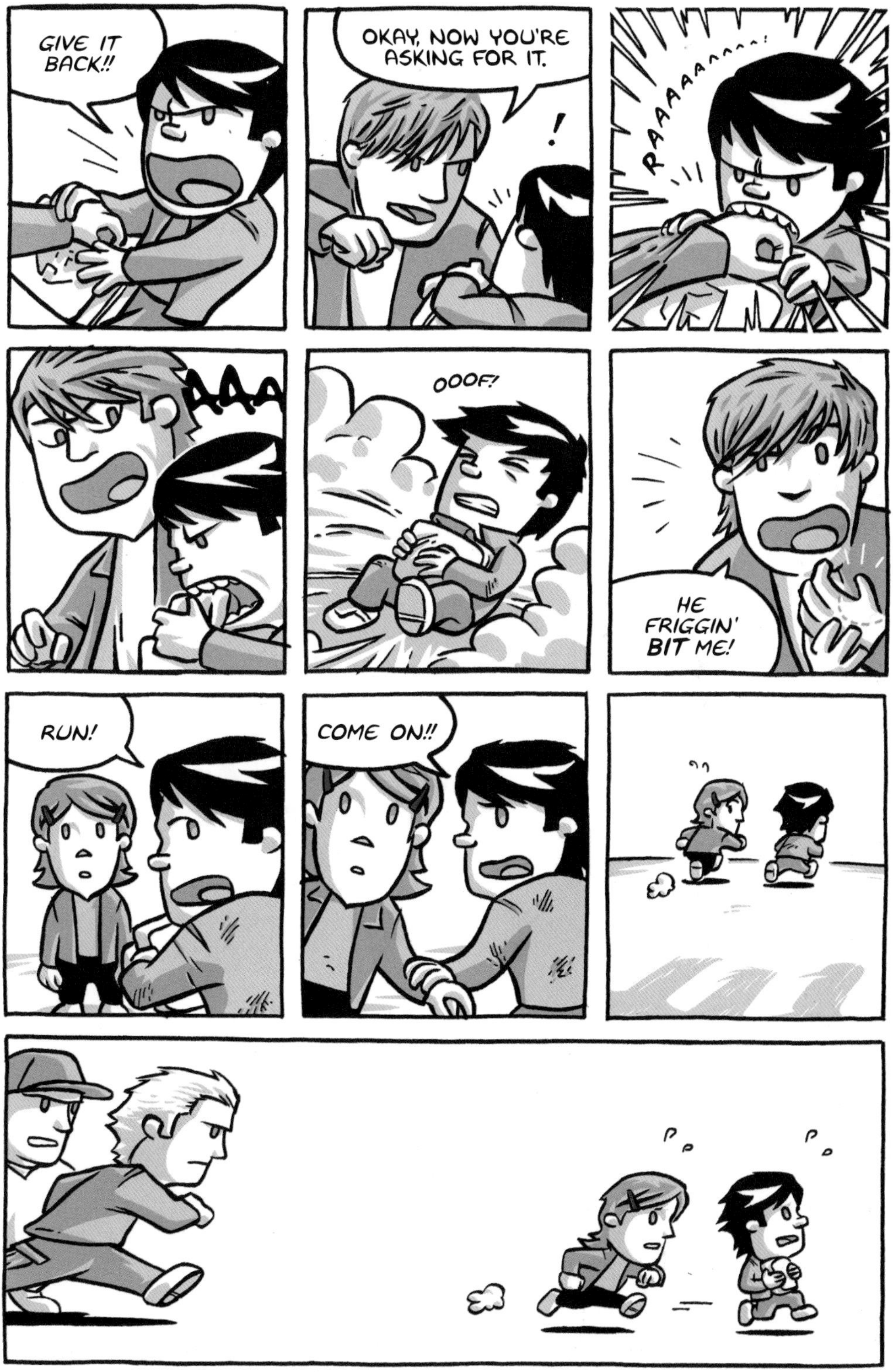
GIVE IT BACK!!
OKAY, NOW YOU'RE ASKING FOR IT.
!
RAAAAAAAAAA!
AAA
OOOF!
HE FRIGGIN' BIT ME!
RUN!
COME ON!!

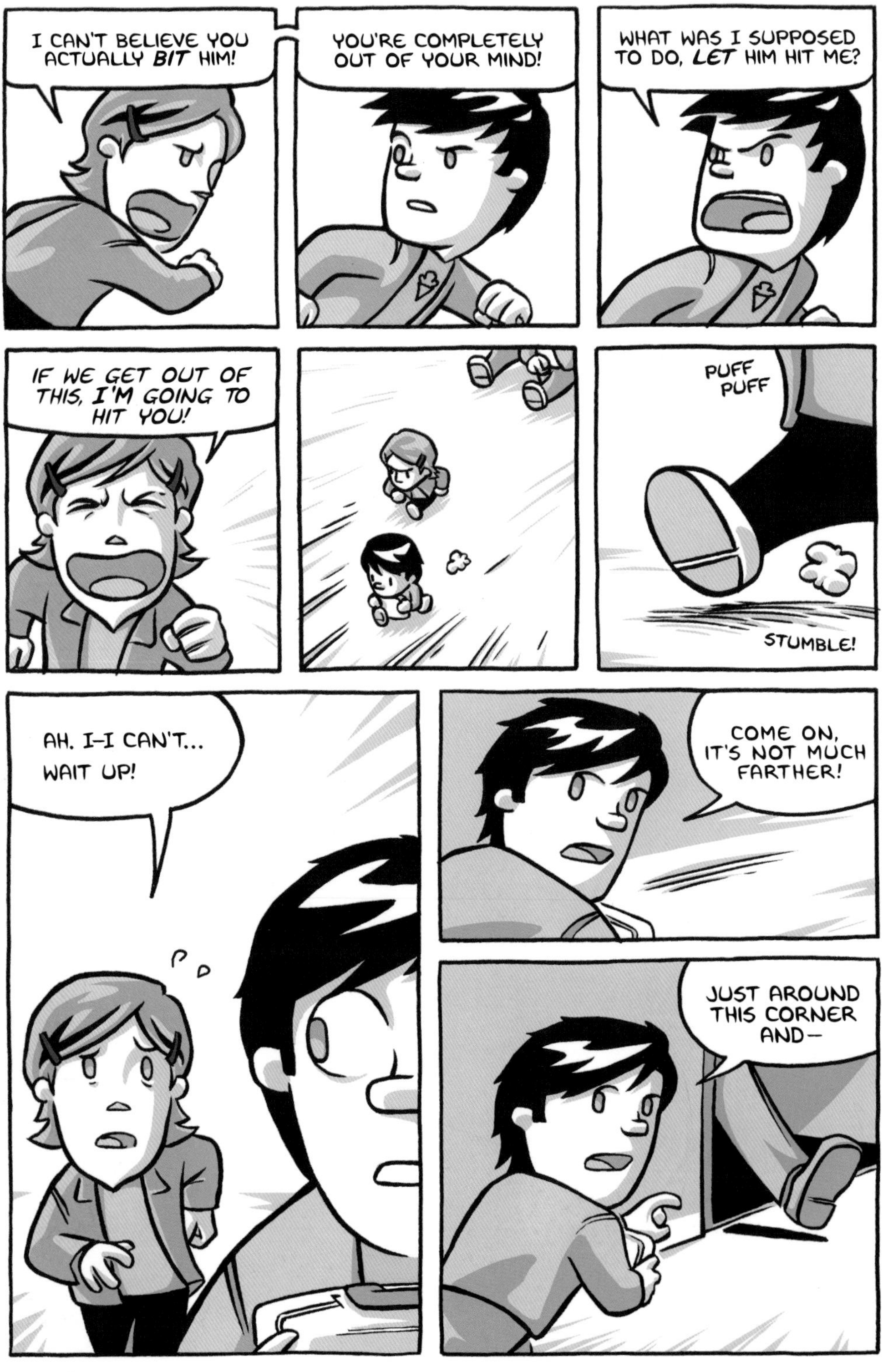
I CAN'T BELIEVE YOU ACTUALLY *BIT* HIM!
YOU'RE COMPLETELY OUT OF YOUR MIND!
WHAT WAS I SUPPOSED TO DO, *LET* HIM HIT ME?
IF WE GET OUT OF THIS, I'M GOING TO HIT YOU!
PUFF
PUFF
STUMBLE!
AH. I-I CAN'T...
WAIT UP!
COME ON, IT'S NOT MUCH FARTHER!
JUST AROUND THIS CORNER AND—

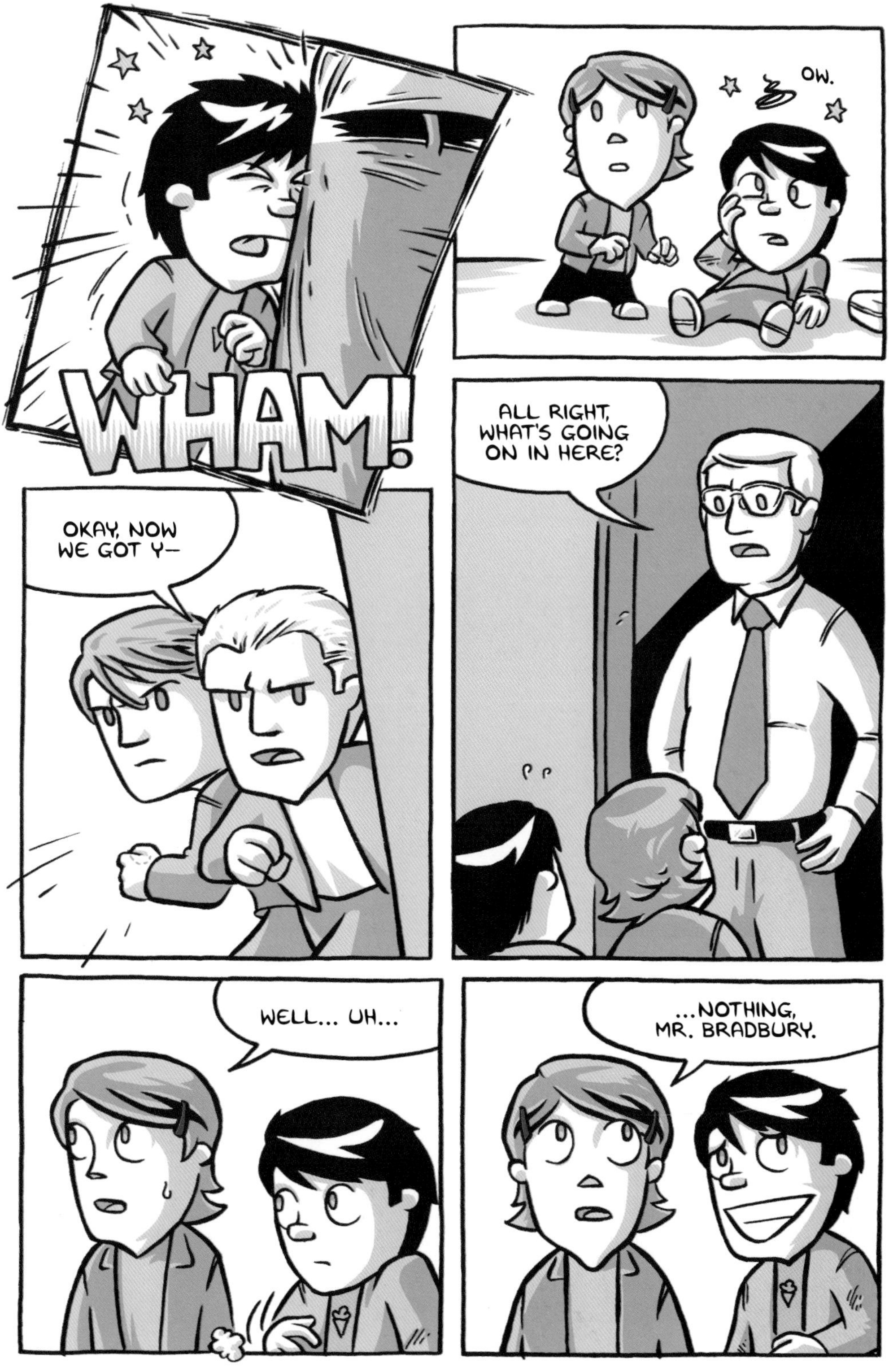
WHAM!
OW.
OKAY, NOW WE GOT Y—
ALL RIGHT, WHAT'S GOING ON IN HERE?
WELL... UH...
...NOTHING, MR. BRADBURY.

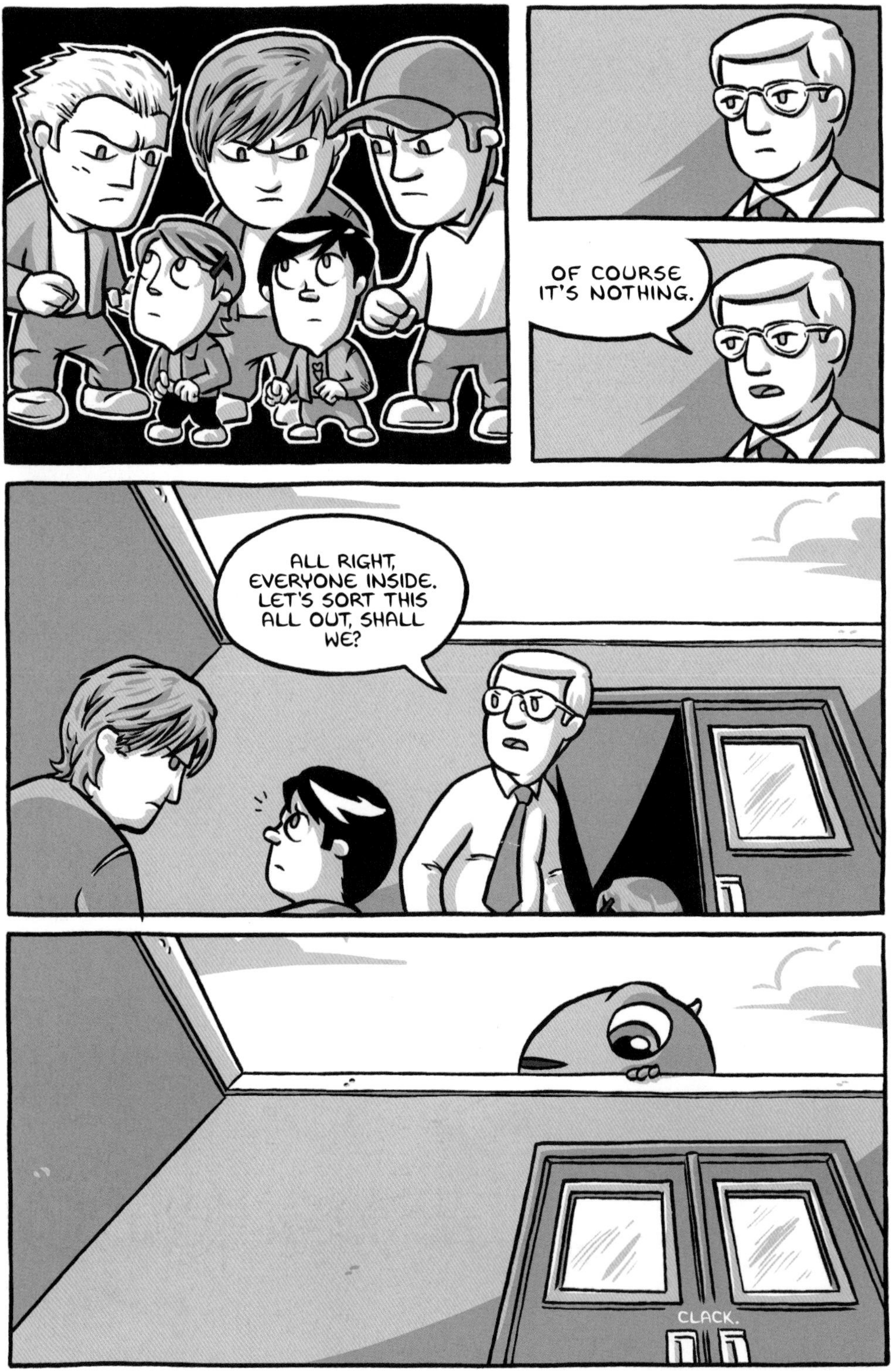
OF COURSE IT'S NOTHING.
ALL RIGHT, EVERYONE INSIDE. LET'S SORT THIS ALL OUT, SHALL WE?
CLACK.

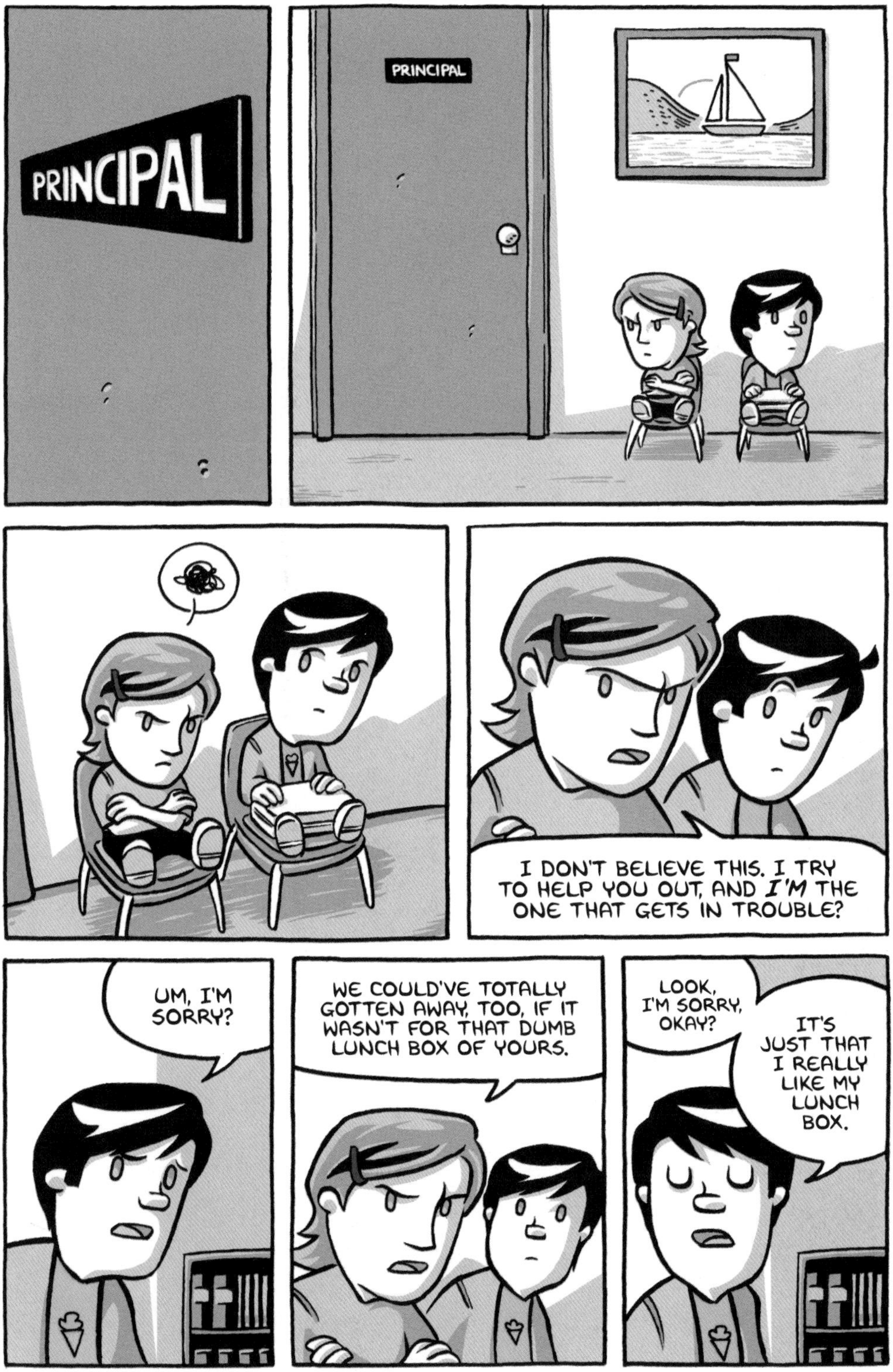
PRINCIPAL
PRINCIPAL
I DON'T BELIEVE THIS. I TRY TO HELP YOU OUT, AND *I'M* THE ONE THAT GETS IN TROUBLE?
UM, I'M SORRY?
WE COULD'VE TOTALLY GOTTEN AWAY, TOO, IF IT WASN'T FOR THAT DUMB LUNCH BOX OF YOURS.
LOOK, I'M SORRY, OKAY?
IT'S JUST THAT I REALLY LIKE MY LUNCH BOX.

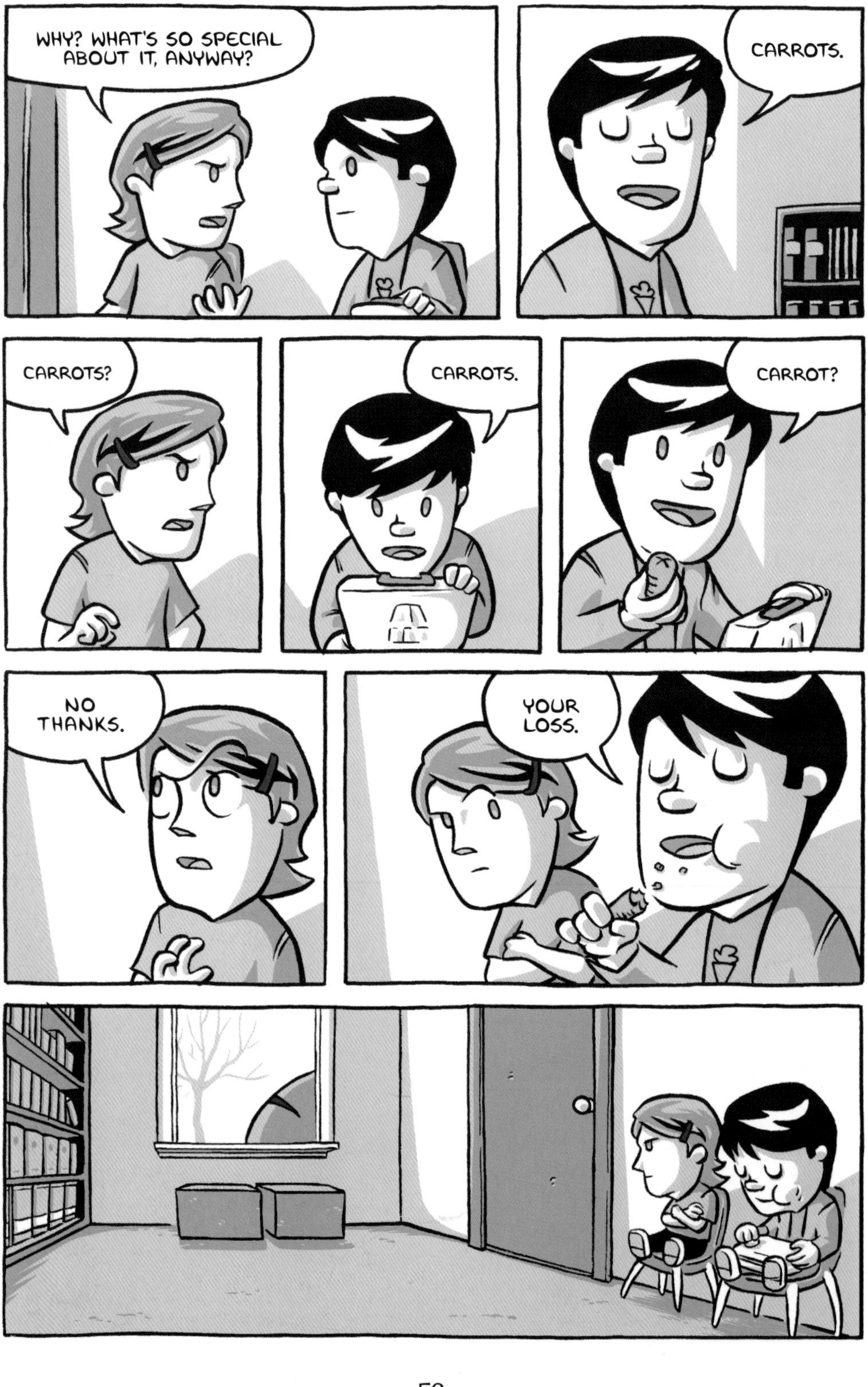
WHY? WHAT'S SO SPECIAL ABOUT IT, ANYWAY?
CARROTS.
CARROTS?
CARROTS.
CARROT?
NO THANKS.
YOUR LOSS.

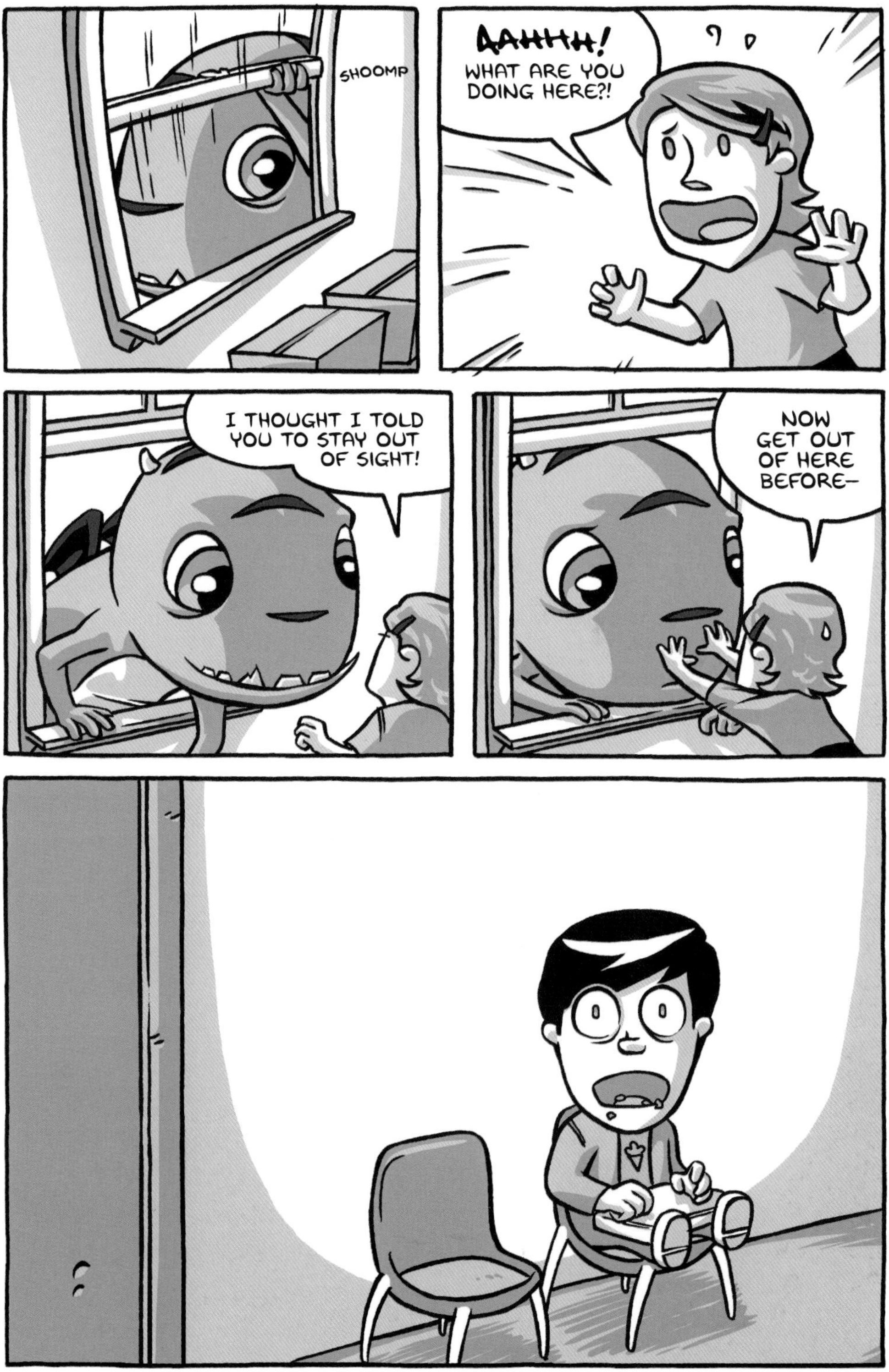
SHOOMP
AAHHH! WHAT ARE YOU DOING HERE?!
I THOUGHT I TOLD YOU TO STAY OUT OF SIGHT!
NOW GET OUT OF HERE BEFORE–

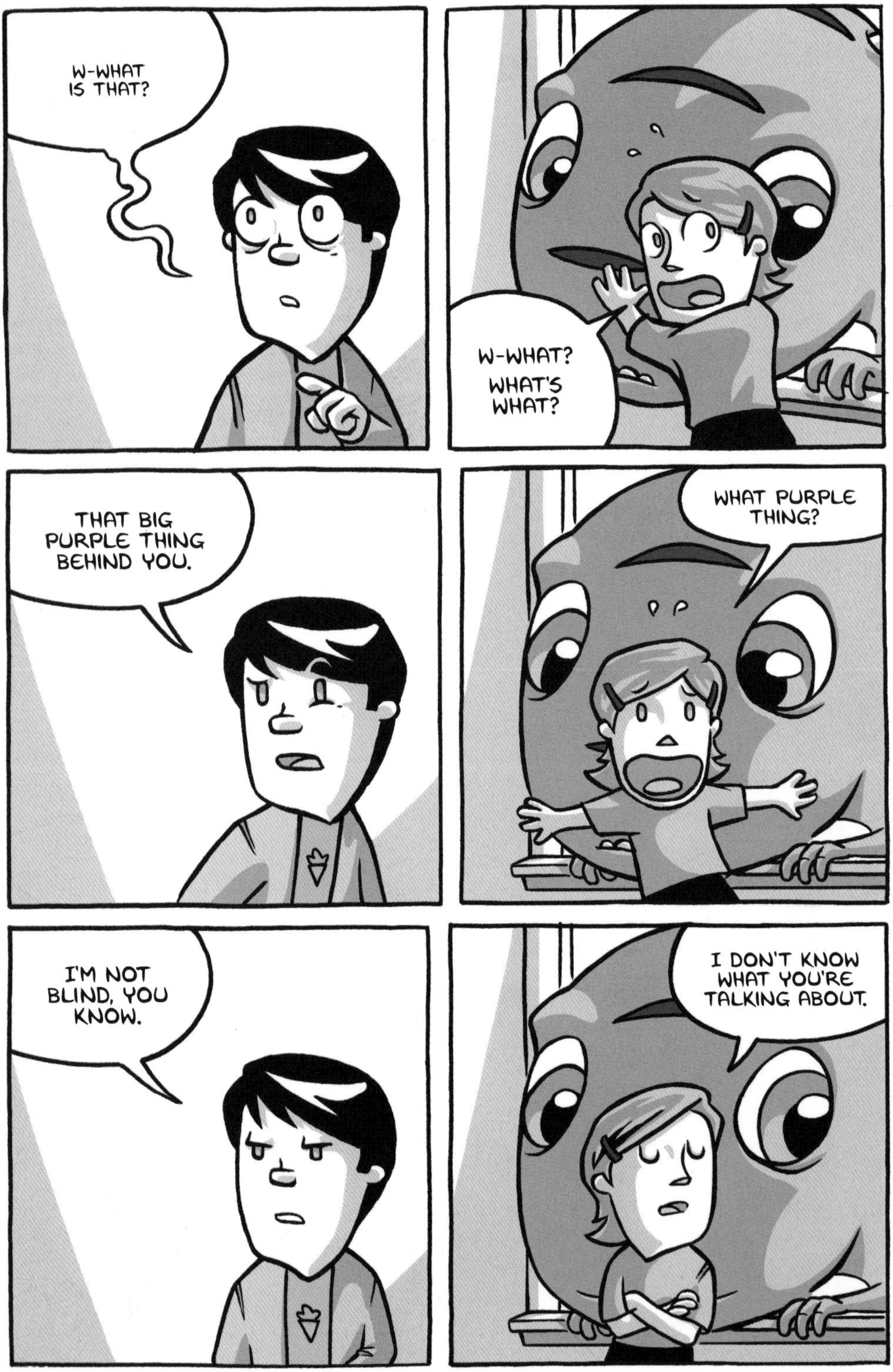
W-WHAT IS THAT?
W-WHAT? WHAT'S WHAT?
THAT BIG PURPLE THING BEHIND YOU.
WHAT PURPLE THING?
I'M NOT BLIND, YOU KNOW.
I DON'T KNOW WHAT YOU'RE TALKING ABOUT.

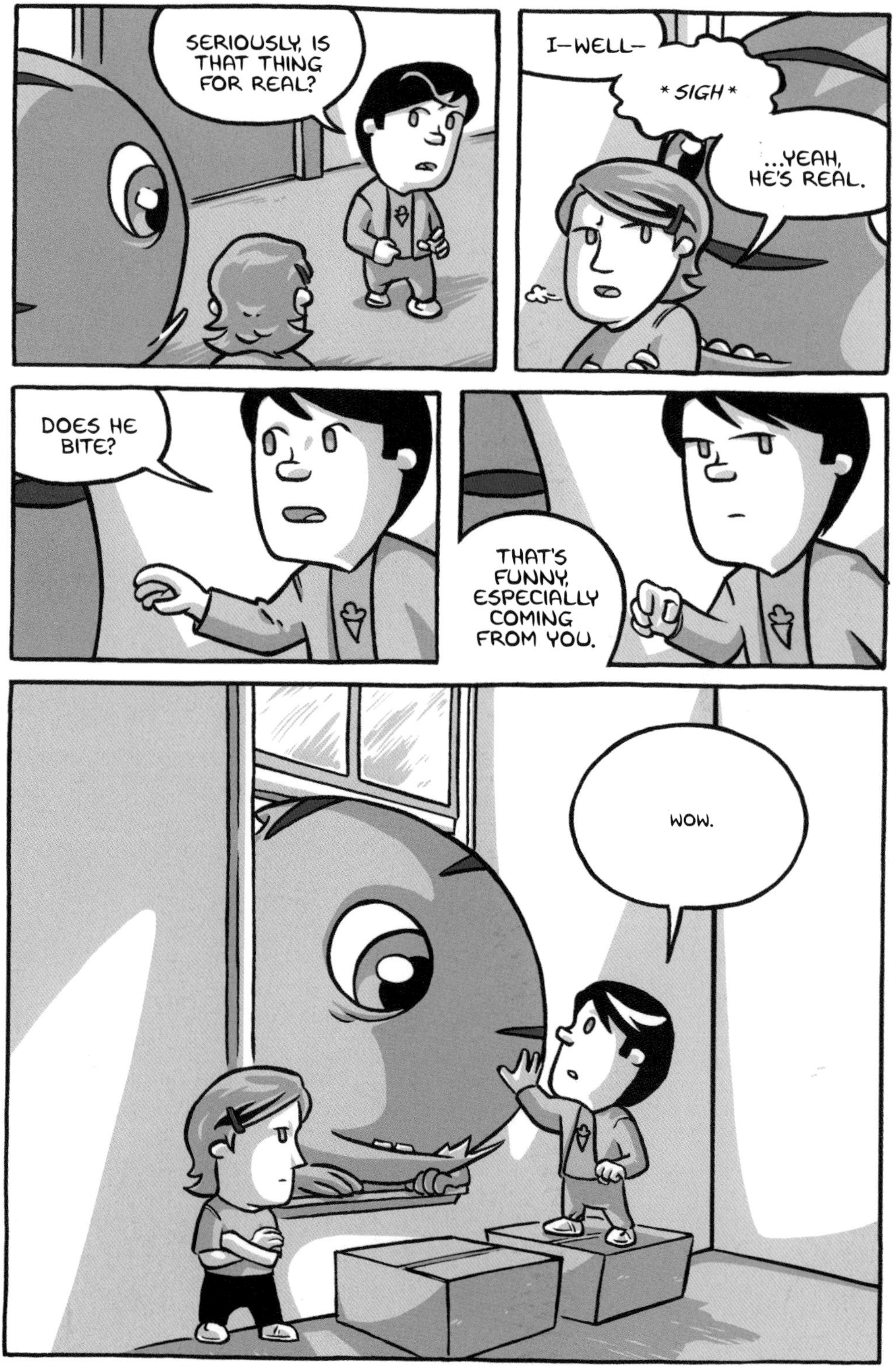
SERIOUSLY, IS THAT THING FOR REAL?
I—WELL—
* SIGH *
...YEAH, HE'S REAL.
DOES HE BITE?
THAT'S FUNNY, ESPECIALLY COMING FROM YOU.
WOW.

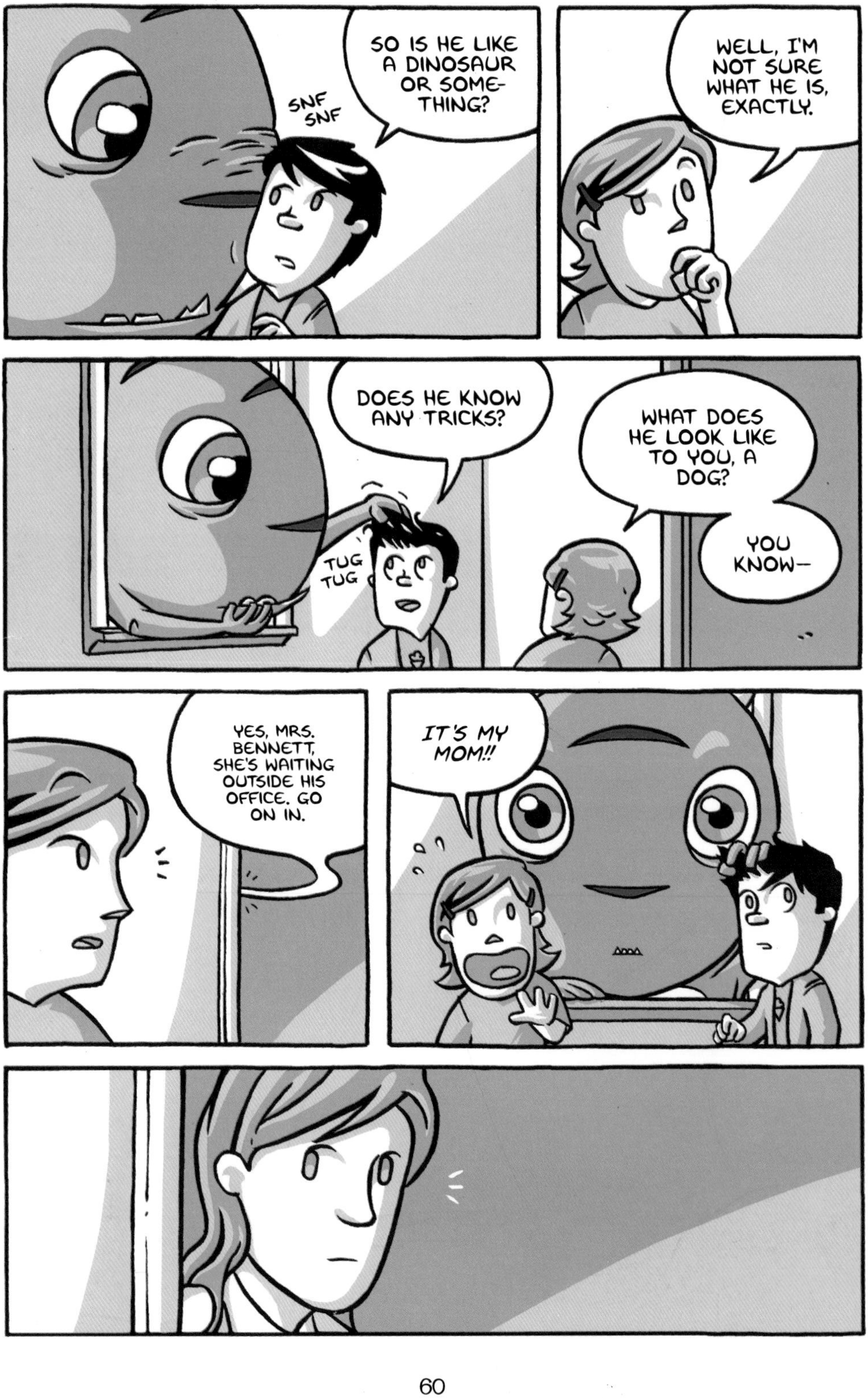
SNF SNF
SO IS HE LIKE A DINOSAUR OR SOME-THING?
WELL, I'M NOT SURE WHAT HE IS, EXACTLY.
DOES HE KNOW ANY TRICKS?
TUG TUG
WHAT DOES HE LOOK LIKE TO YOU, A DOG?
YOU KNOW—
YES, MRS. BENNETT, SHE'S WAITING OUTSIDE HIS OFFICE. GO ON IN.
IT'S MY MOM!!

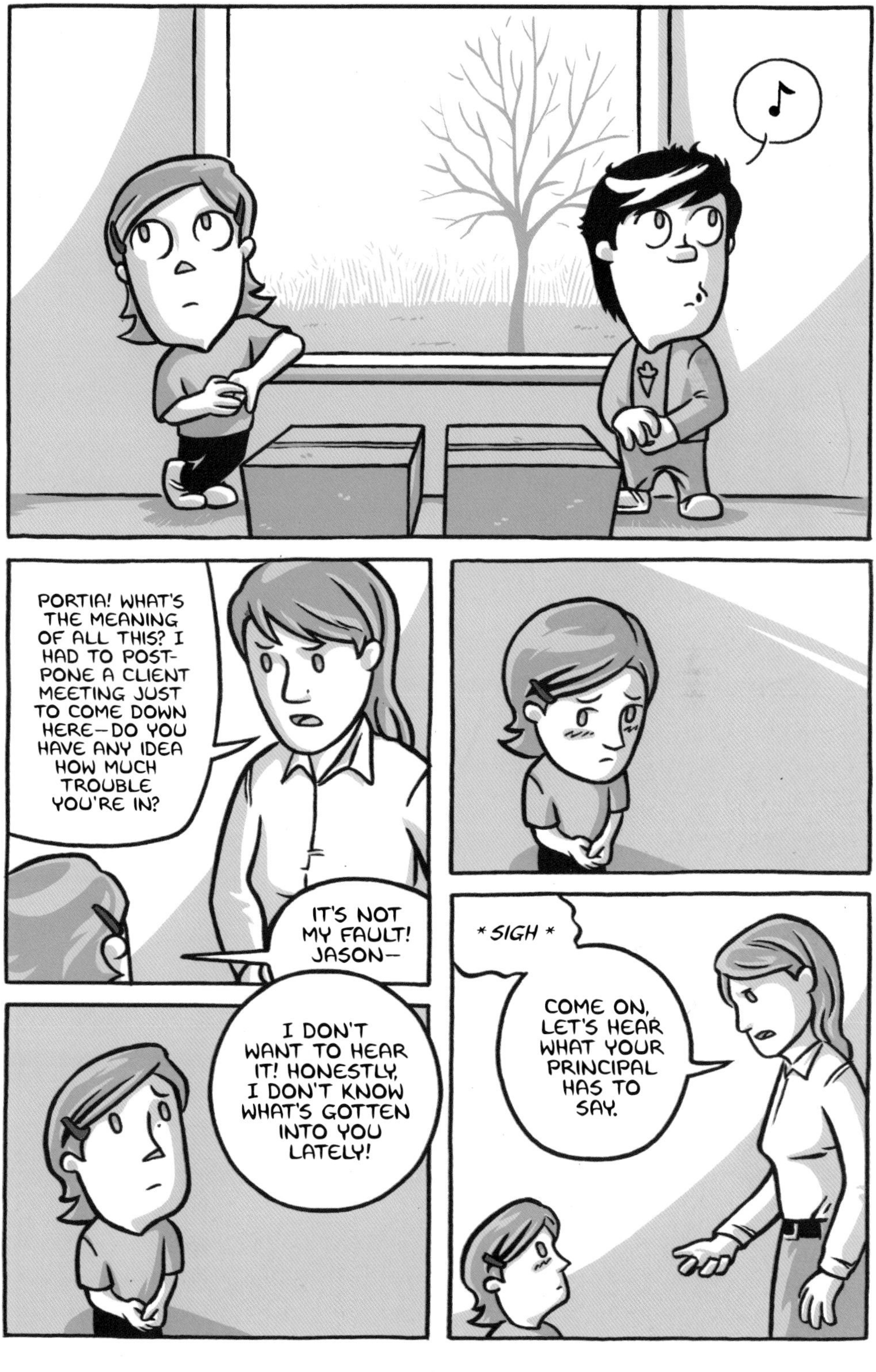
♪
PORTIA! WHAT'S THE MEANING OF ALL THIS? I HAD TO POST-PONE A CLIENT MEETING JUST TO COME DOWN HERE—DO YOU HAVE ANY IDEA HOW MUCH TROUBLE YOU'RE IN?
IT'S NOT MY FAULT! JASON—
I DON'T WANT TO HEAR IT! HONESTLY, I DON'T KNOW WHAT'S GOTTEN INTO YOU LATELY!
SIGH
COME ON, LET'S HEAR WHAT YOUR PRINCIPAL HAS TO SAY.

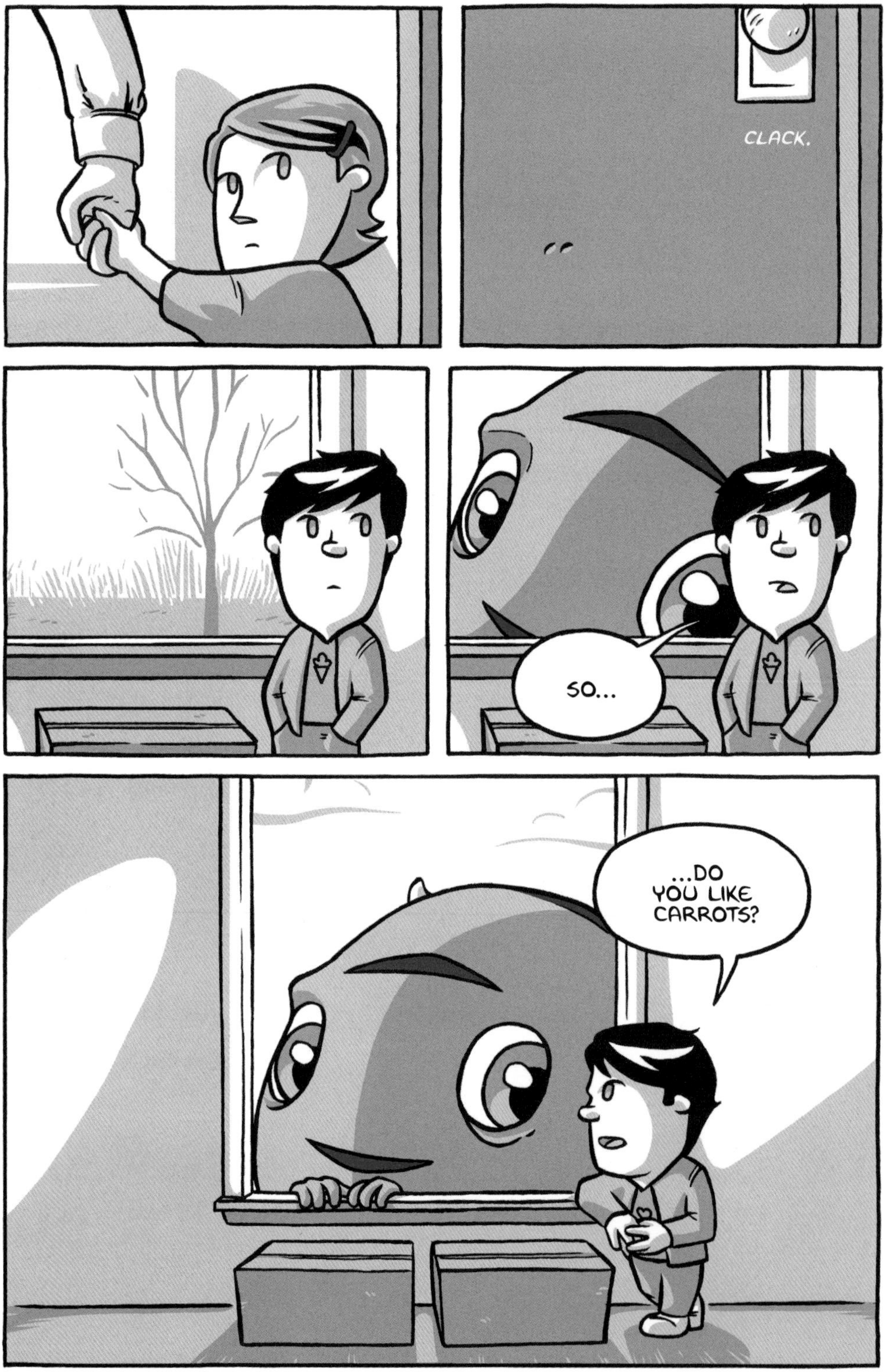
CLACK.
SO...
...DO YOU LIKE CARROTS?

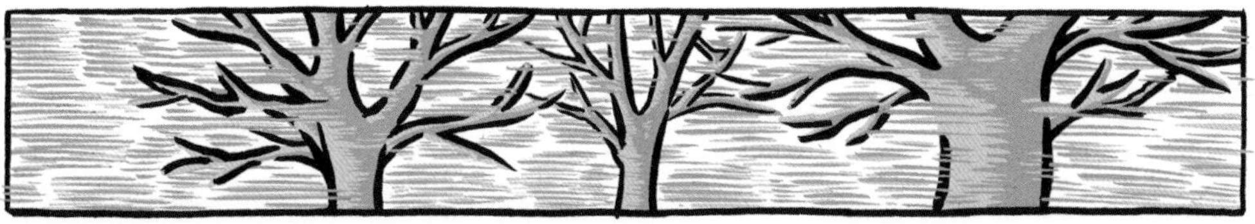

CHAPTER THREE

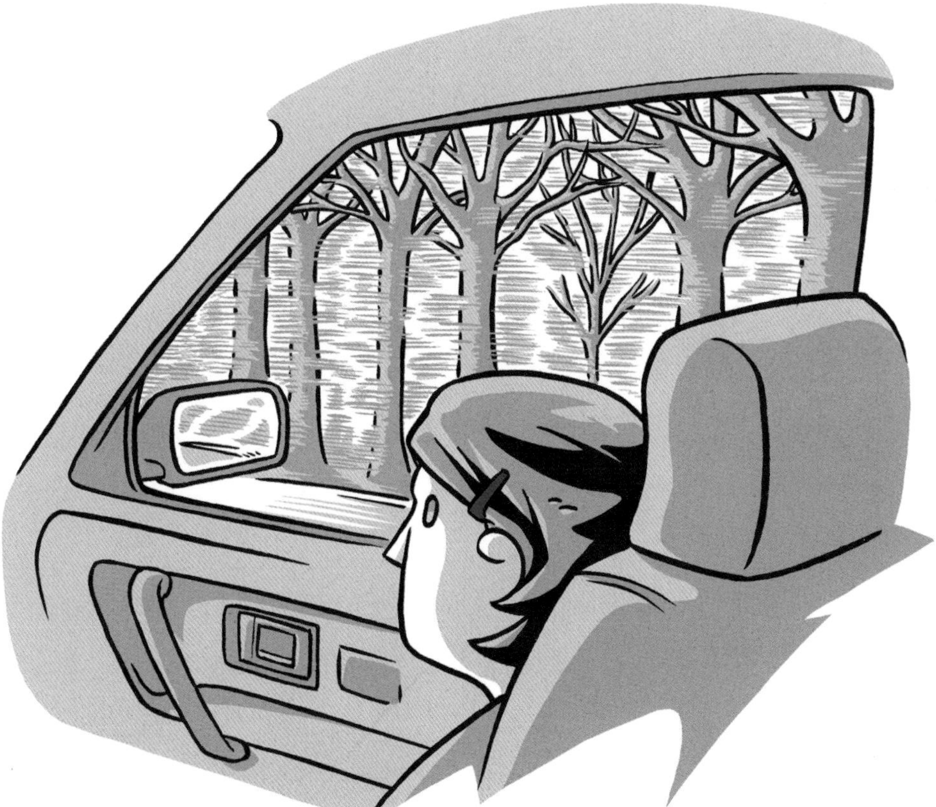

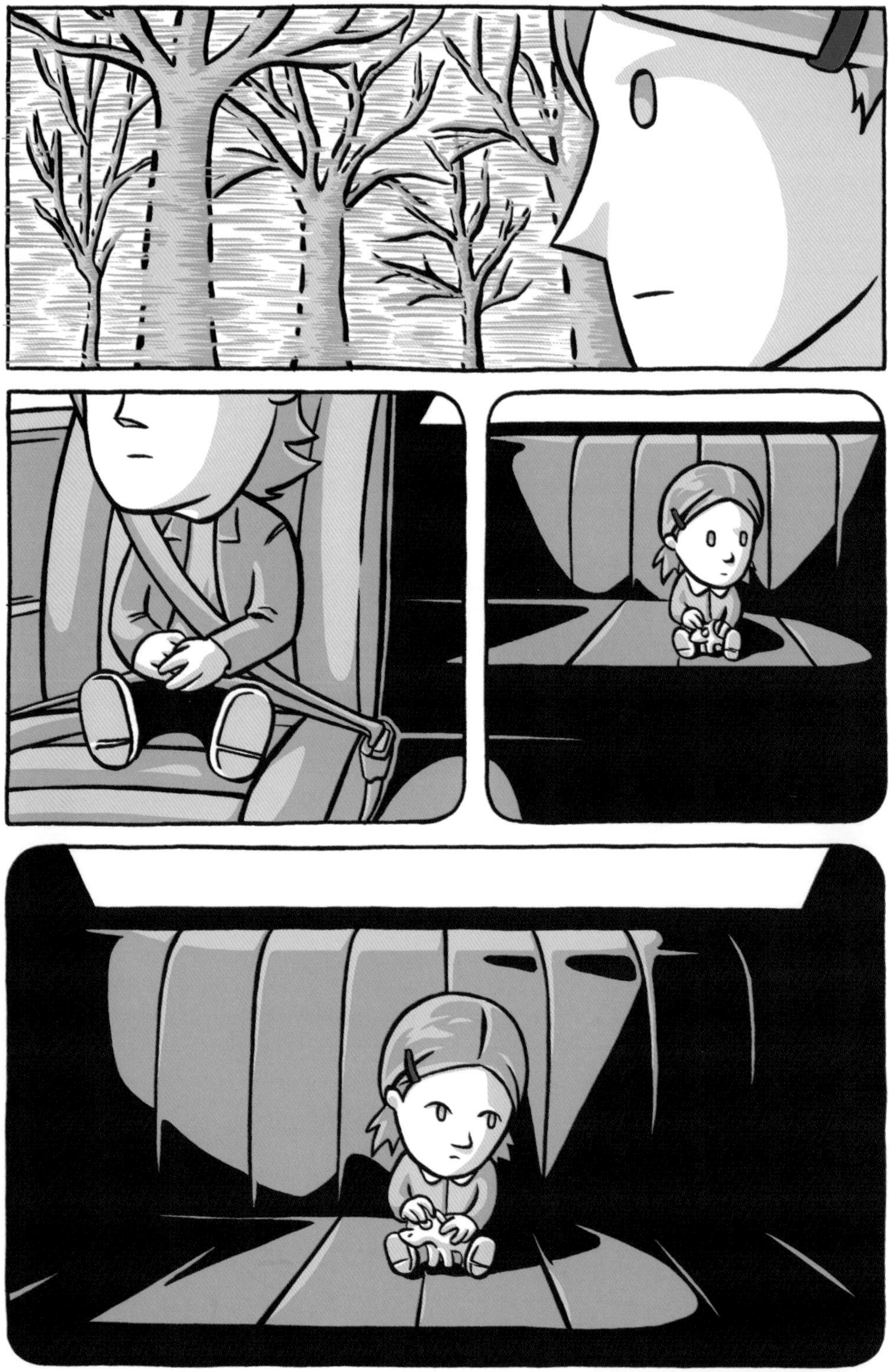

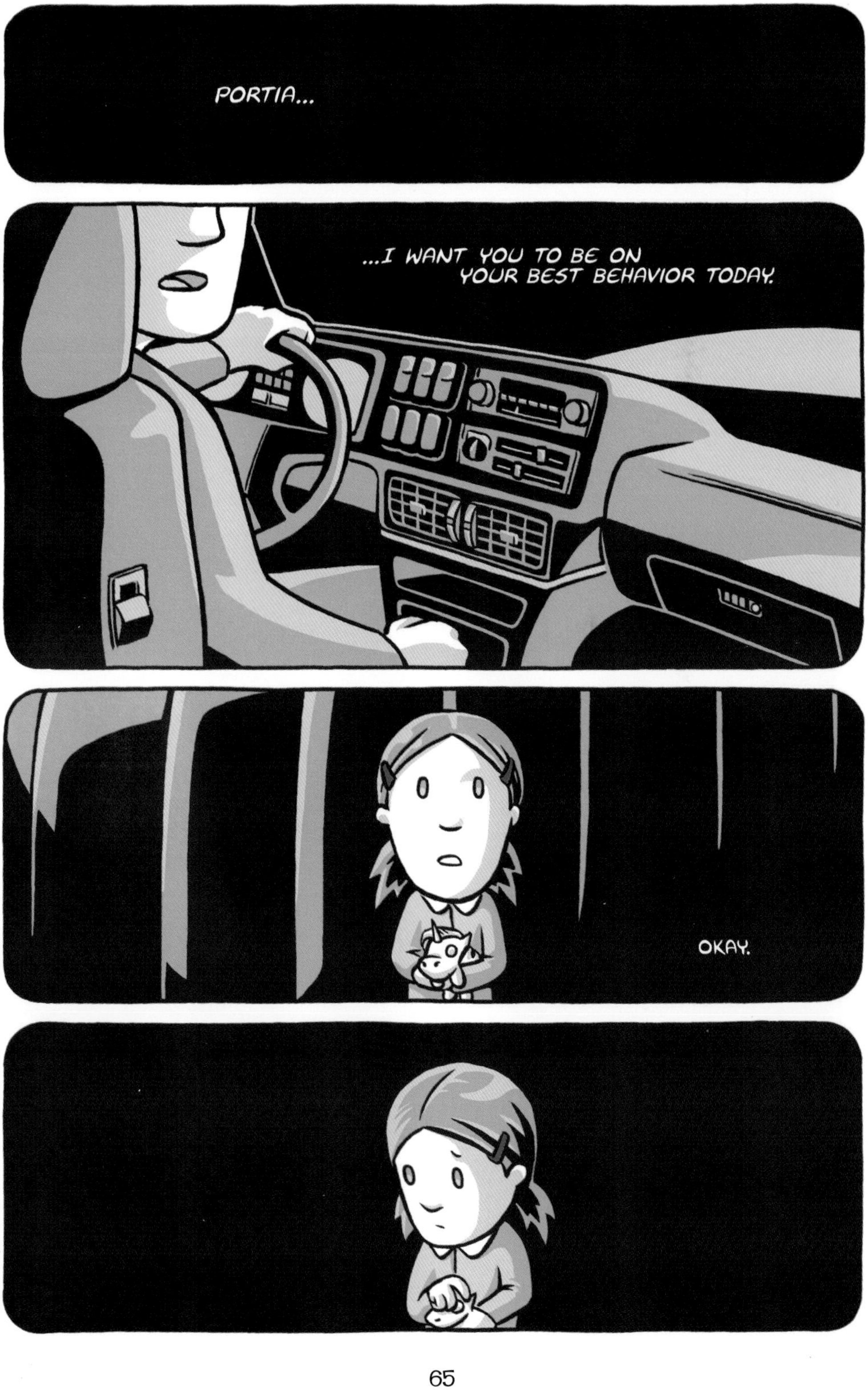
PORTIA...
...I WANT YOU TO BE ON YOUR BEST BEHAVIOR TODAY.
OKAY.

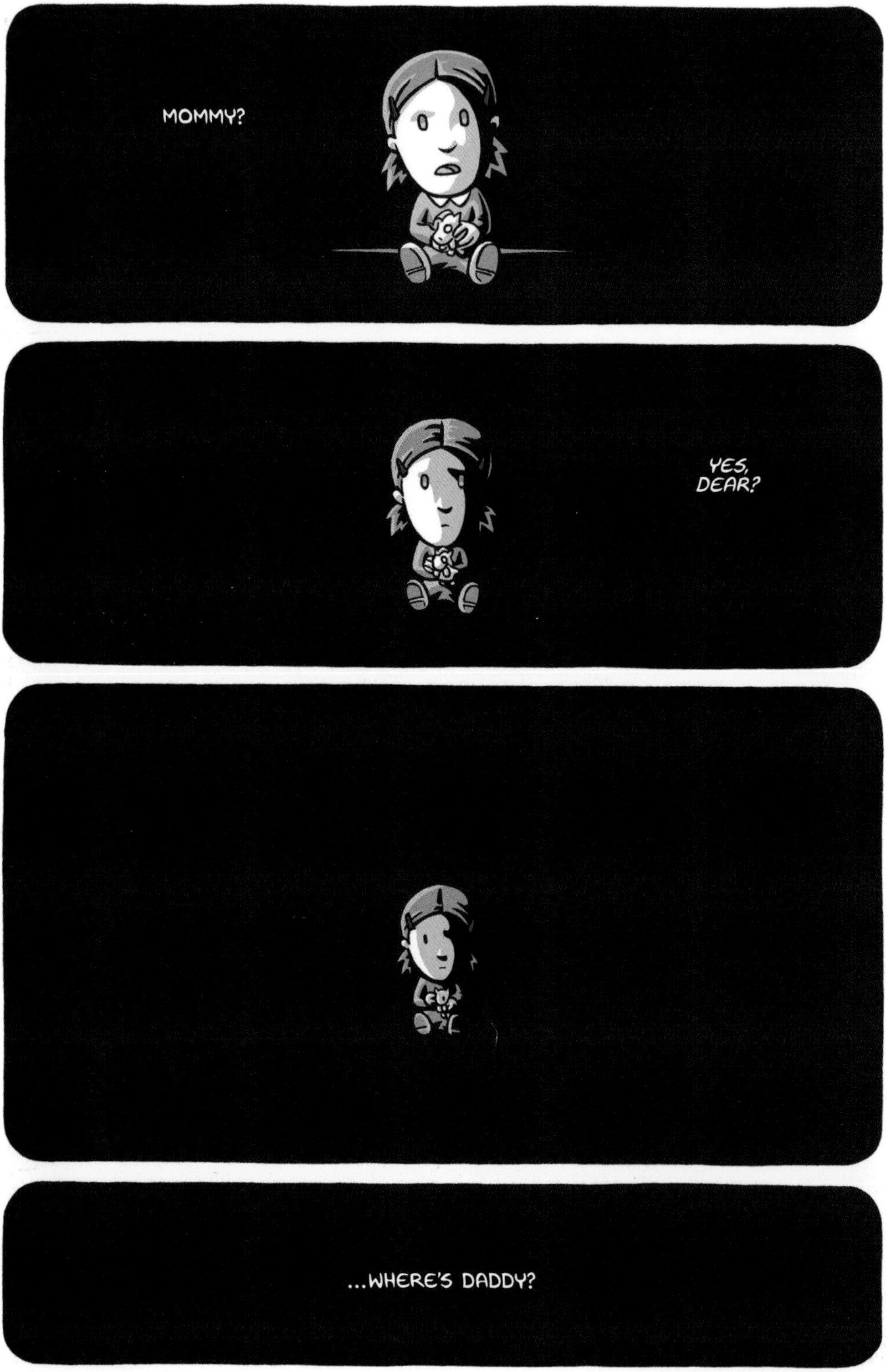
MOMMY?
YES, DEAR?
...WHERE'S DADDY?

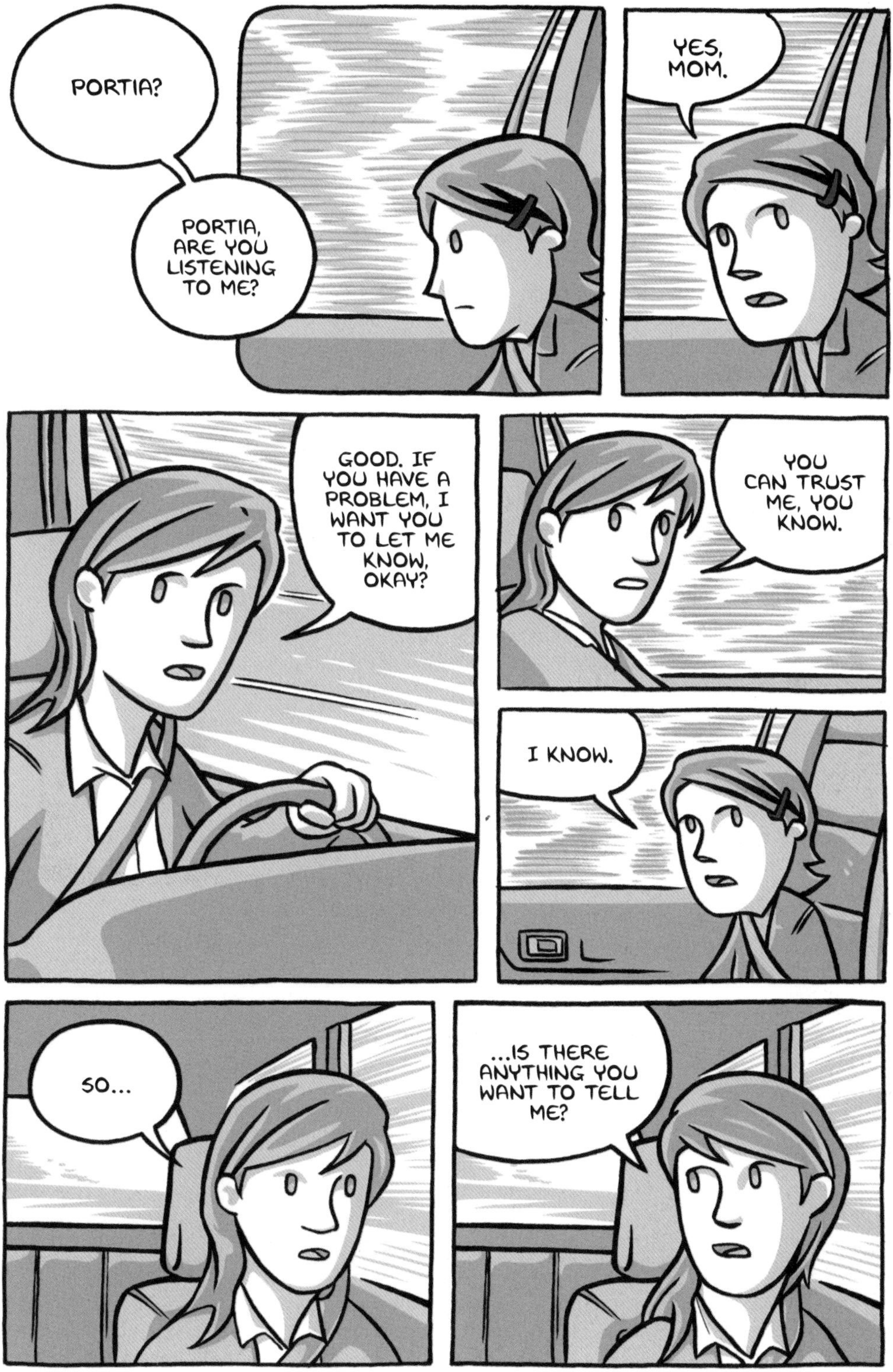
PORTIA?
PORTIA, ARE YOU LISTENING TO ME?
YES, MOM.
GOOD. IF YOU HAVE A PROBLEM, I WANT YOU TO LET ME KNOW, OKAY?
YOU CAN TRUST ME, YOU KNOW.
I KNOW.
SO...
...IS THERE ANYTHING YOU WANT TO TELL ME?

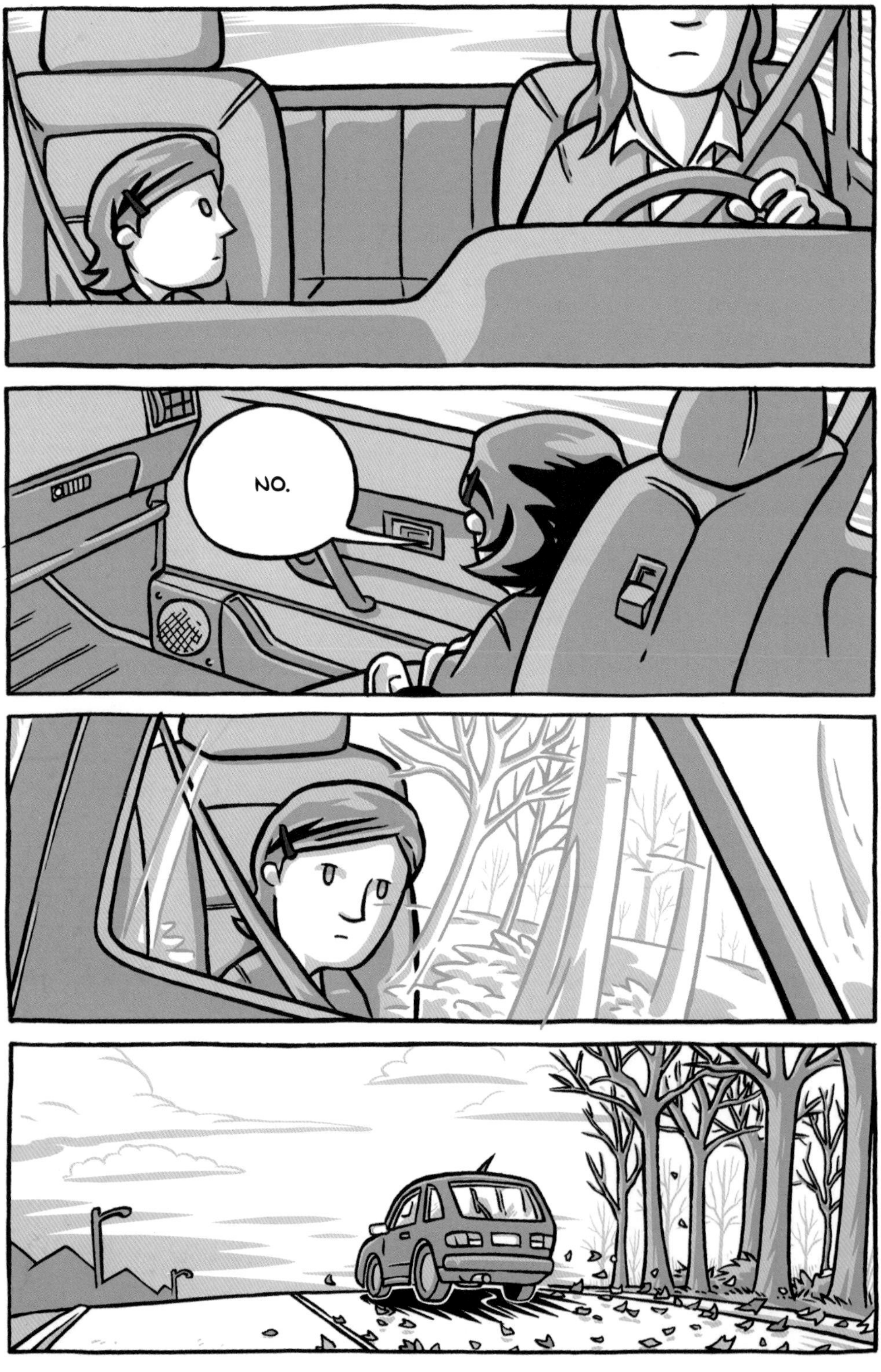
NO.

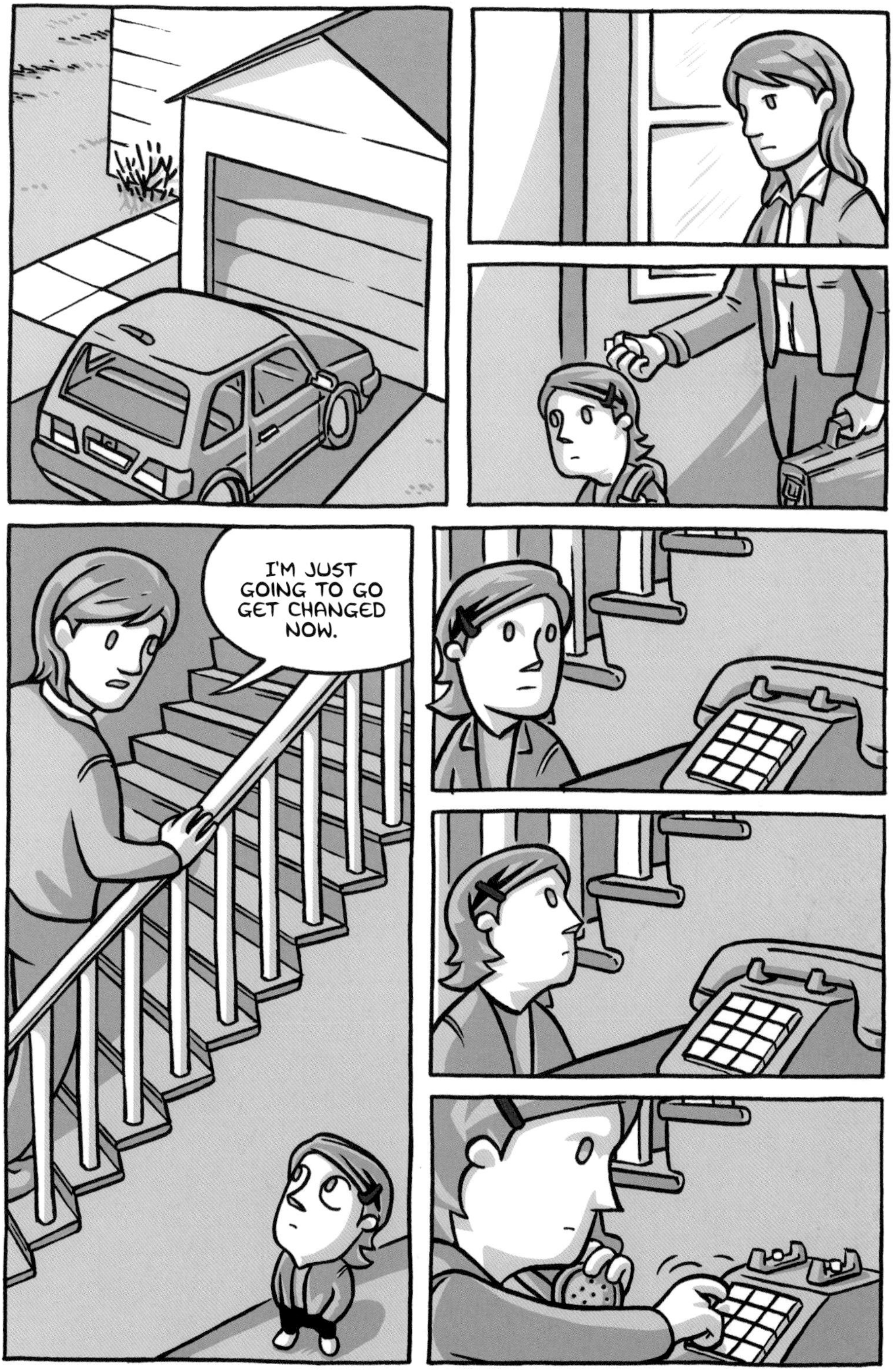
I'M JUST GOING TO GO GET CHANGED NOW.

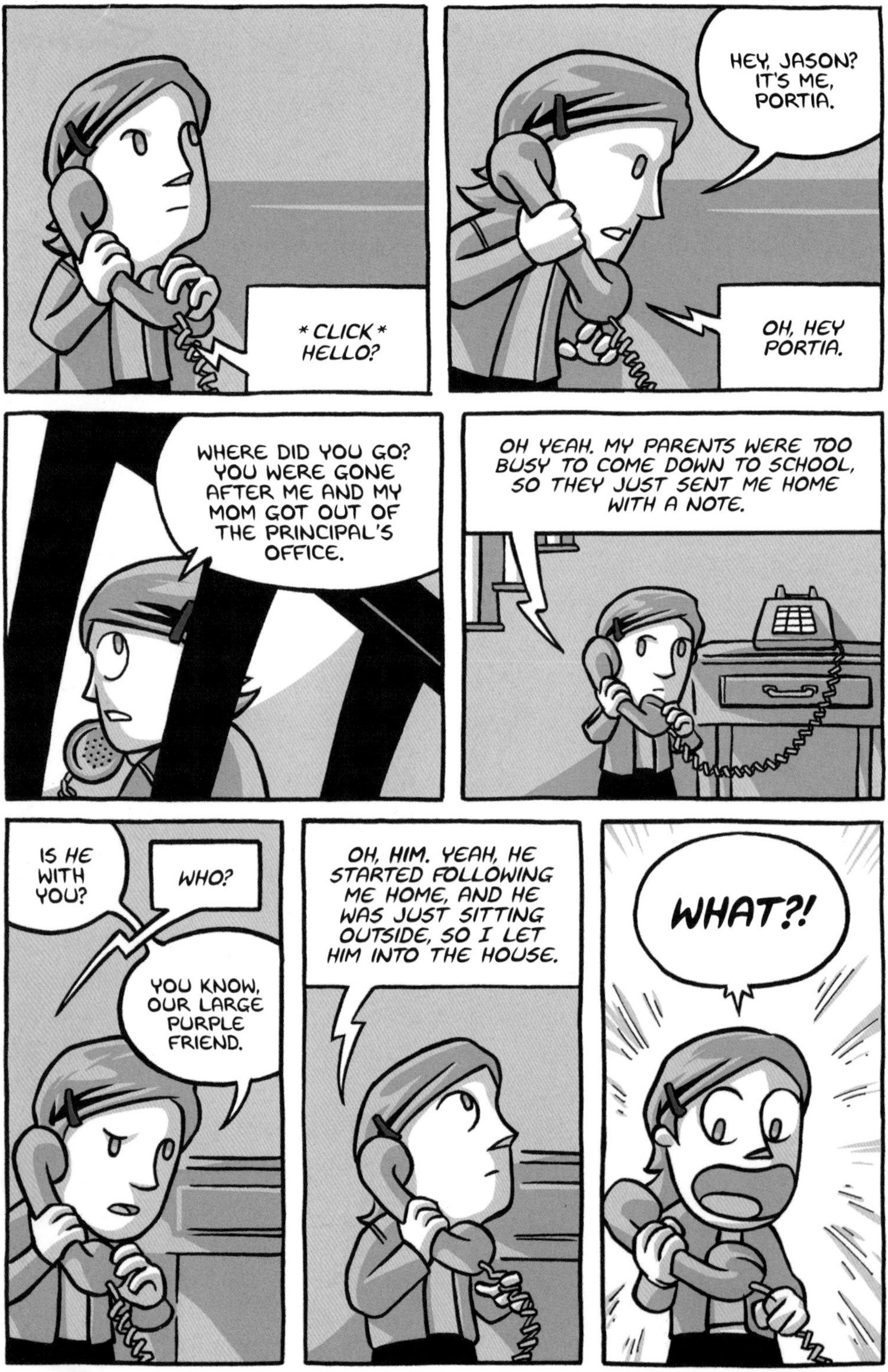
CLICK HELLO?
HEY, JASON? IT'S ME, PORTIA.
OH, HEY PORTIA.
WHERE DID YOU GO? YOU WERE GONE AFTER ME AND MY MOM GOT OUT OF THE PRINCIPAL'S OFFICE.
OH YEAH. MY PARENTS WERE TOO BUSY TO COME DOWN TO SCHOOL, SO THEY JUST SENT ME HOME WITH A NOTE.
IS HE WITH YOU?
WHO?
YOU KNOW, OUR LARGE PURPLE FRIEND.
OH, HIM. YEAH, HE STARTED FOLLOWING ME HOME, AND HE WAS JUST SITTING OUTSIDE, SO I LET HIM INTO THE HOUSE.
WHAT?!

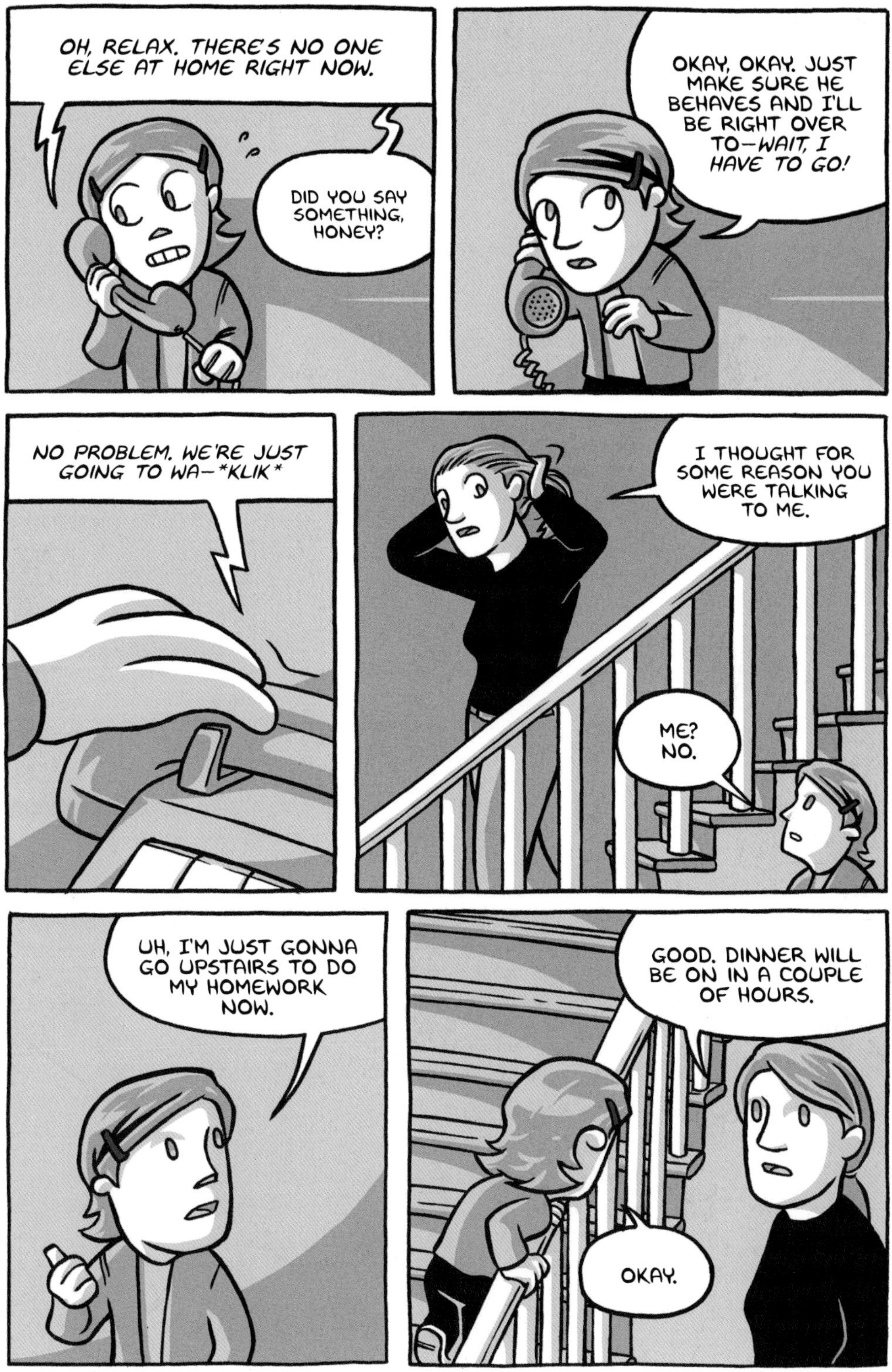
OH, RELAX. THERE'S NO ONE ELSE AT HOME RIGHT NOW.
DID YOU SAY SOMETHING, HONEY?
OKAY, OKAY. JUST MAKE SURE HE BEHAVES AND I'LL BE RIGHT OVER TO—WAIT, I HAVE TO GO!
NO PROBLEM. WE'RE JUST GOING TO WA— *KLIK*
I THOUGHT FOR SOME REASON YOU WERE TALKING TO ME.
ME? NO.
UH, I'M JUST GONNA GO UPSTAIRS TO DO MY HOMEWORK NOW.
GOOD. DINNER WILL BE ON IN A COUPLE OF HOURS.
OKAY.

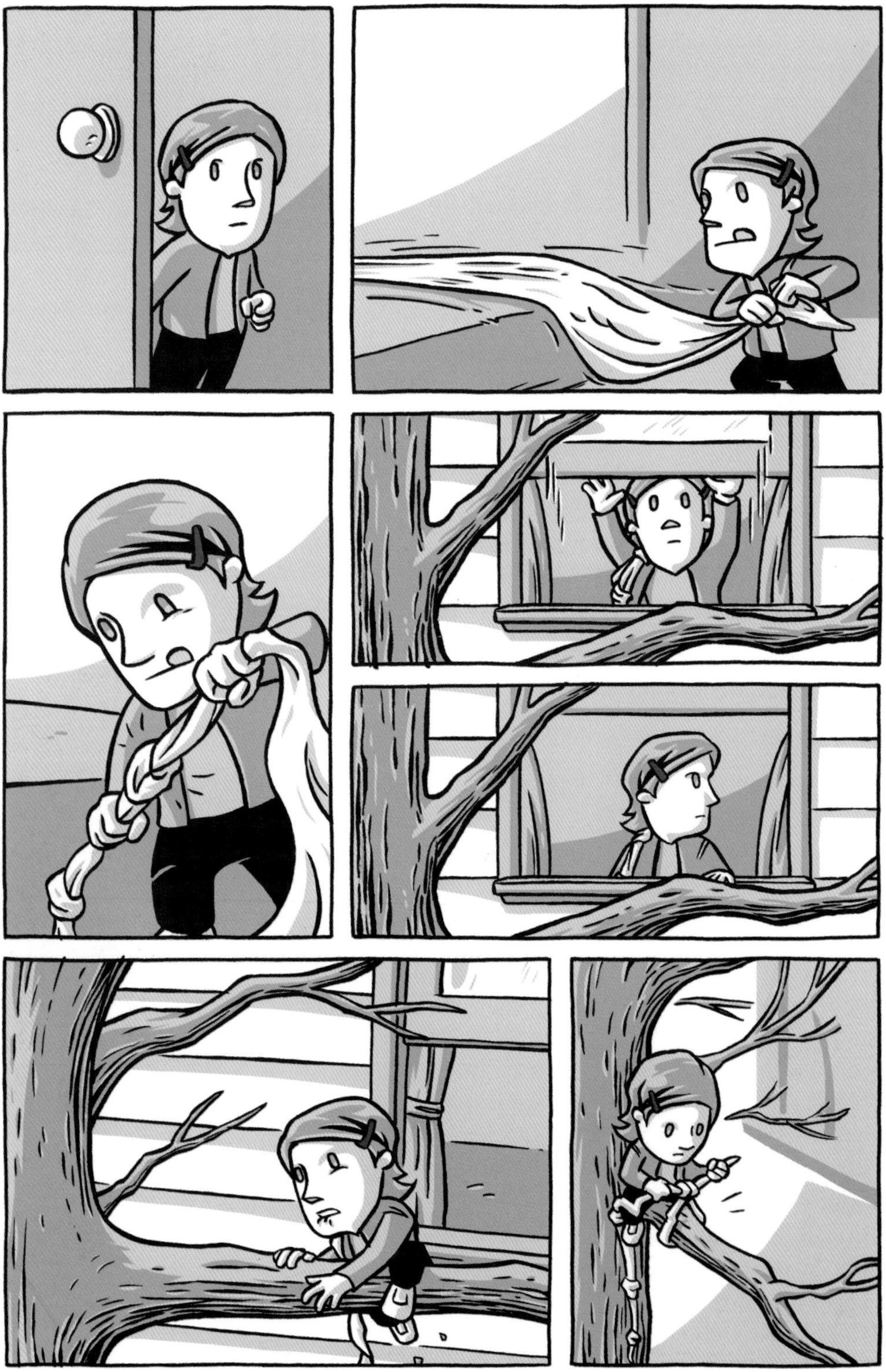

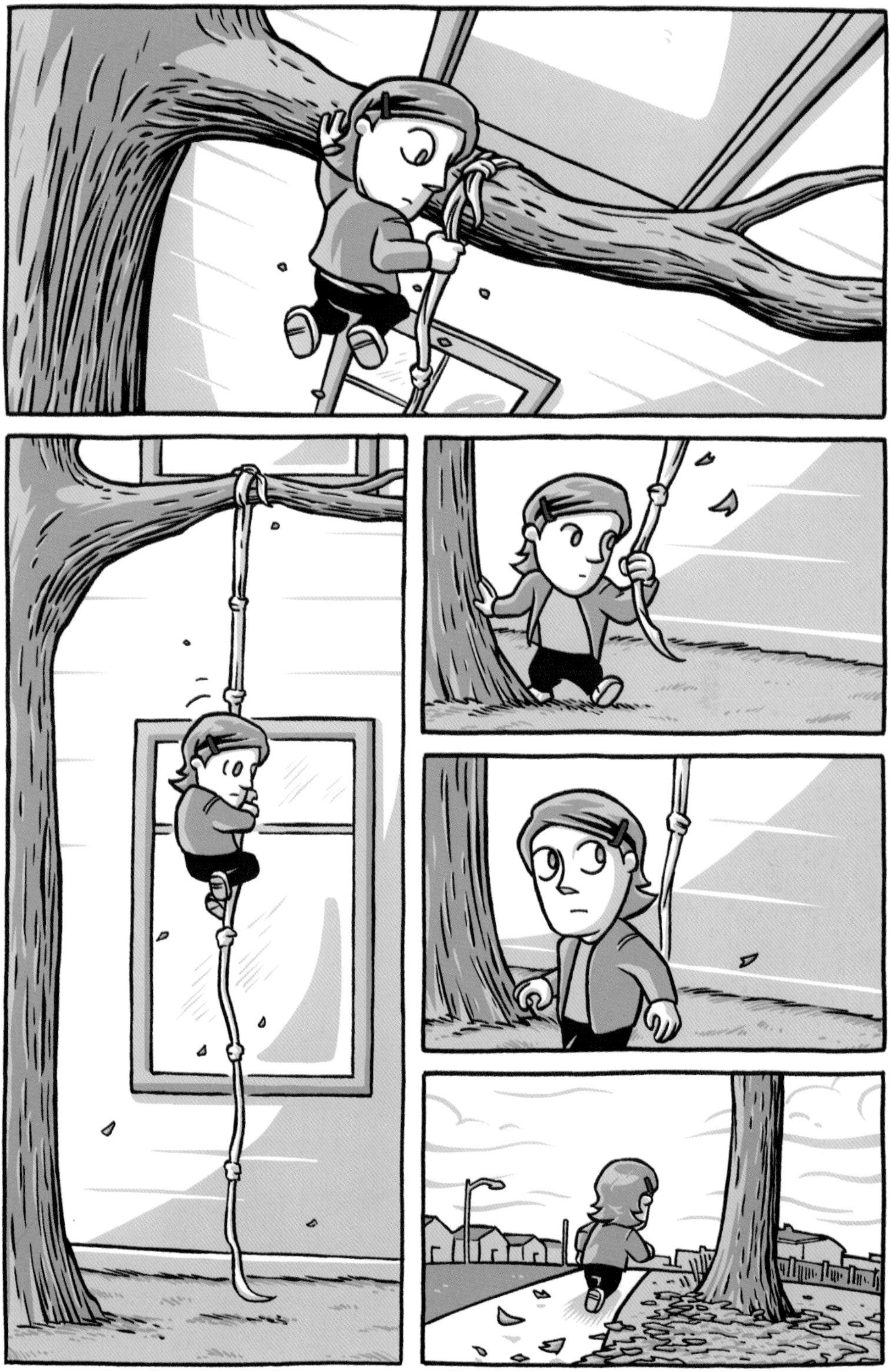

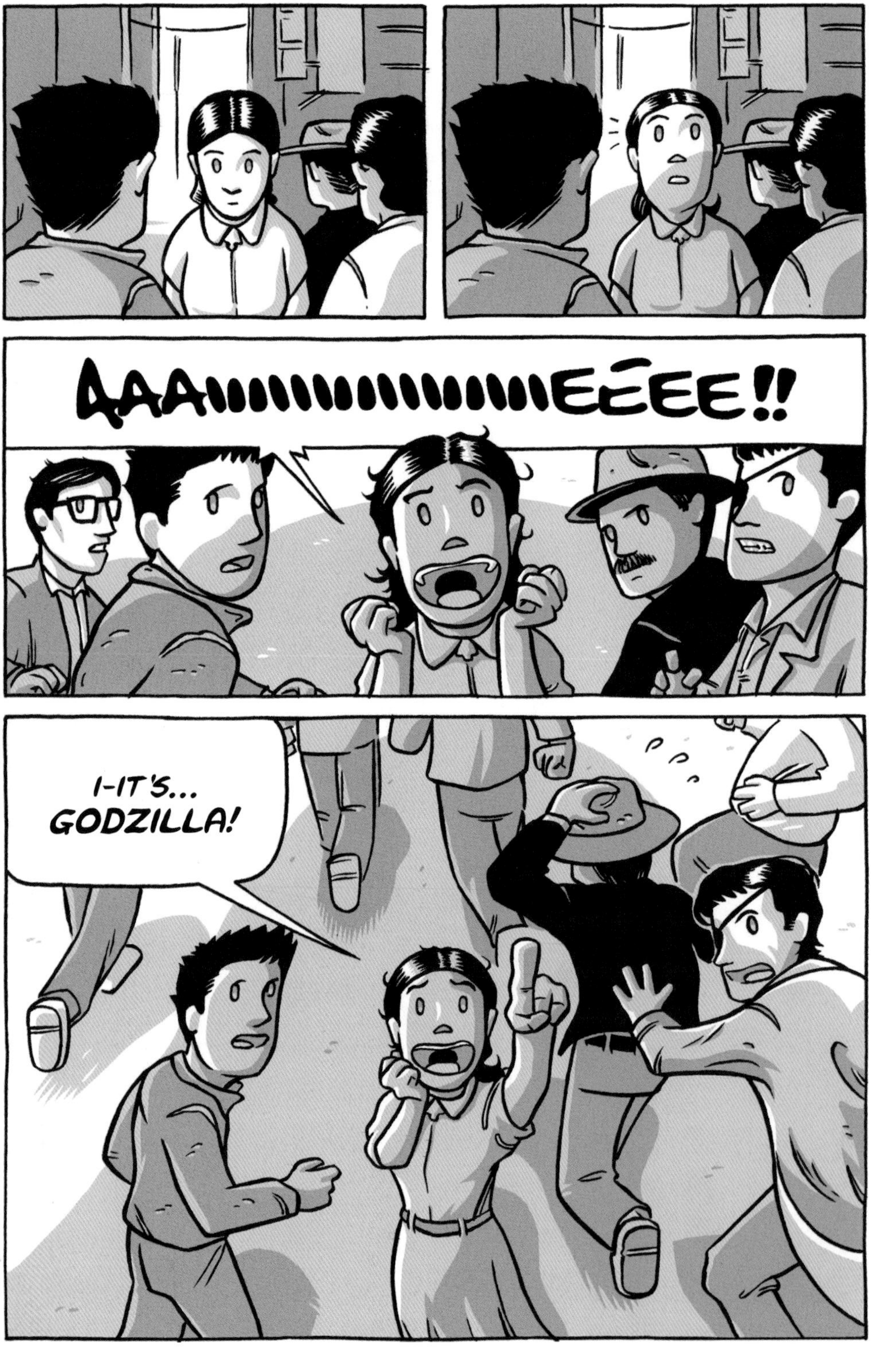
AAAIIIIIIIIIIIIIIIIIIEEEE!!
I-IT'S... GODZILLA!

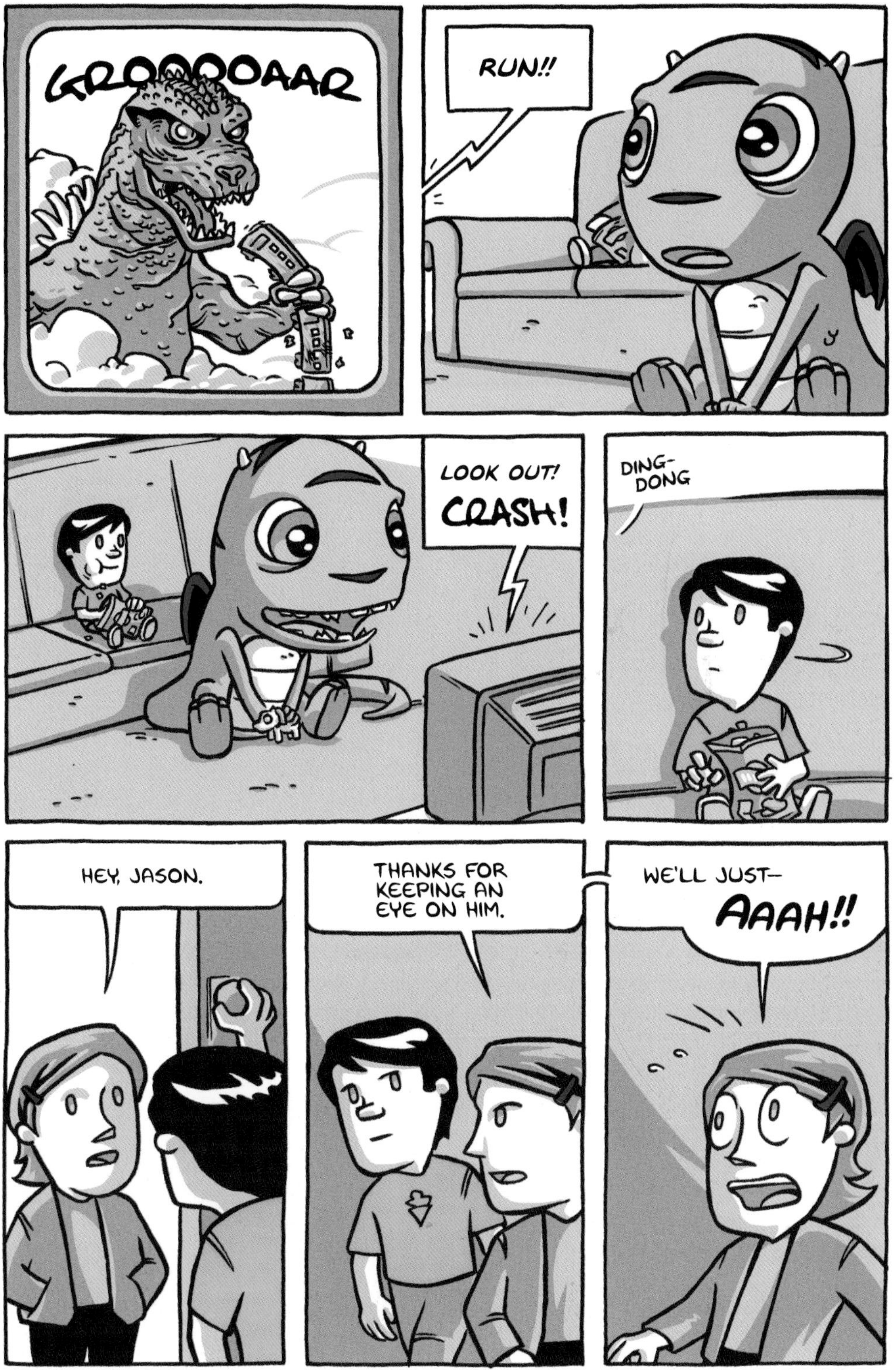

GROOOOOAAR
RUN!!
LOOK OUT!
CRASH!
DING-
DONG
HEY, JASON.
THANKS FOR
KEEPING AN
EYE ON HIM.
WE'LL JUST—
AAAH!!

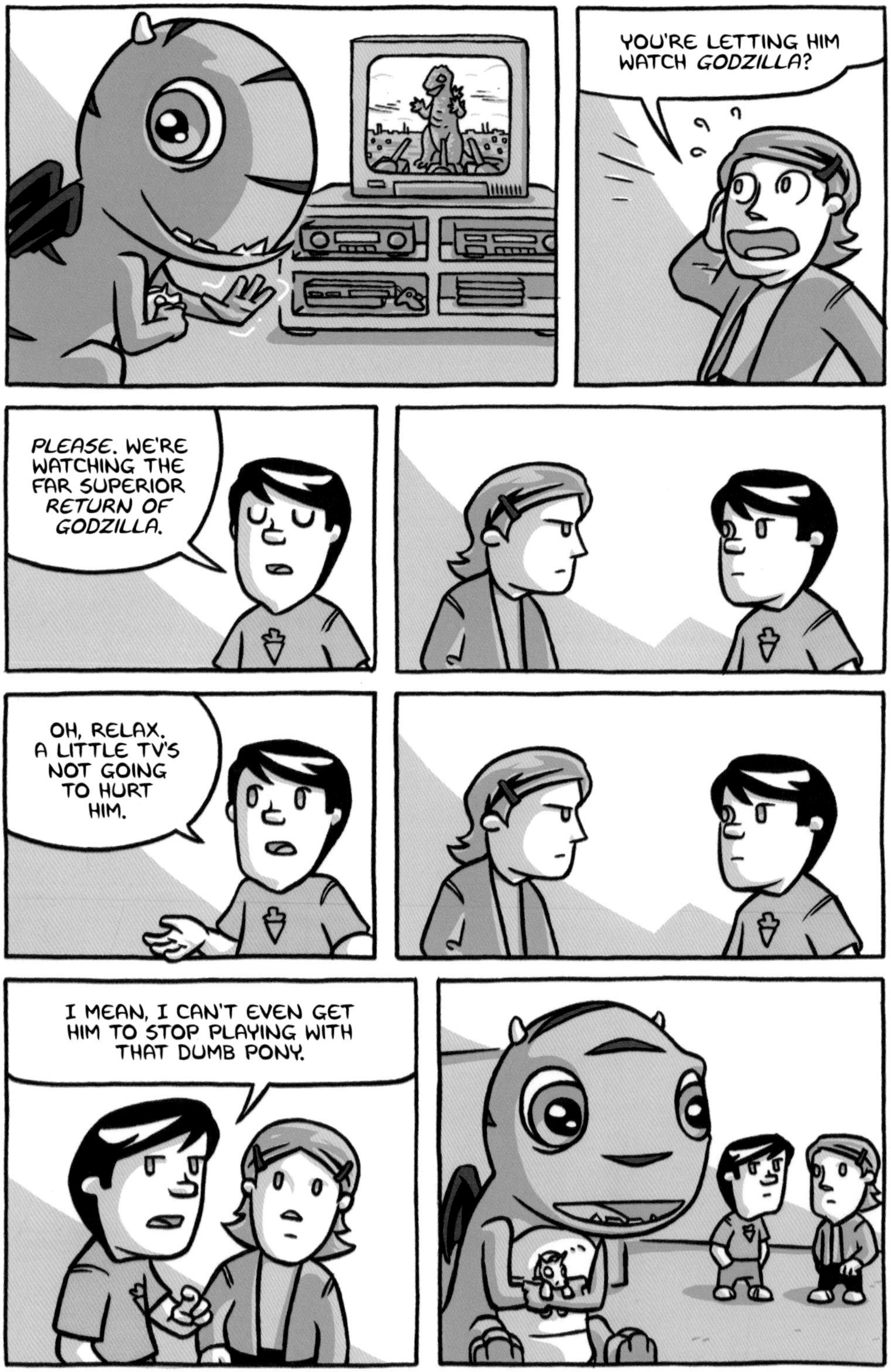
YOU'RE LETTING HIM WATCH *GODZILLA*?
PLEASE. WE'RE WATCHING THE FAR SUPERIOR *RETURN OF GODZILLA*.
OH, RELAX. A LITTLE TV'S NOT GOING TO HURT HIM.
I MEAN, I CAN'T EVEN GET HIM TO STOP PLAYING WITH THAT DUMB PONY.

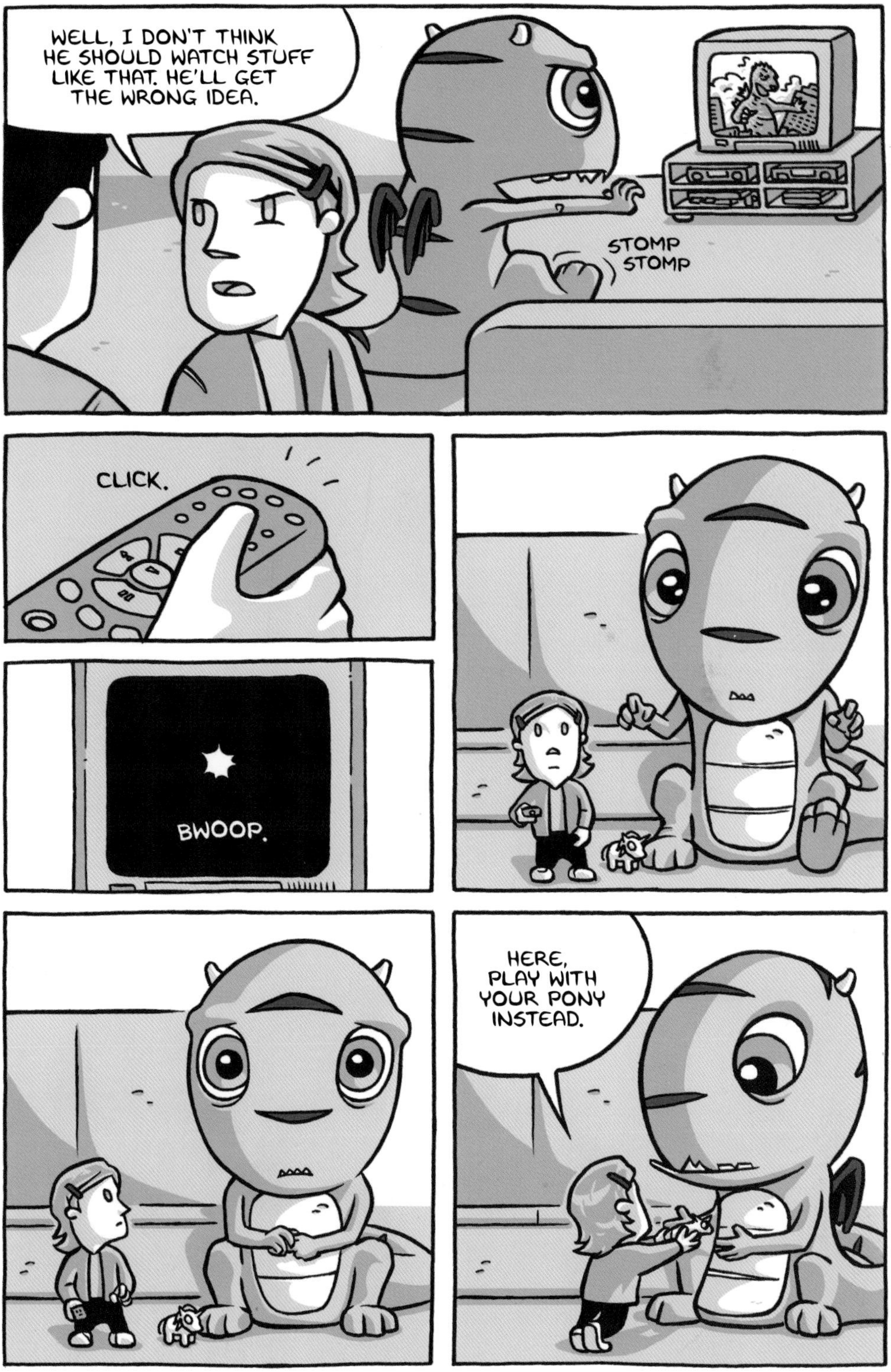

WELL, I DON'T THINK HE SHOULD WATCH STUFF LIKE THAT. HE'LL GET THE WRONG IDEA.
STOMP STOMP
CLICK.
BWOOP.
HERE, PLAY WITH YOUR PONY INSTEAD.

78

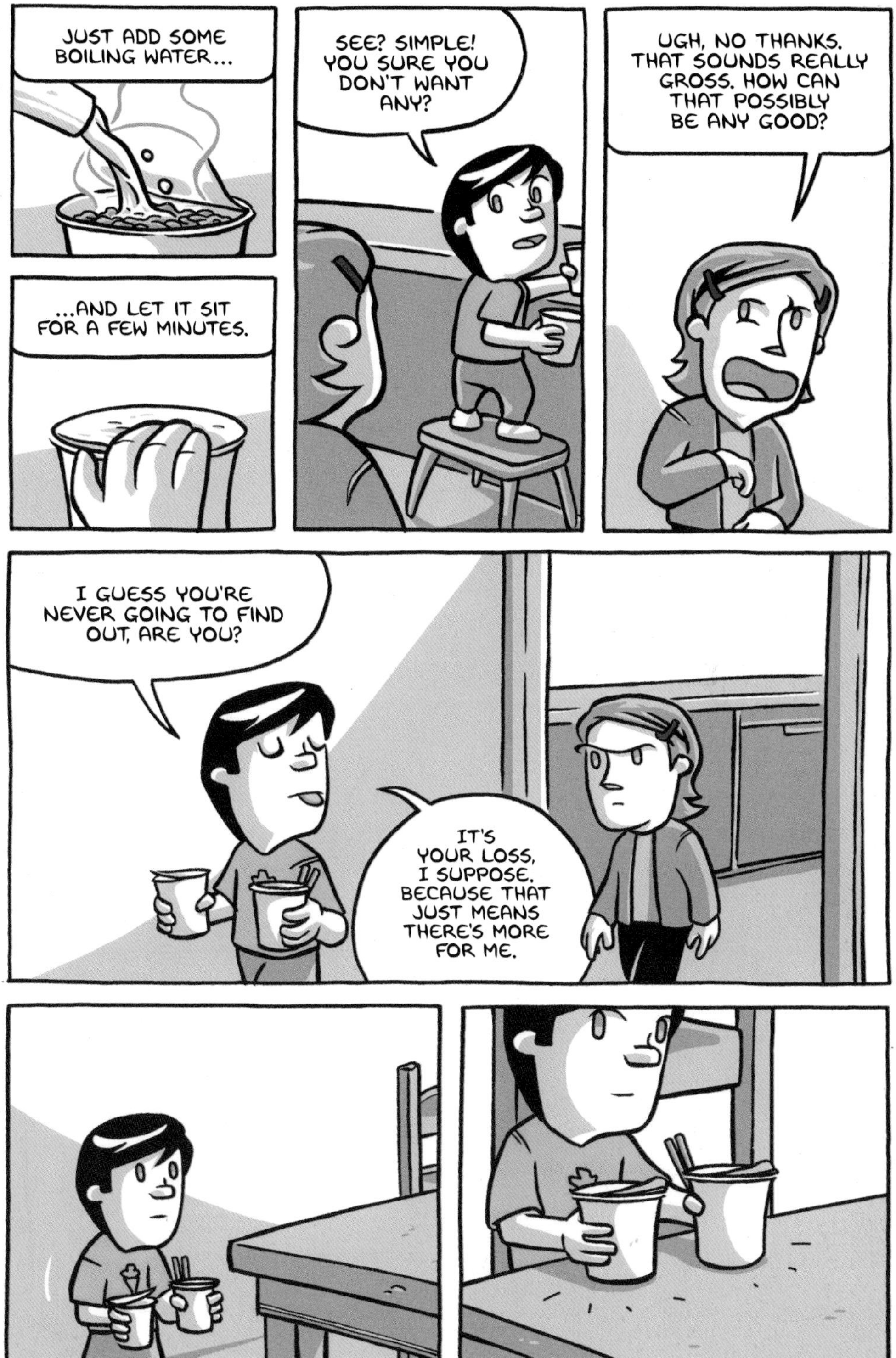
JUST ADD SOME BOILING WATER...
...AND LET IT SIT FOR A FEW MINUTES.
SEE? SIMPLE! YOU SURE YOU DON'T WANT ANY?
UGH, NO THANKS. THAT SOUNDS REALLY GROSS. HOW CAN THAT POSSIBLY BE ANY GOOD?
I GUESS YOU'RE NEVER GOING TO FIND OUT, ARE YOU?
IT'S YOUR LOSS, I SUPPOSE. BECAUSE THAT JUST MEANS THERE'S MORE FOR ME.

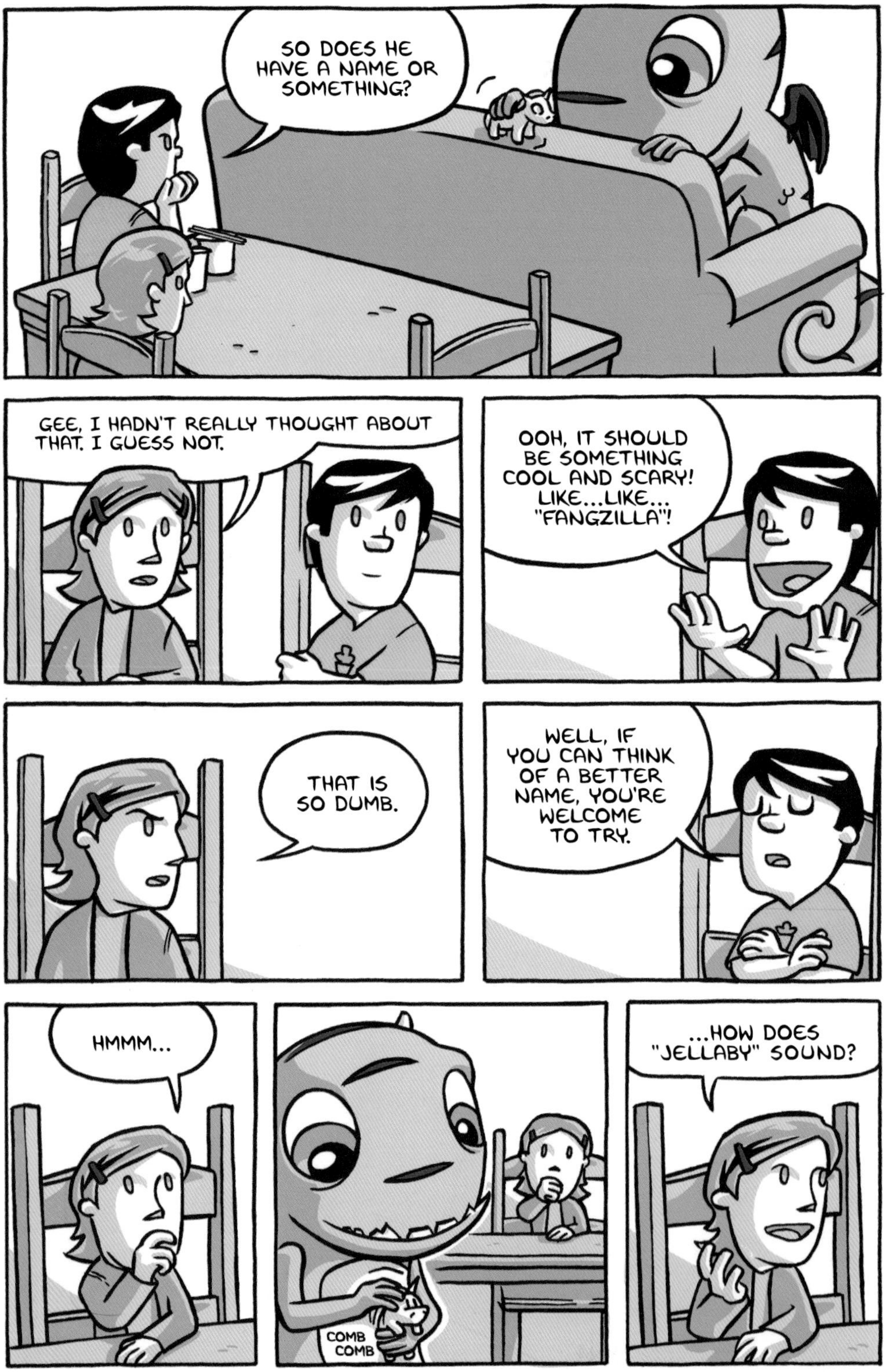
SO DOES HE HAVE A NAME OR SOMETHING?
GEE, I HADN'T REALLY THOUGHT ABOUT THAT. I GUESS NOT.
OOH, IT SHOULD BE SOMETHING COOL AND SCARY! LIKE...LIKE... "FANGZILLA"!
THAT IS SO DUMB.
WELL, IF YOU CAN THINK OF A BETTER NAME, YOU'RE WELCOME TO TRY.
HMMM...
COMB COMB
...HOW DOES "JELLABY" SOUND?

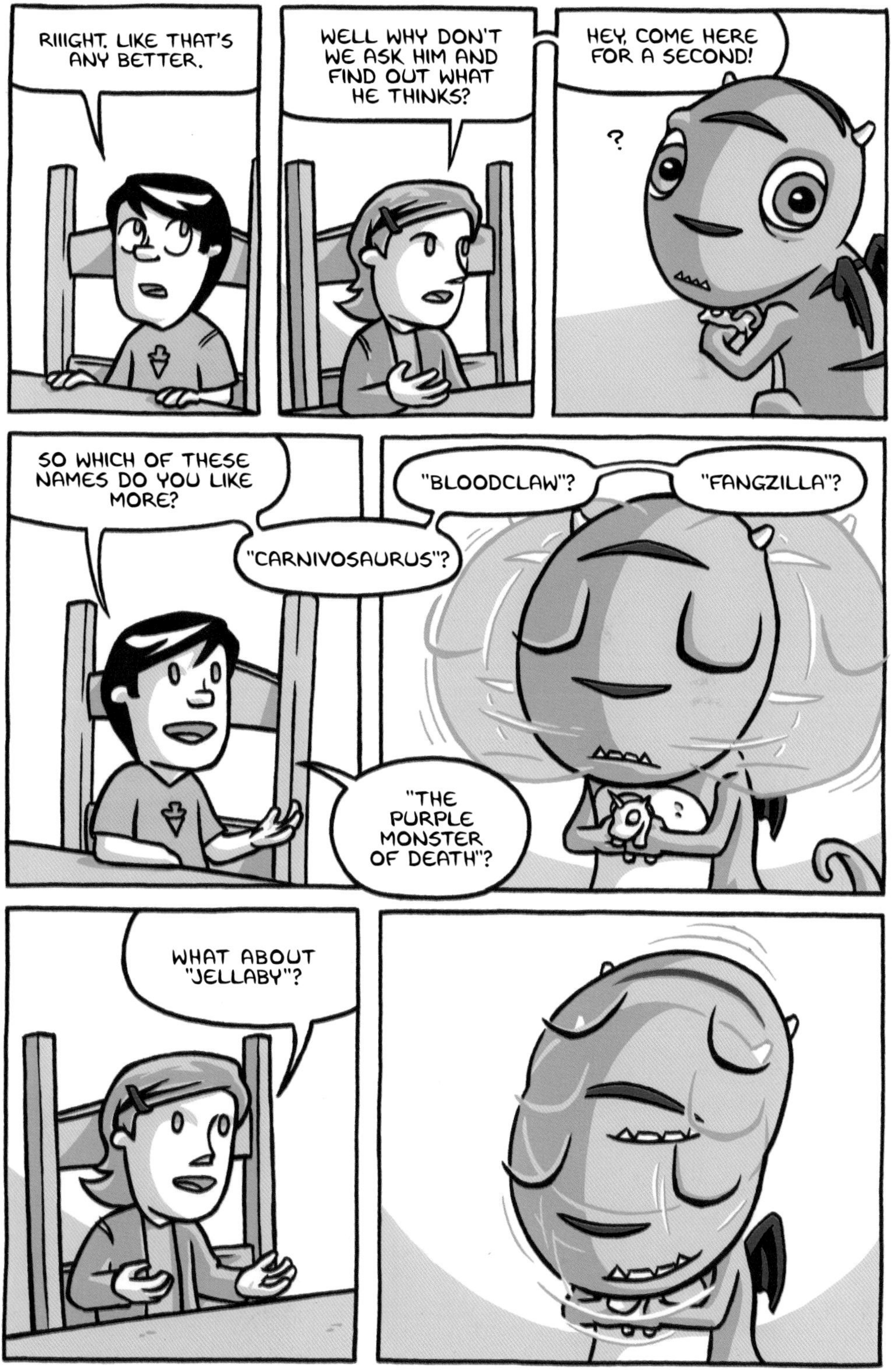
RIIIGHT. LIKE THAT'S ANY BETTER.
WELL WHY DON'T WE ASK HIM AND FIND OUT WHAT HE THINKS?
HEY, COME HERE FOR A SECOND!
?
SO WHICH OF THESE NAMES DO YOU LIKE MORE?
"CARNIVOSAURUS"?
"BLOODCLAW"?
"FANGZILLA"?
"THE PURPLE MONSTER OF DEATH"?
WHAT ABOUT "JELLABY"?

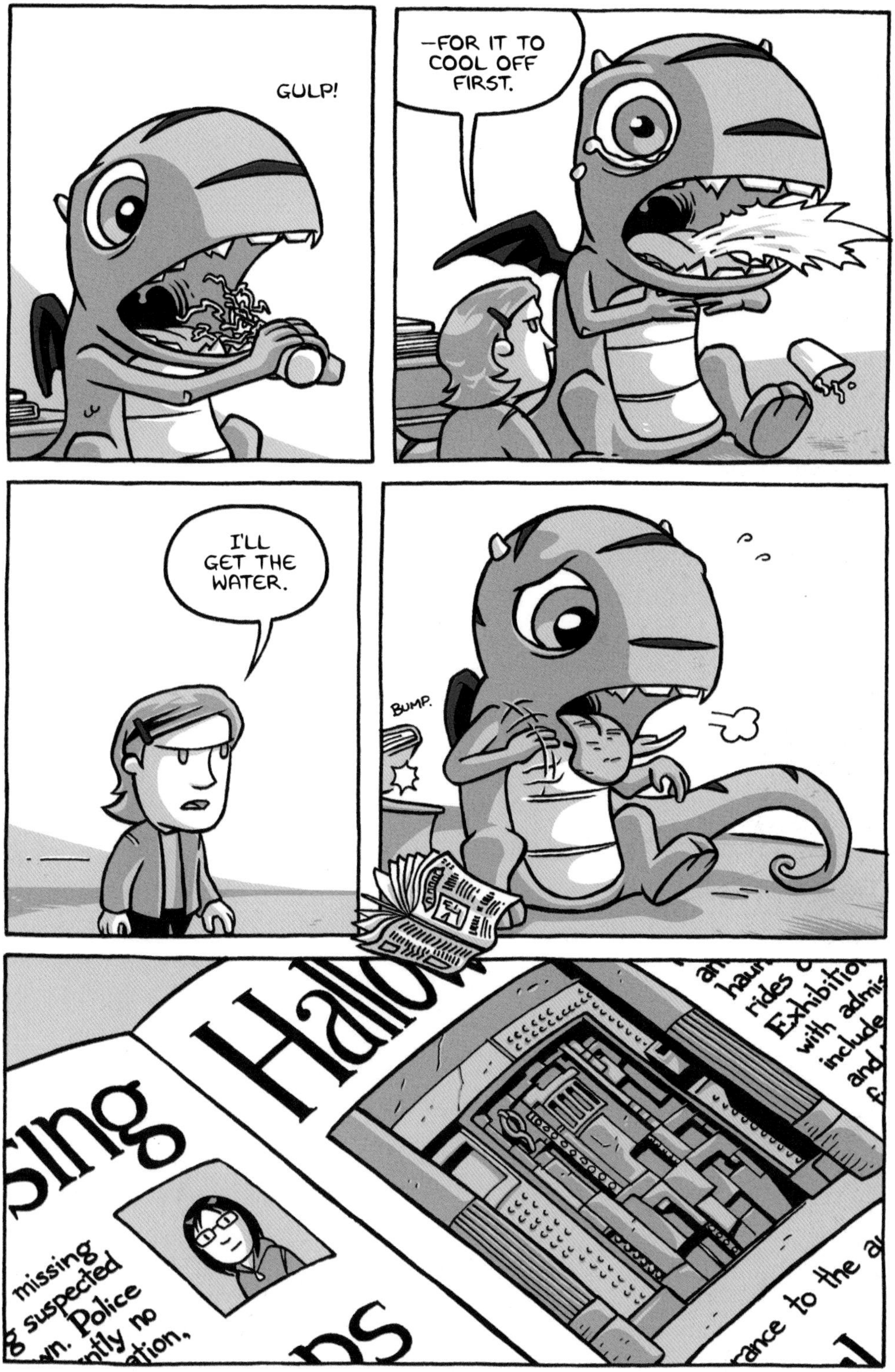
GULP!
—FOR IT TO COOL OFF FIRST.
I'LL GET THE WATER.
BUMP.
Hallo
sing
missing
g suspected
wn. Police
ntly no
ation.
ps
an
haun
rides o
Exhibitio
with admis
include
and
rance to the a

85

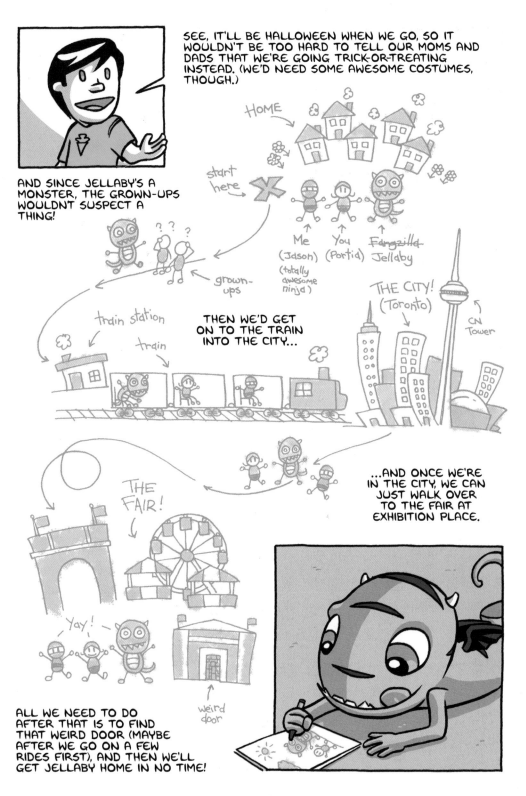

SEE, IT'LL BE HALLOWEEN WHEN WE GO, SO IT WOULDN'T BE TOO HARD TO TELL OUR MOMS AND DADS THAT WE'RE GOING TRICK-OR-TREATING INSTEAD. (WE'D NEED SOME AWESOME COSTUMES, THOUGH.)

AND SINCE JELLABY'S A MONSTER, THE GROWN-UPS WOULDN'T SUSPECT A THING!

THEN WE'D GET ON TO THE TRAIN INTO THE CITY...

...AND ONCE WE'RE IN THE CITY, WE CAN JUST WALK OVER TO THE FAIR AT EXHIBITION PLACE.

ALL WE NEED TO DO AFTER THAT IS TO FIND THAT WEIRD DOOR (MAYBE AFTER WE GO ON A FEW RIDES FIRST), AND THEN WE'LL GET JELLABY HOME IN NO TIME!

87

90

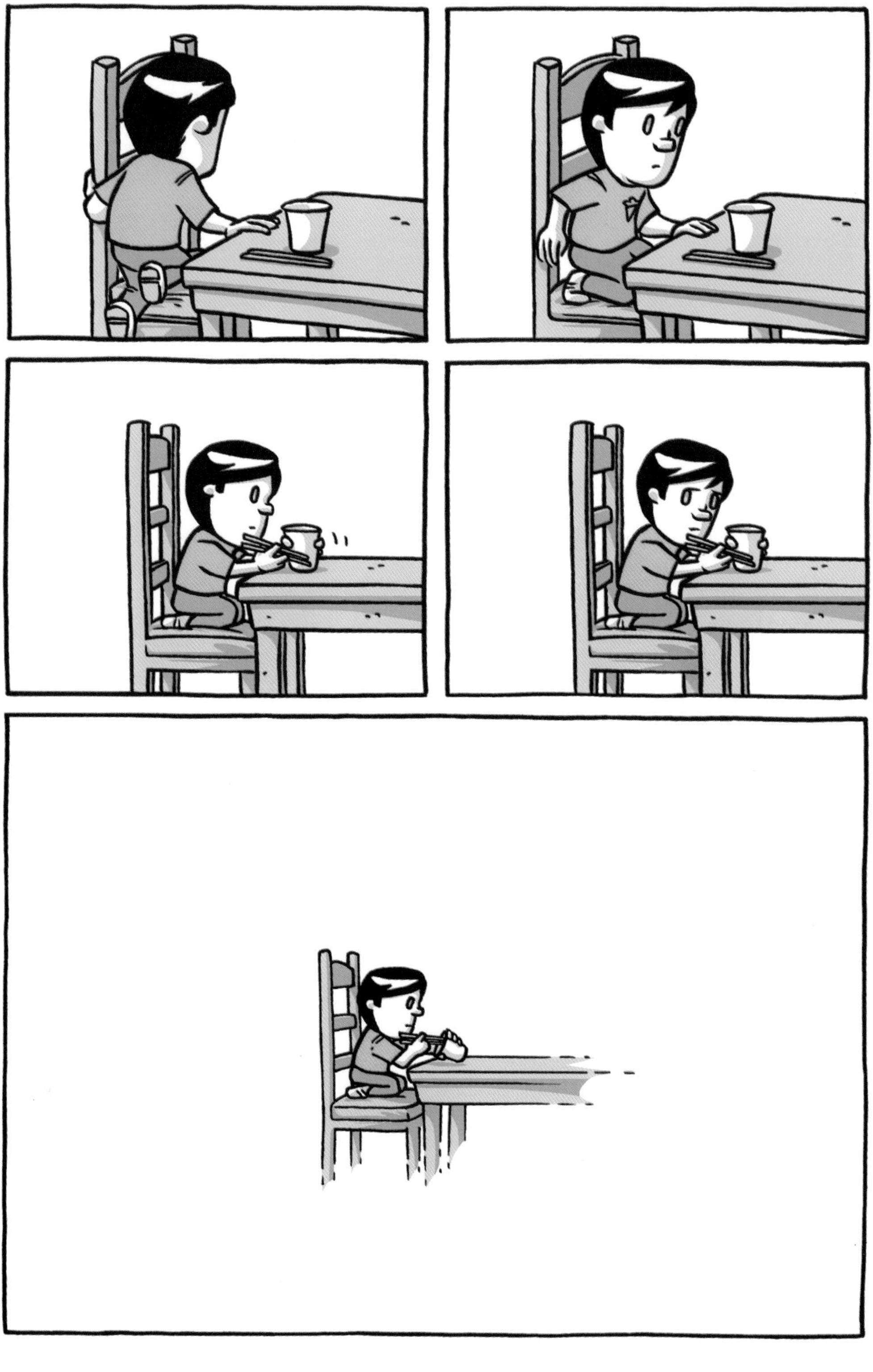

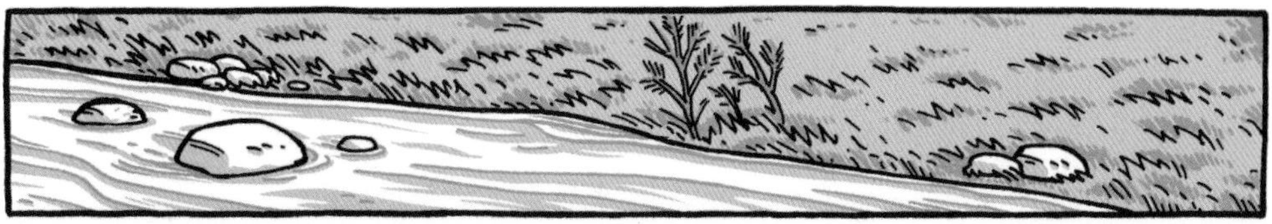

CHAPTER FOUR

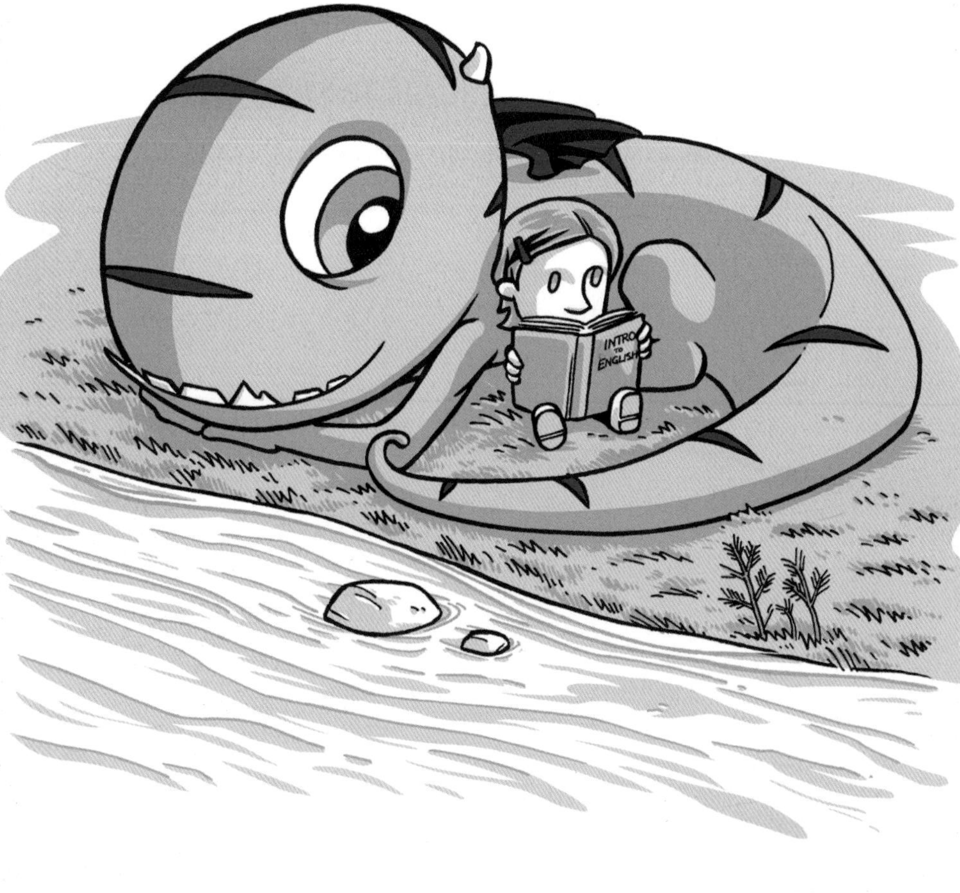
INTRO
TO
ENGLISH

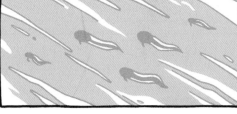

THAT'S ENOUGH FOR TODAY, I GUESS.

97

98

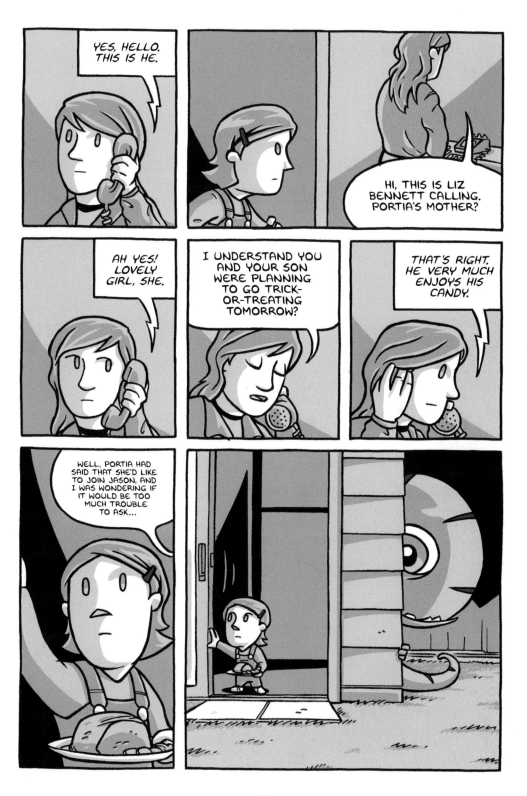

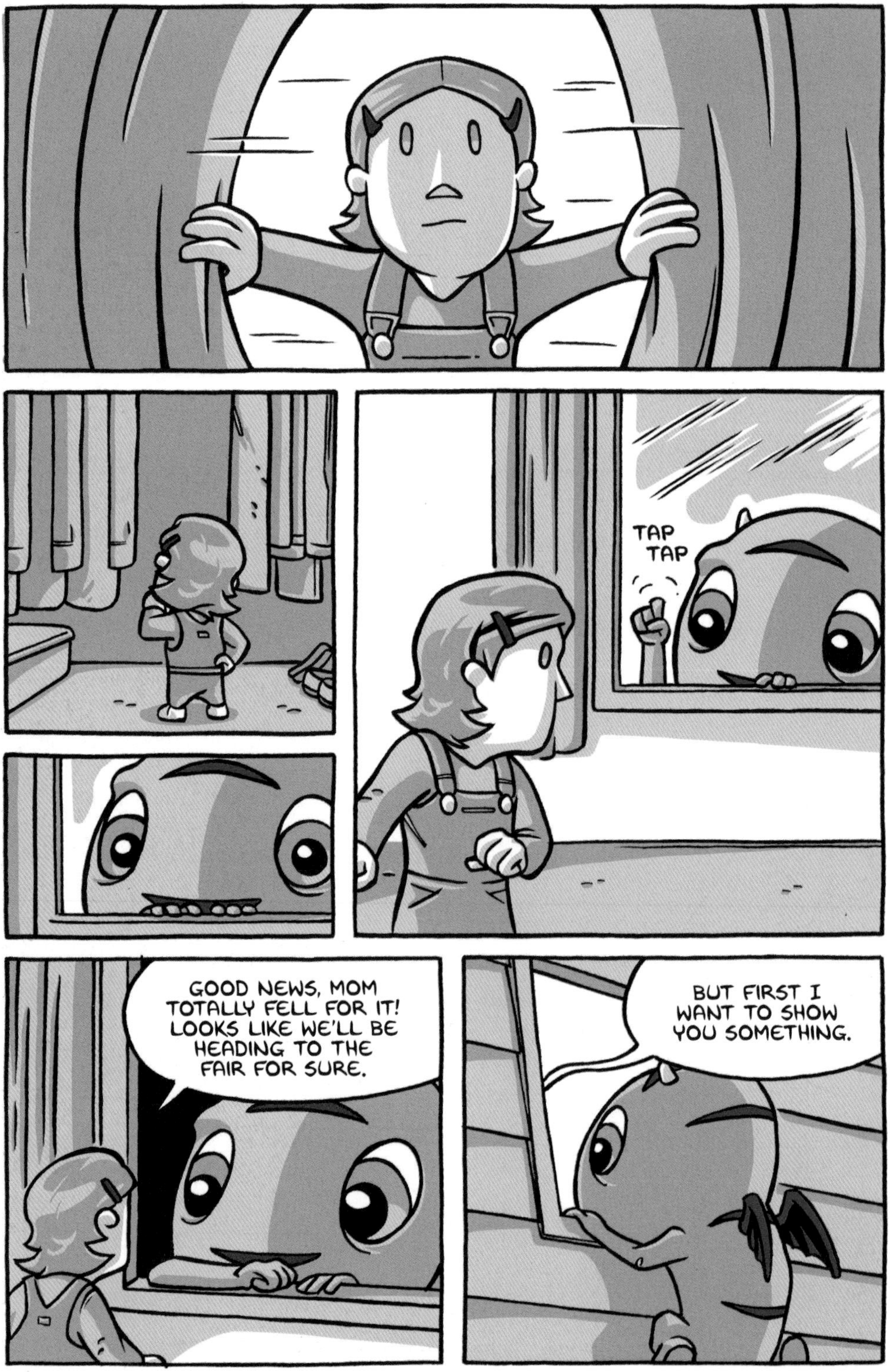
TAP
TAP
GOOD NEWS, MOM TOTALLY FELL FOR IT! LOOKS LIKE WE'LL BE HEADING TO THE FAIR FOR SURE.
BUT FIRST I WANT TO SHOW YOU SOMETHING.

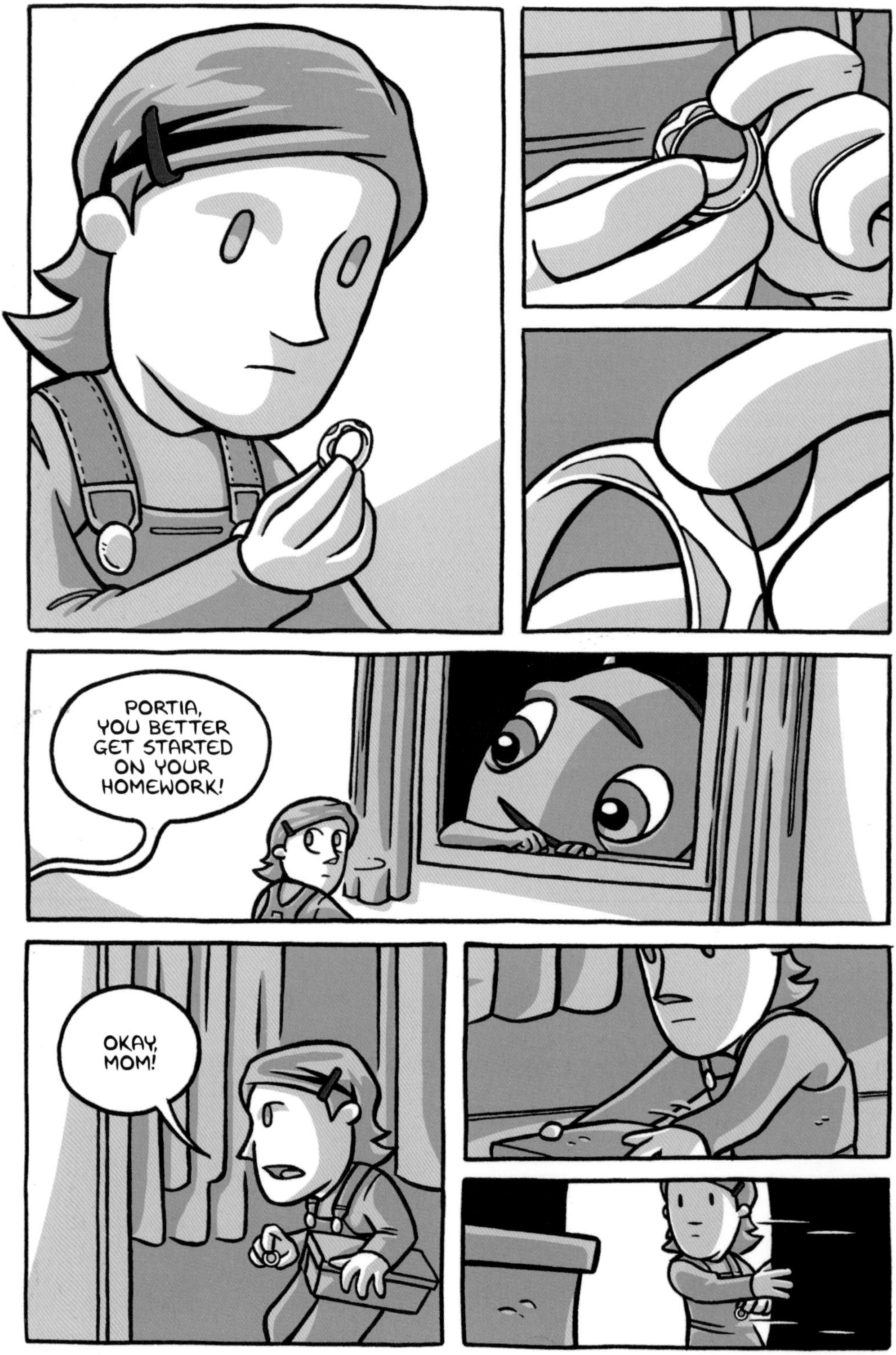
PORTIA, YOU BETTER GET STARTED ON YOUR HOMEWORK!
OKAY, MOM!

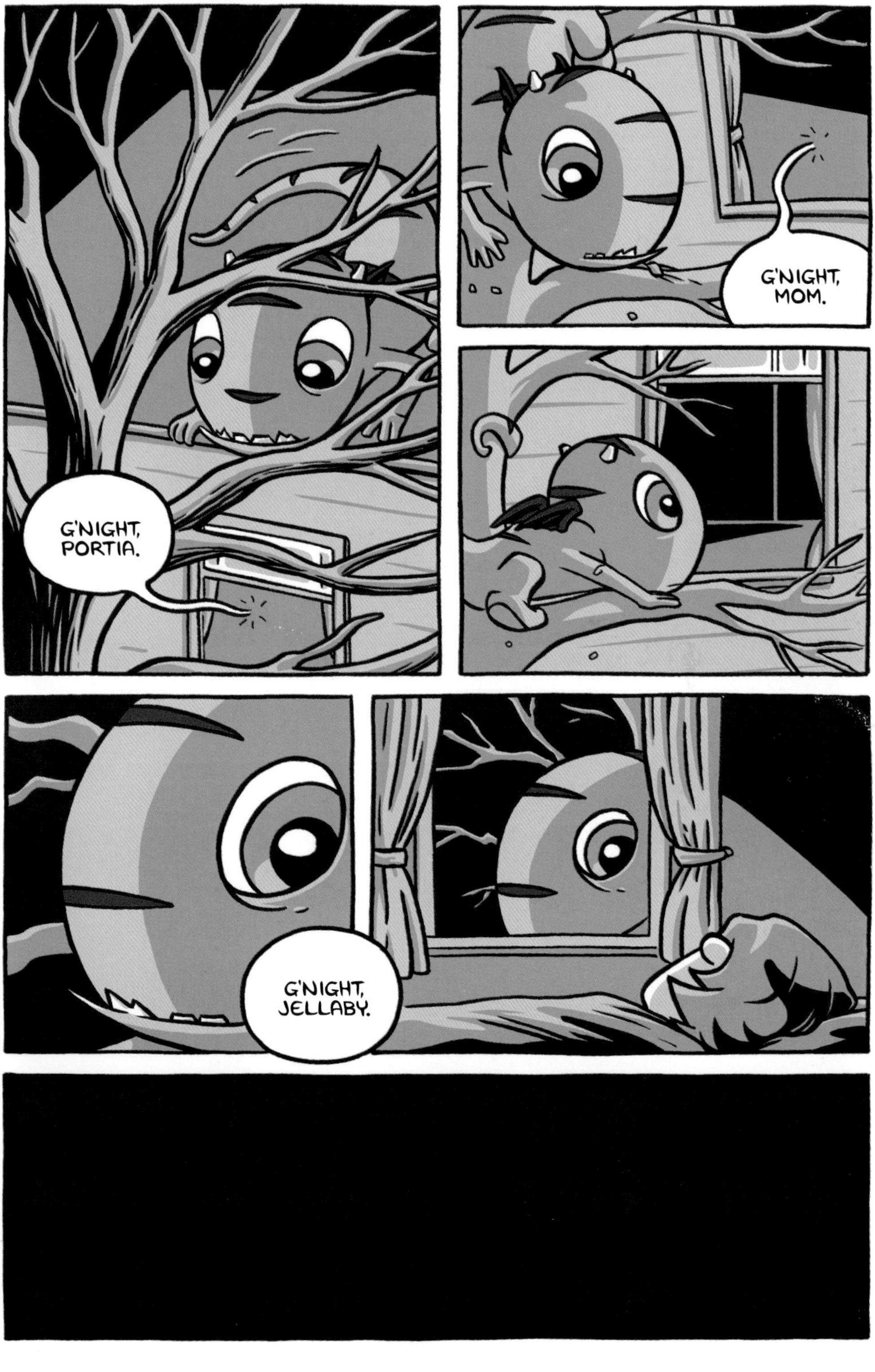
G'NIGHT, PORTIA.
G'NIGHT, MOM.
G'NIGHT, JELLABY.

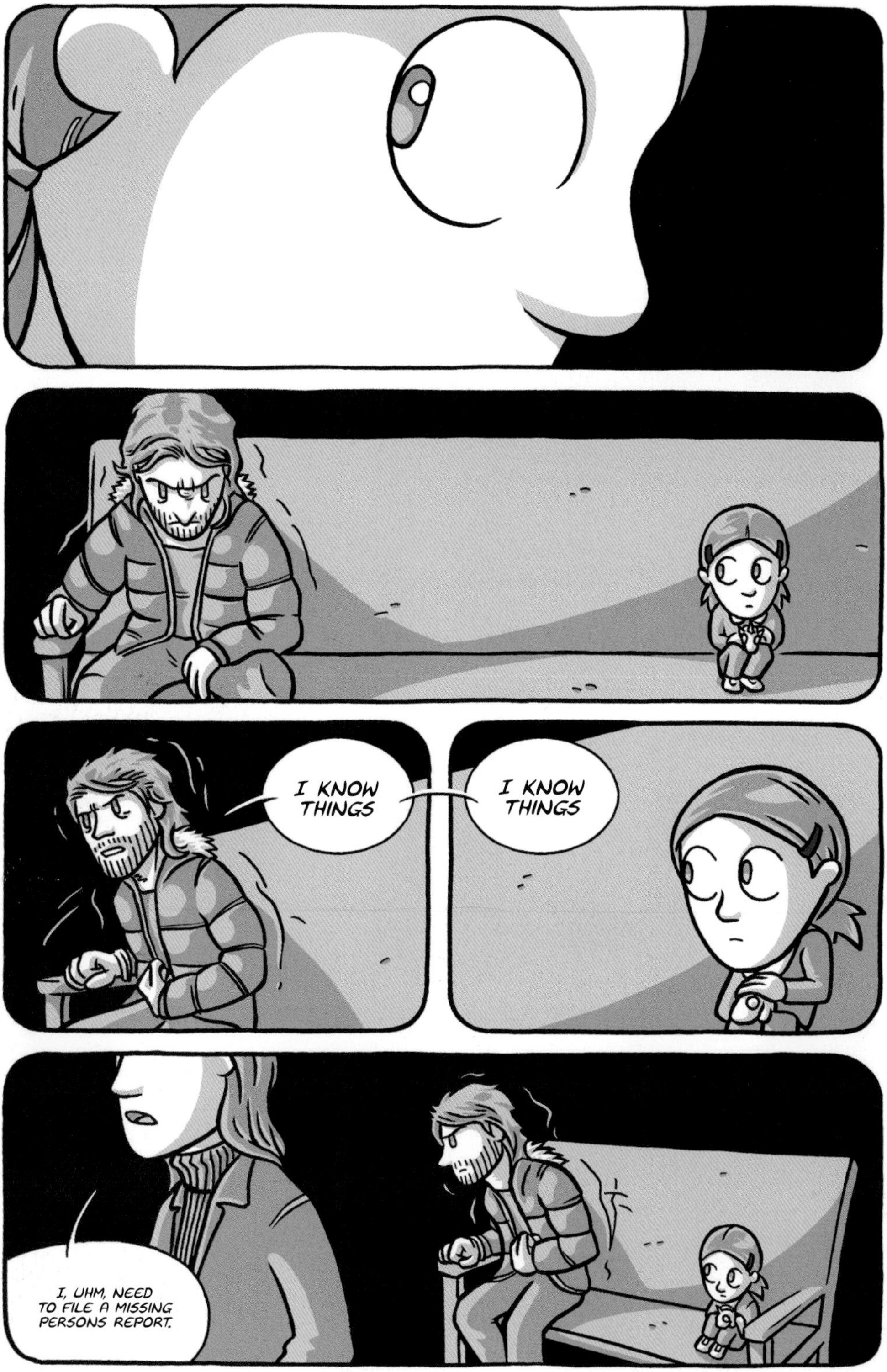
I KNOW THINGS
I KNOW THINGS
I, UHM, NEED TO FILE A MISSING PERSONS REPORT.

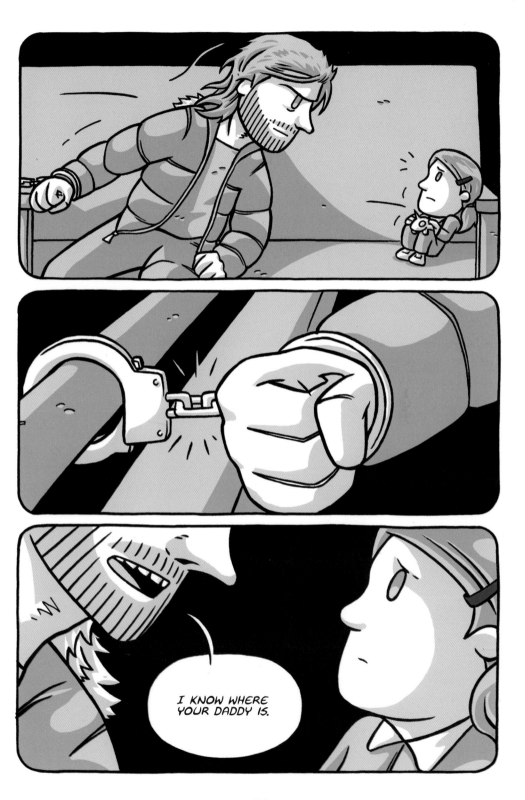

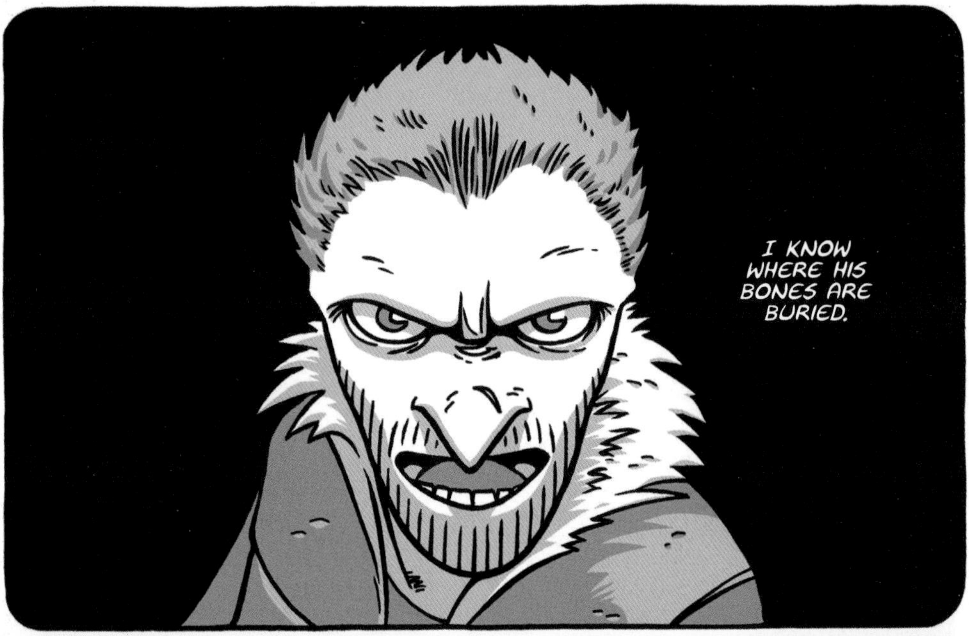
I KNOW WHERE HIS BONES ARE BURIED.

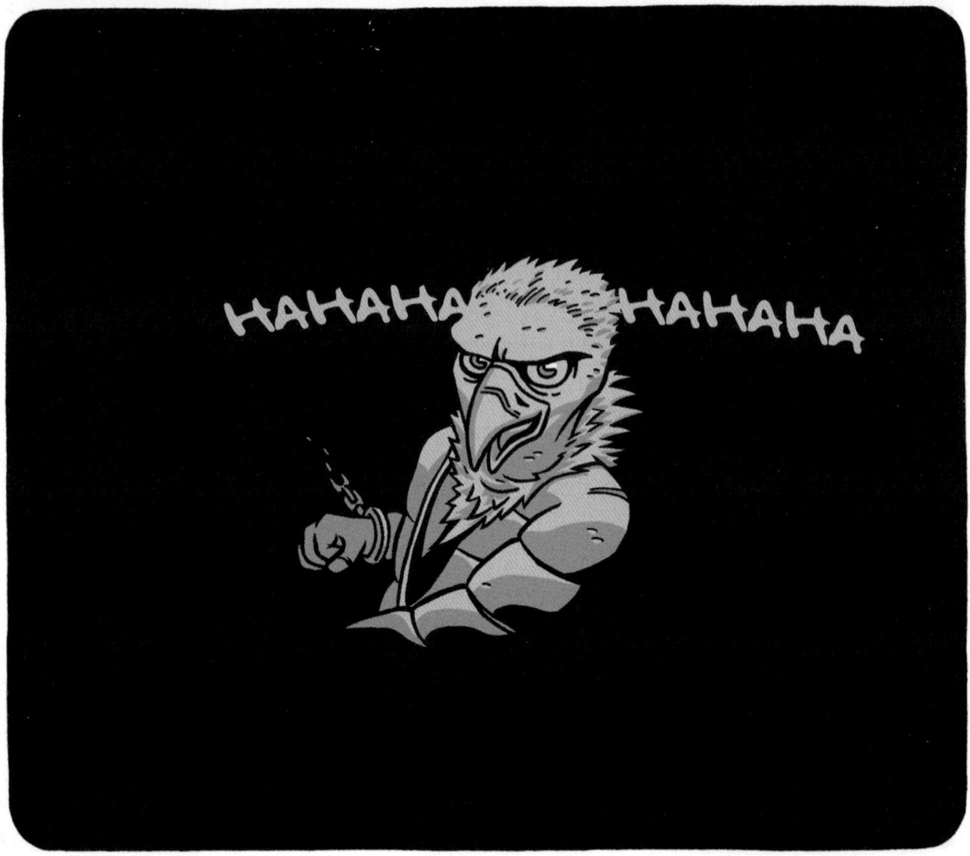
HAHAHA HAHAHA

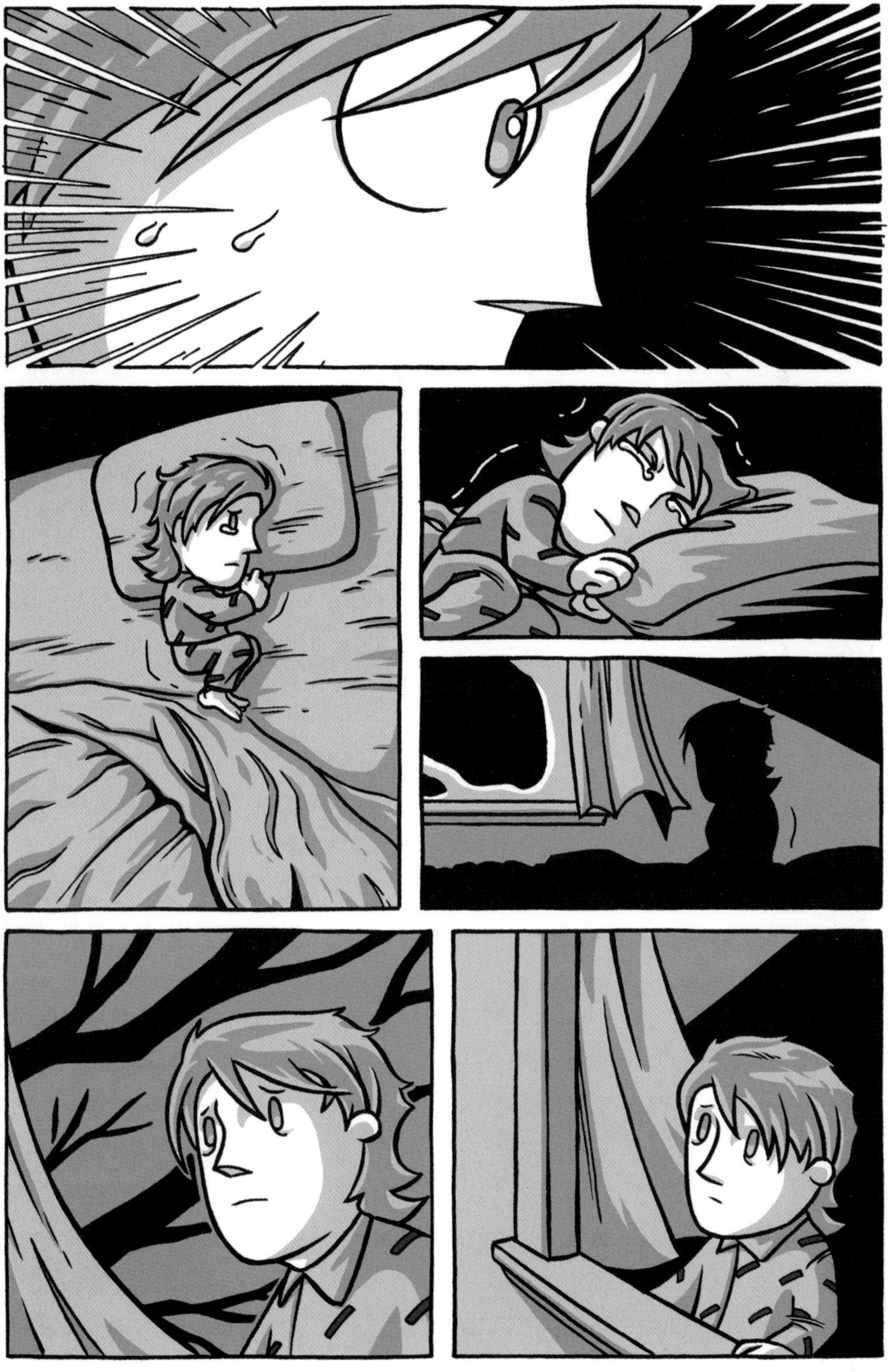

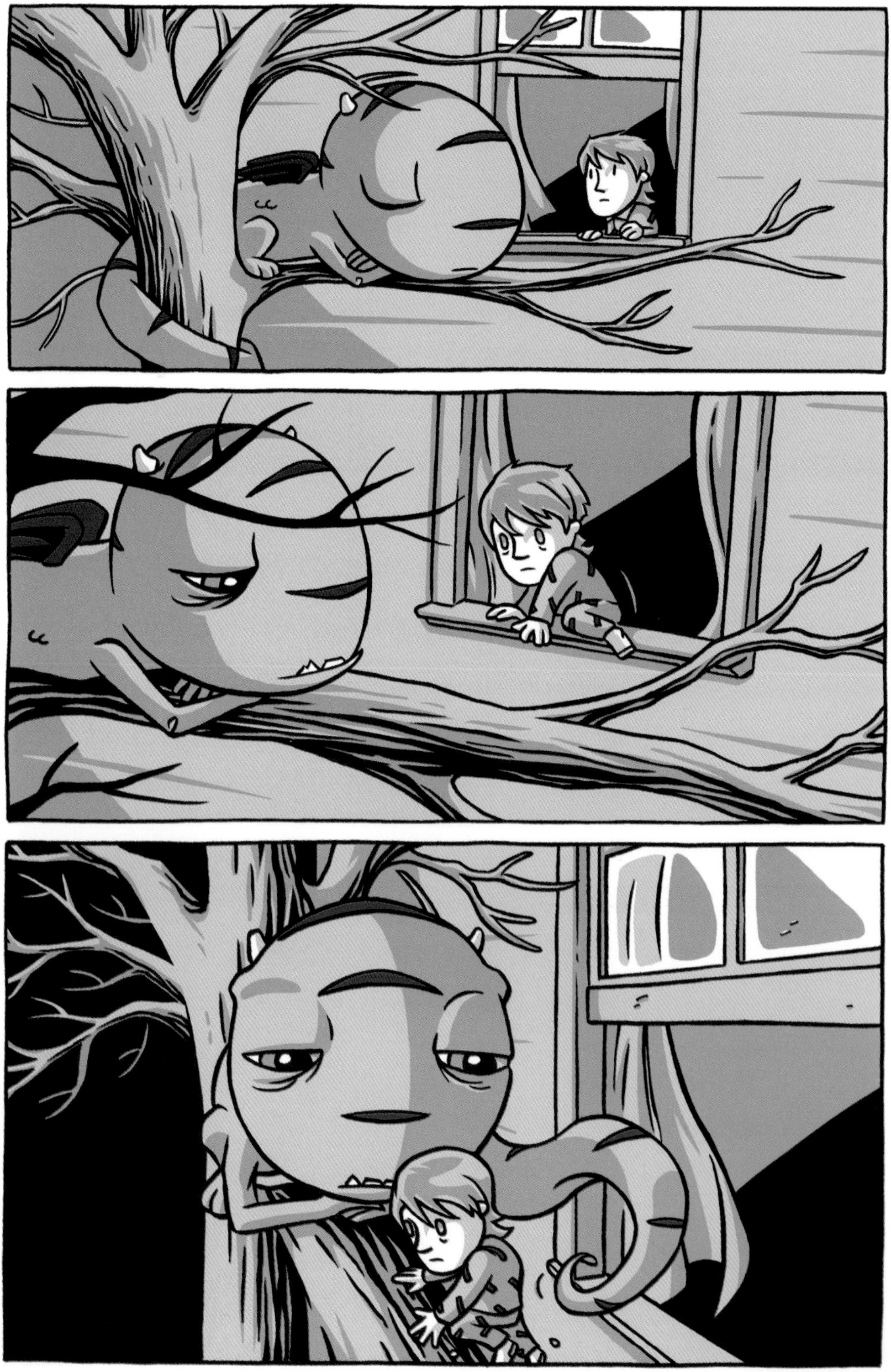

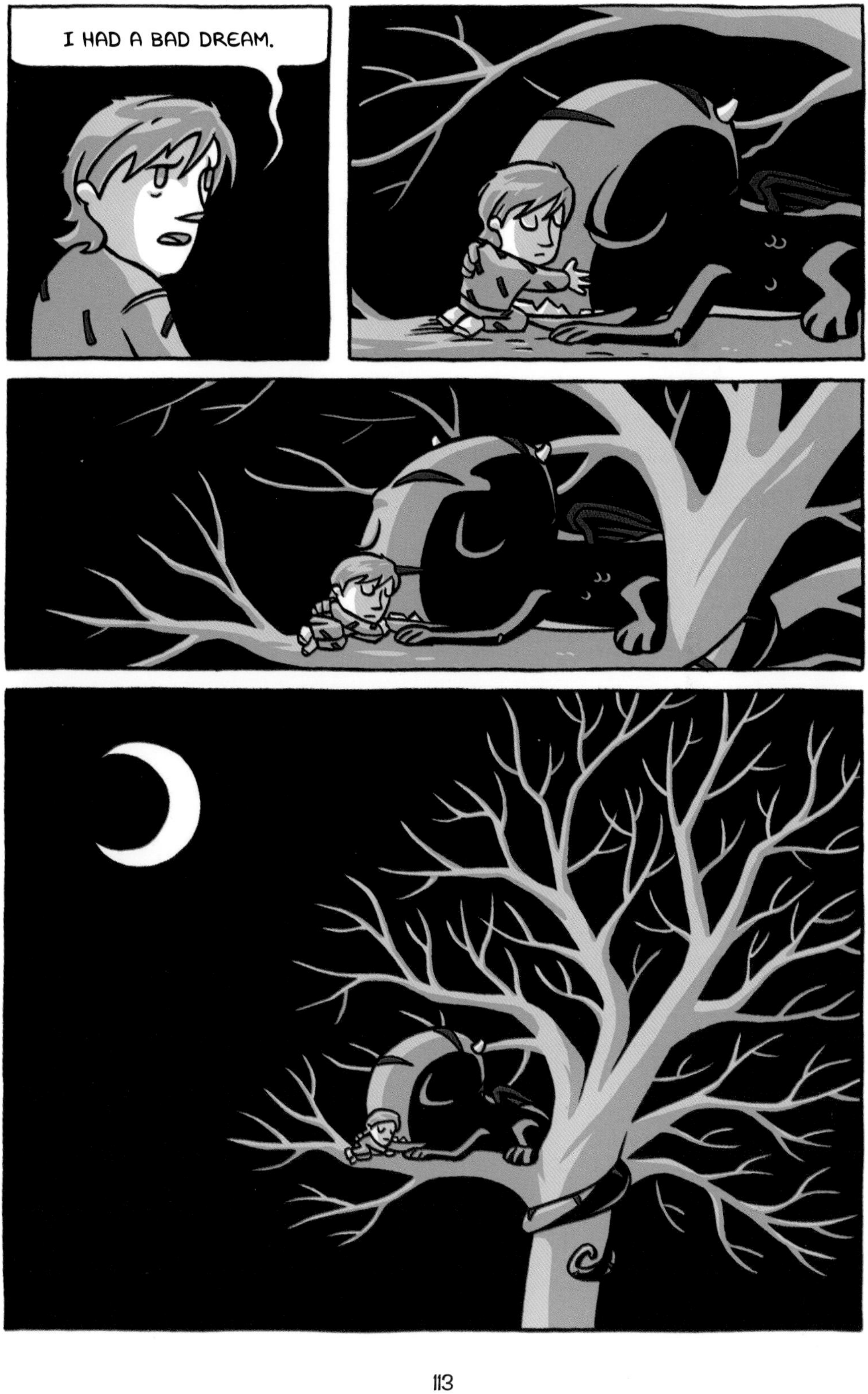
I HAD A BAD DREAM.

CHAPTER FIVE

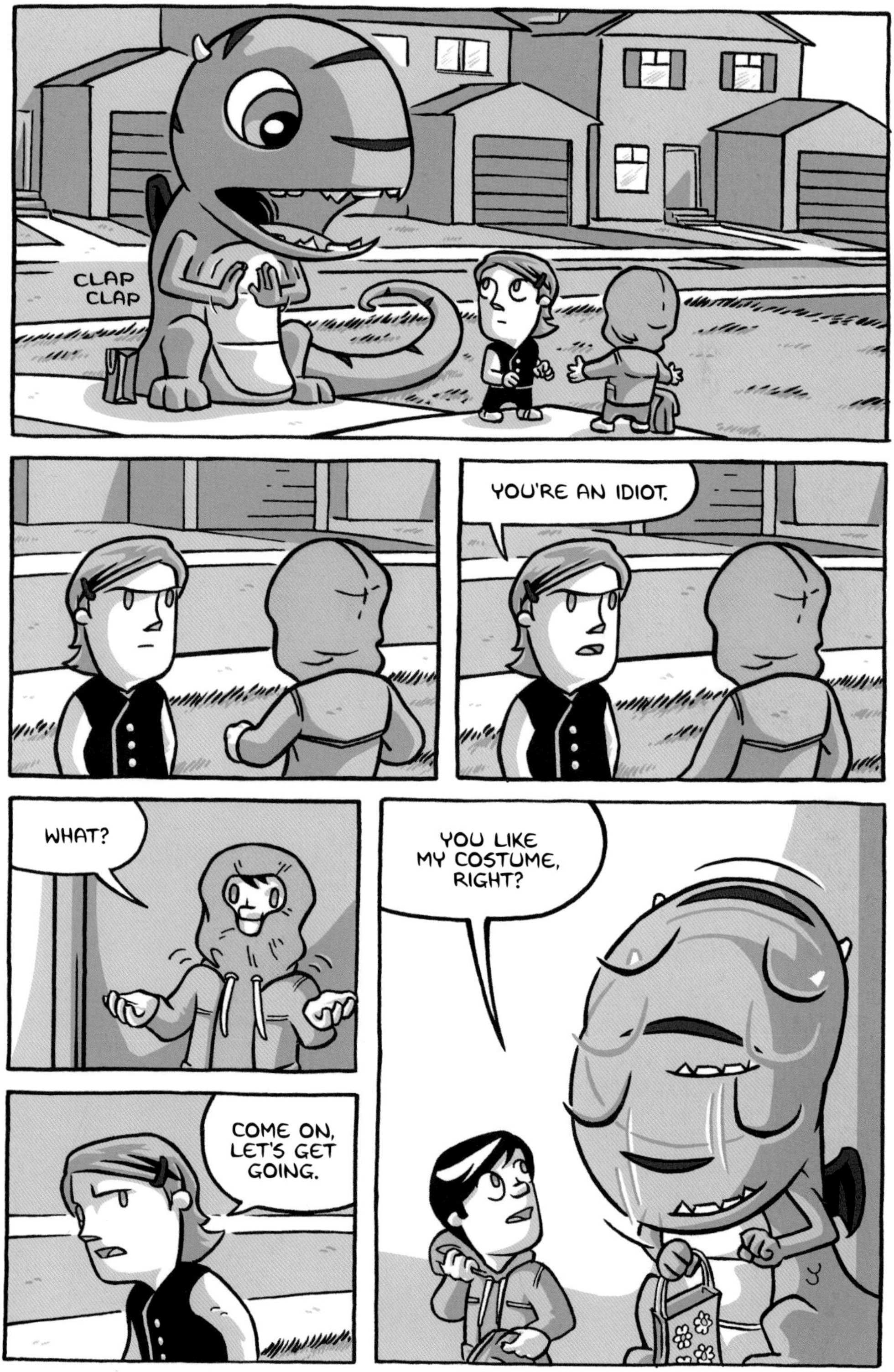
CLAP
CLAP
YOU'RE AN IDIOT.
WHAT?
COME ON, LET'S GET GOING.
YOU LIKE MY COSTUME, RIGHT?

119

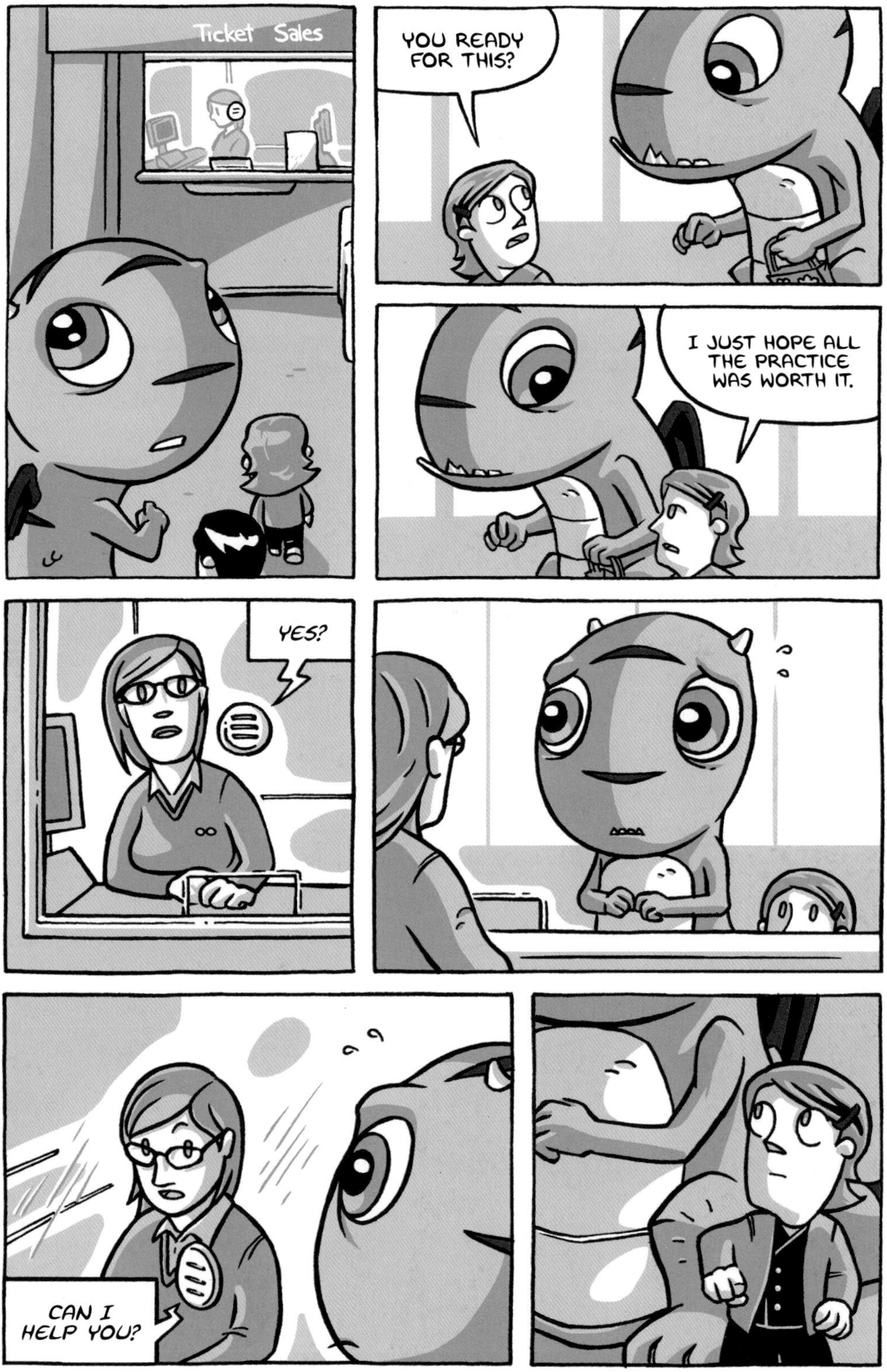
Ticket Sales
YOU READY FOR THIS?
I JUST HOPE ALL THE PRACTICE WAS WORTH IT.
YES?
CAN I HELP YOU?

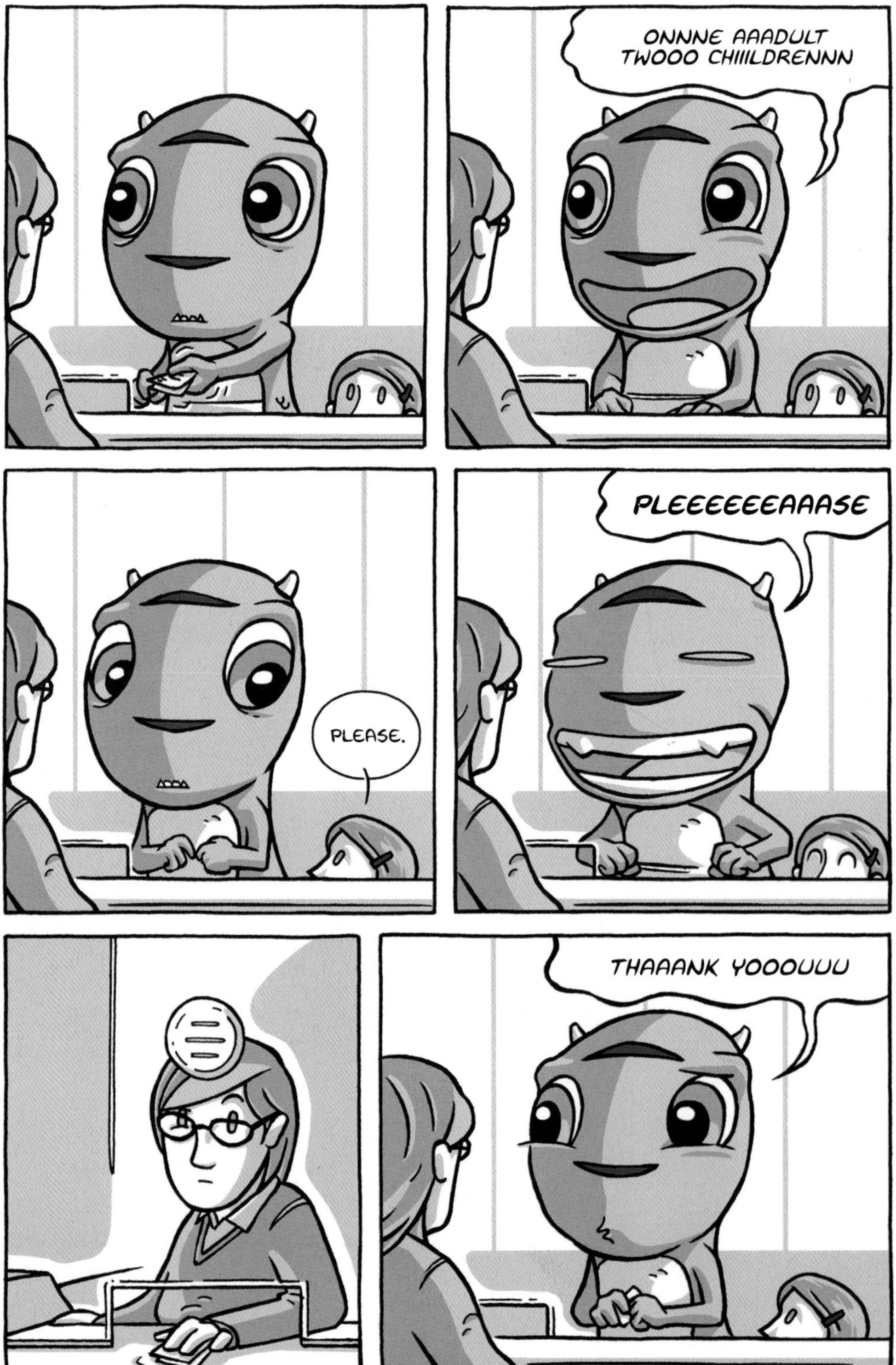
ONNNE AAADULT TWOOO CHIIILDRENNN
PLEASE.
PLEEEEEEEAAASE
THAAANK YOOOUUU

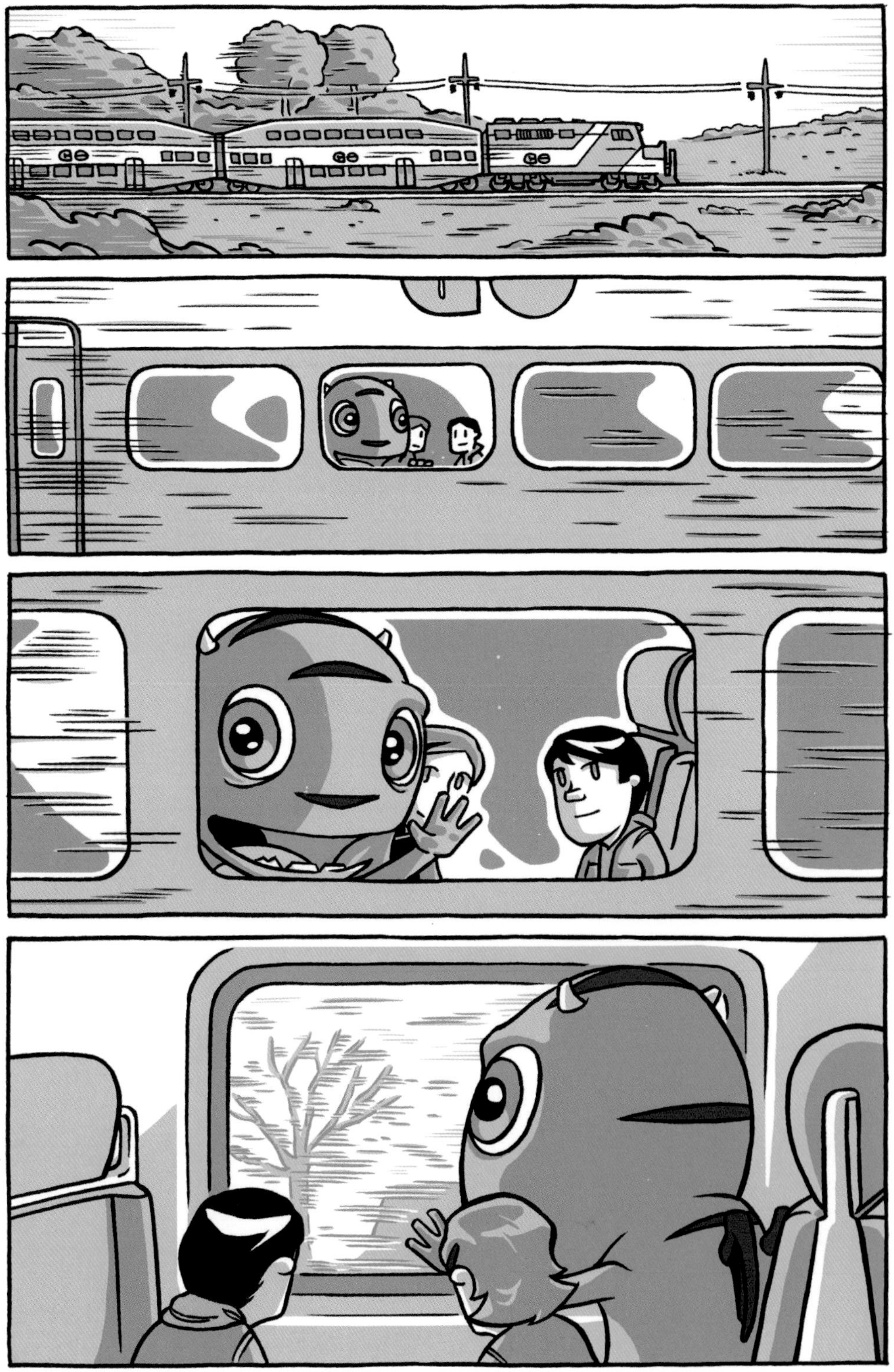

125

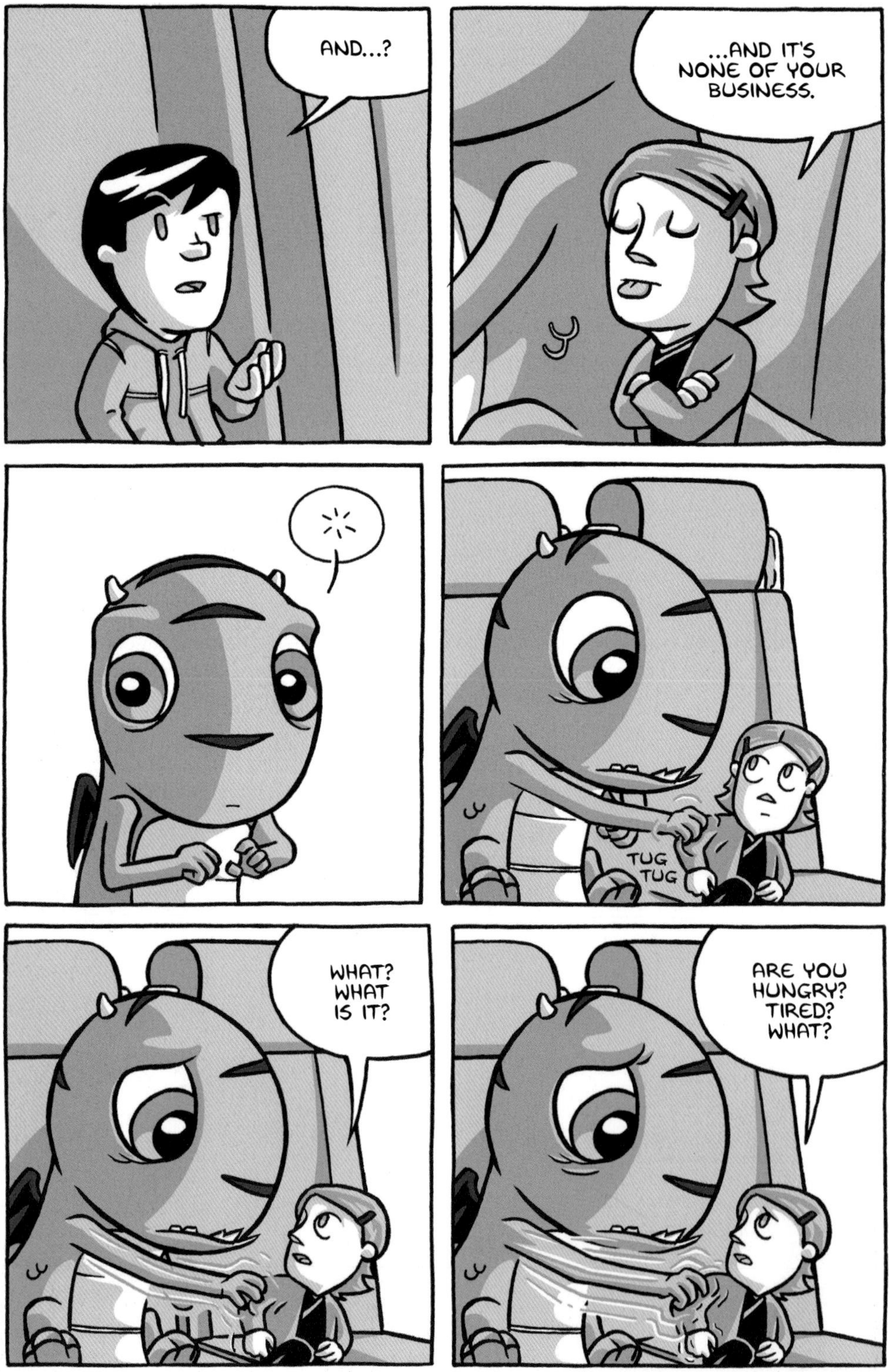
AND...?
...AND IT'S NONE OF YOUR BUSINESS.
TUG TUG
WHAT? WHAT IS IT?
ARE YOU HUNGRY? TIRED? WHAT?

127

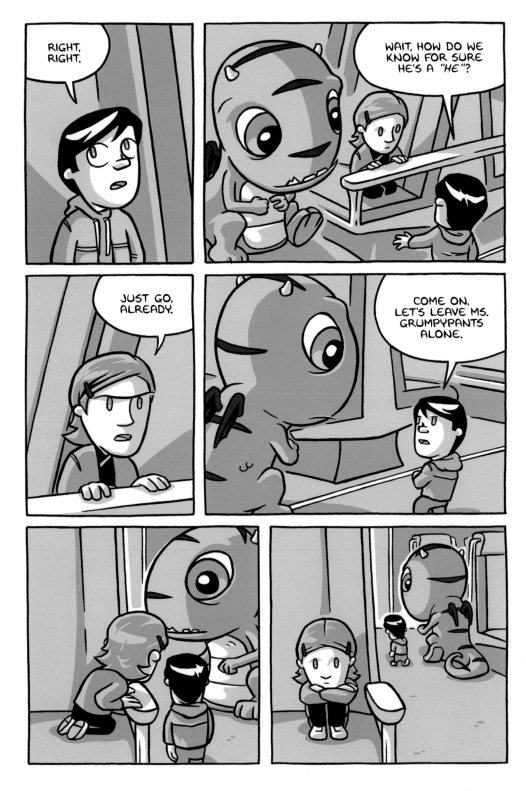

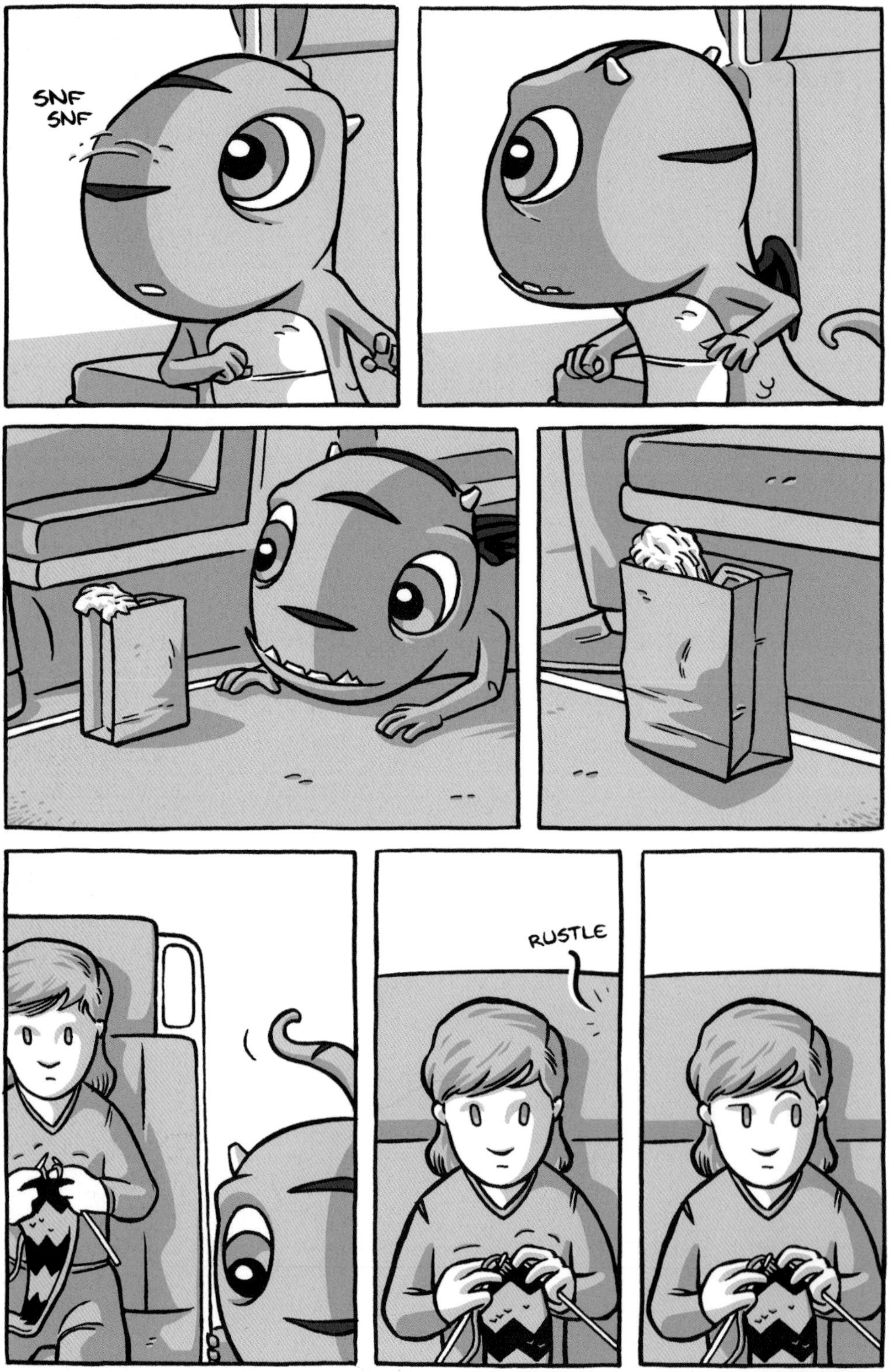
SNF
SNF
RUSTLE

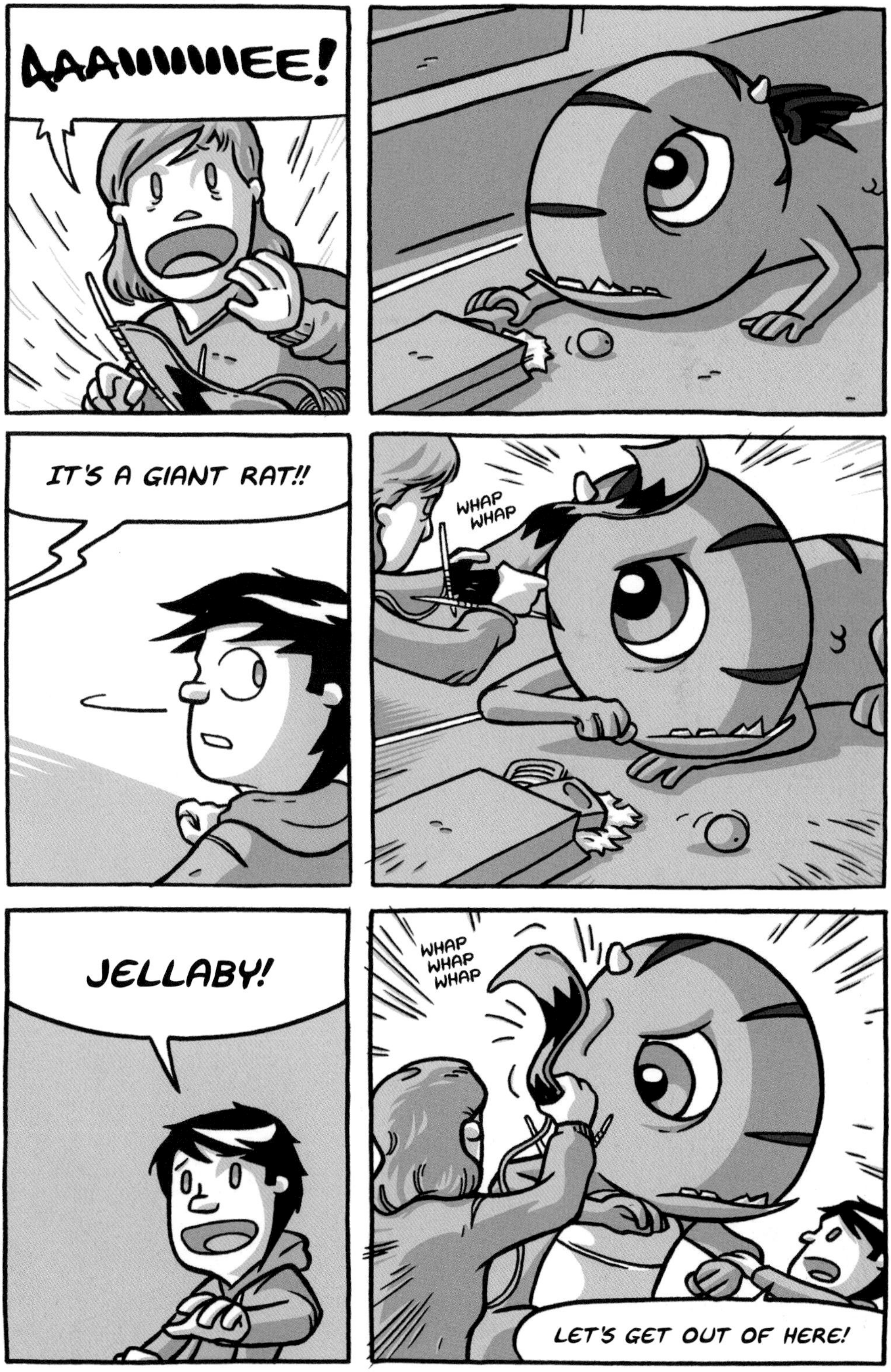
AAAIIIIIIIEE!
IT'S A GIANT RAT!!
WHAP WHAP
JELLABY!
WHAP WHAP WHAP
LET'S GET OUT OF HERE!

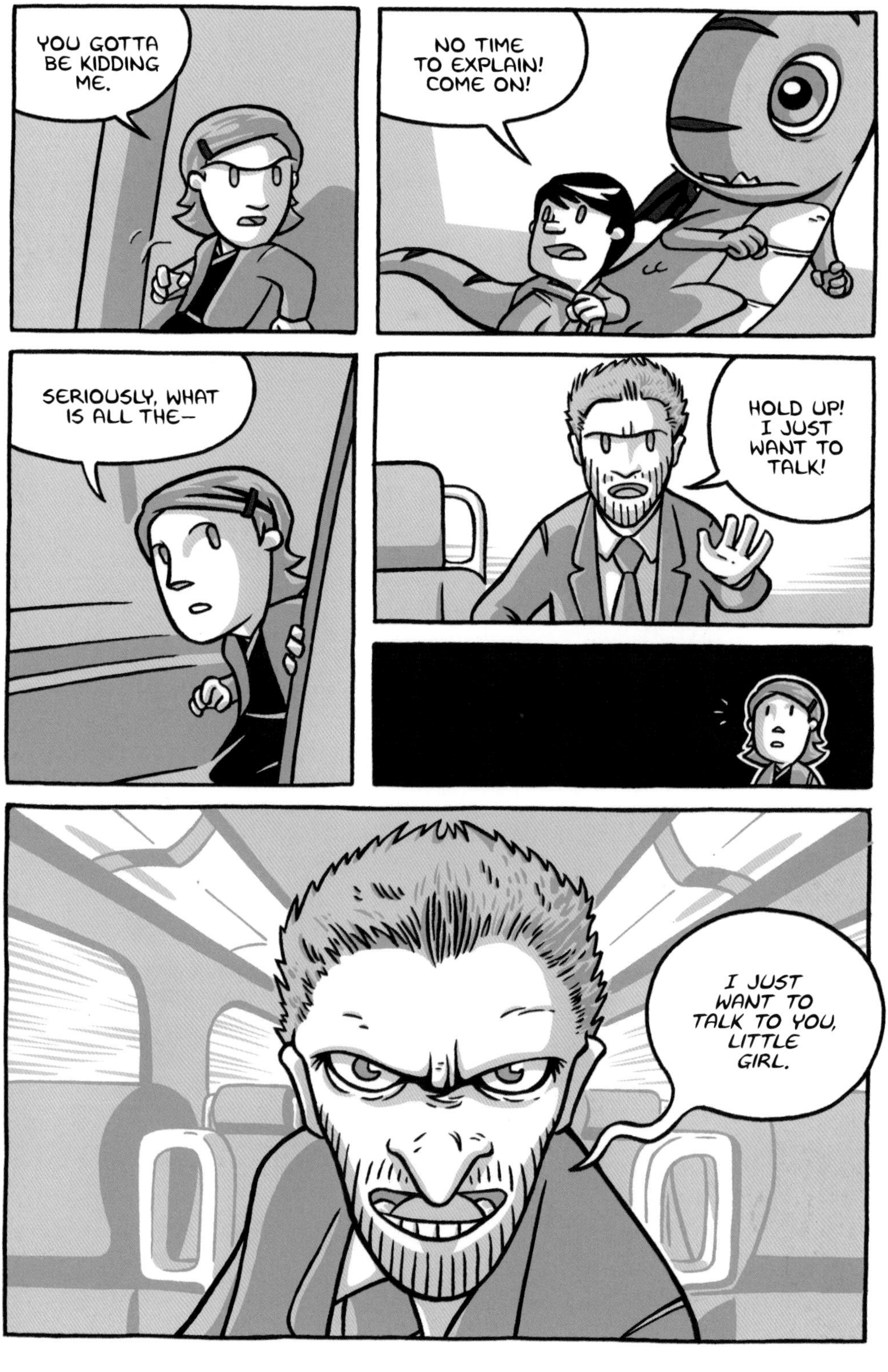
YOU GOTTA BE KIDDING ME.
NO TIME TO EXPLAIN! COME ON!
SERIOUSLY, WHAT IS ALL THE—
HOLD UP! I JUST WANT TO TALK!
I JUST WANT TO TALK TO YOU, LITTLE GIRL.

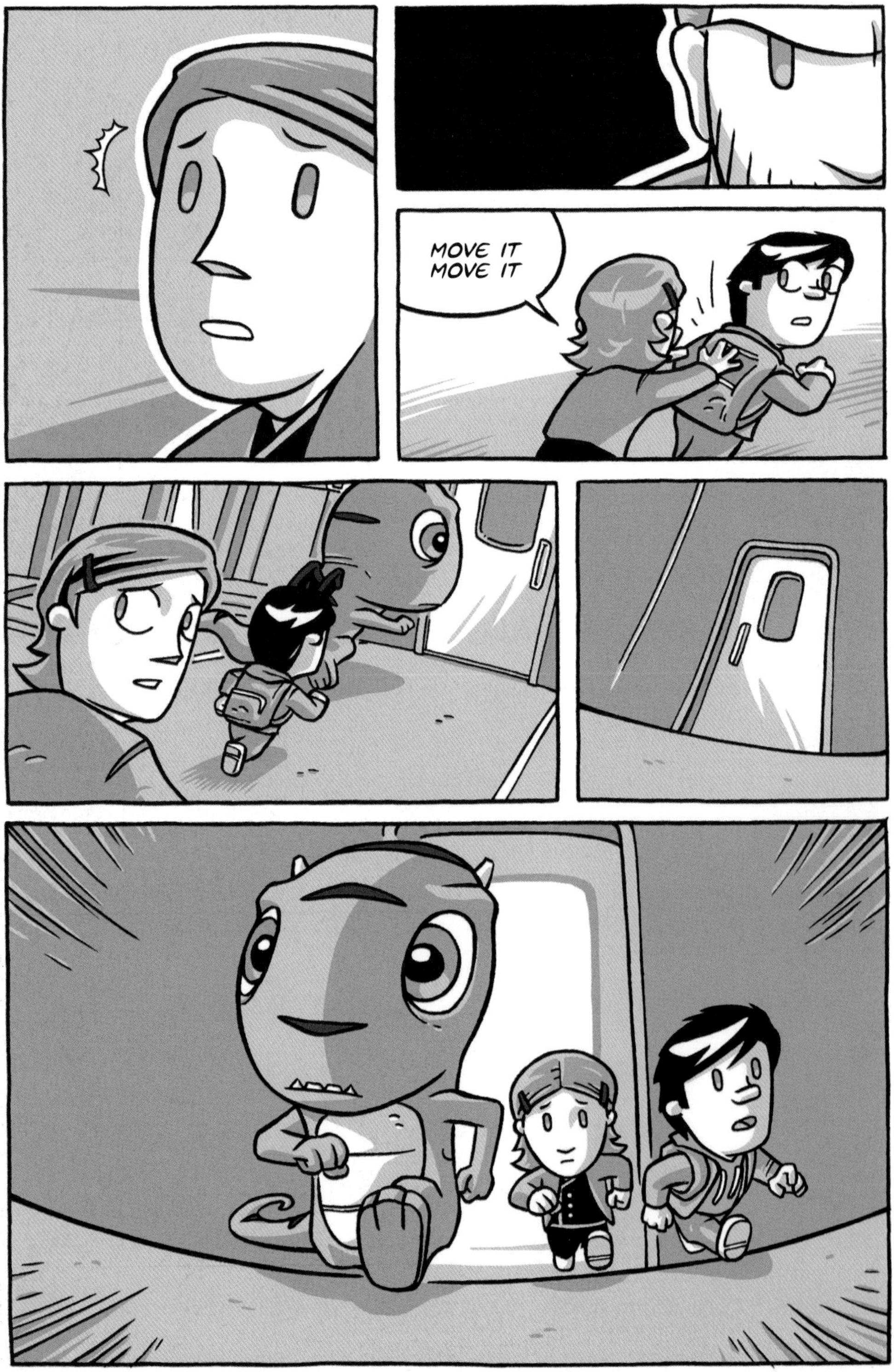
MOVE IT
MOVE IT

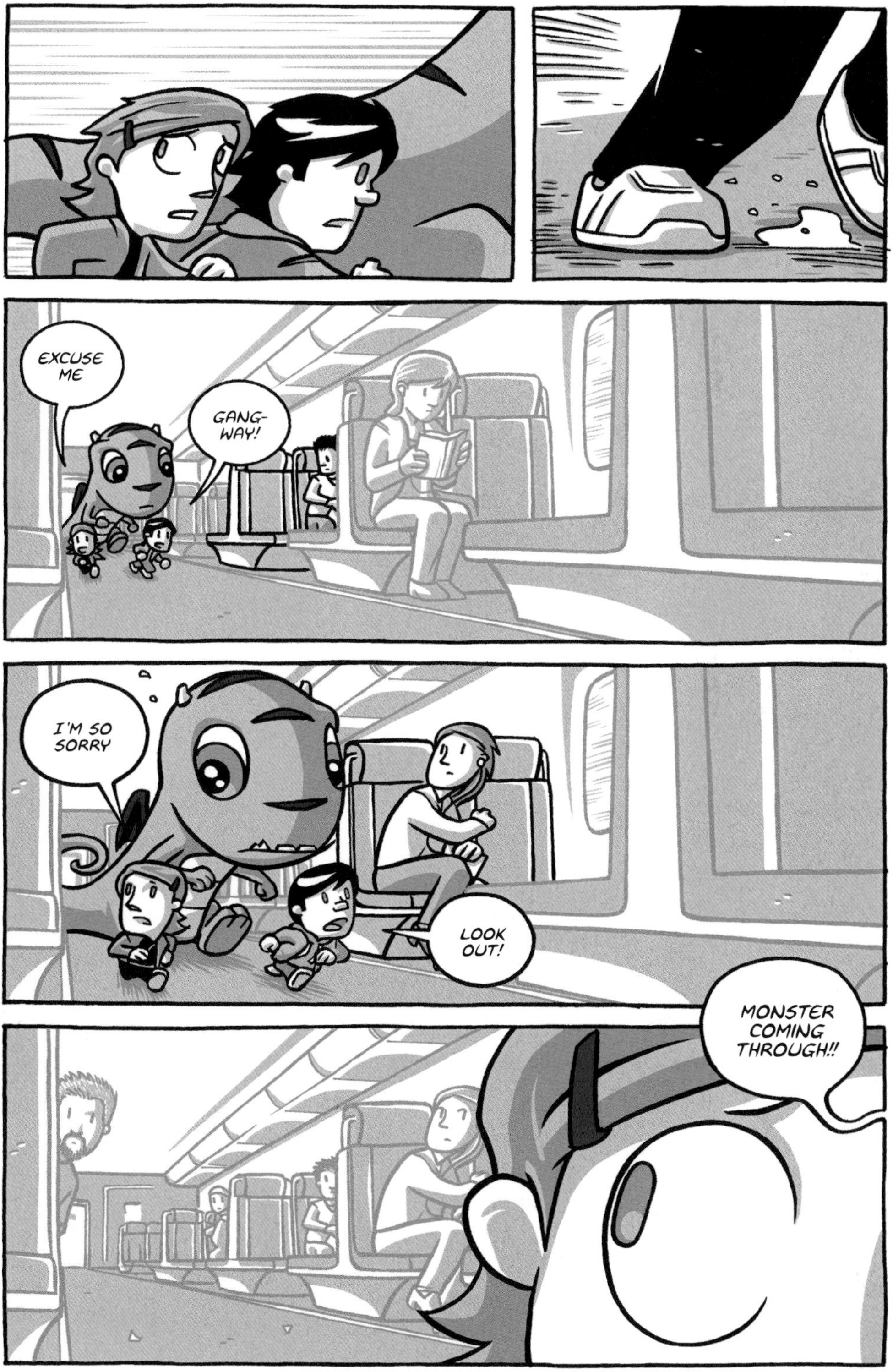
EXCUSE ME
GANG-WAY!
I'M SO SORRY
LOOK OUT!
MONSTER COMING THROUGH!!

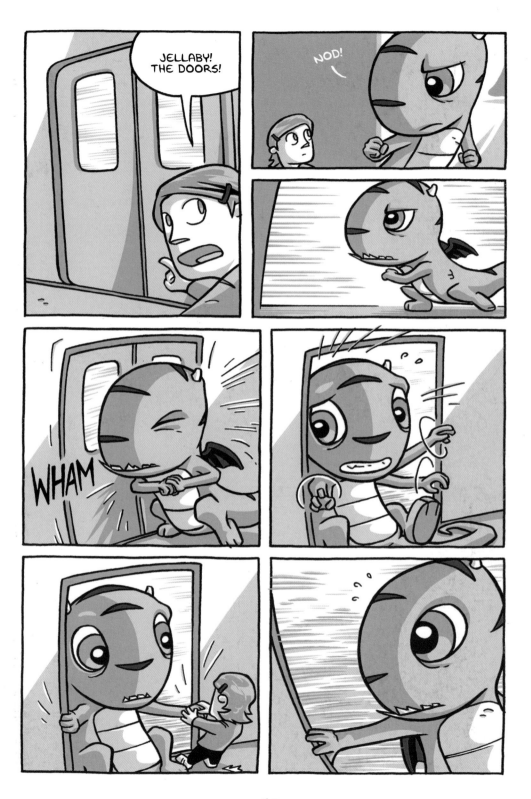

138

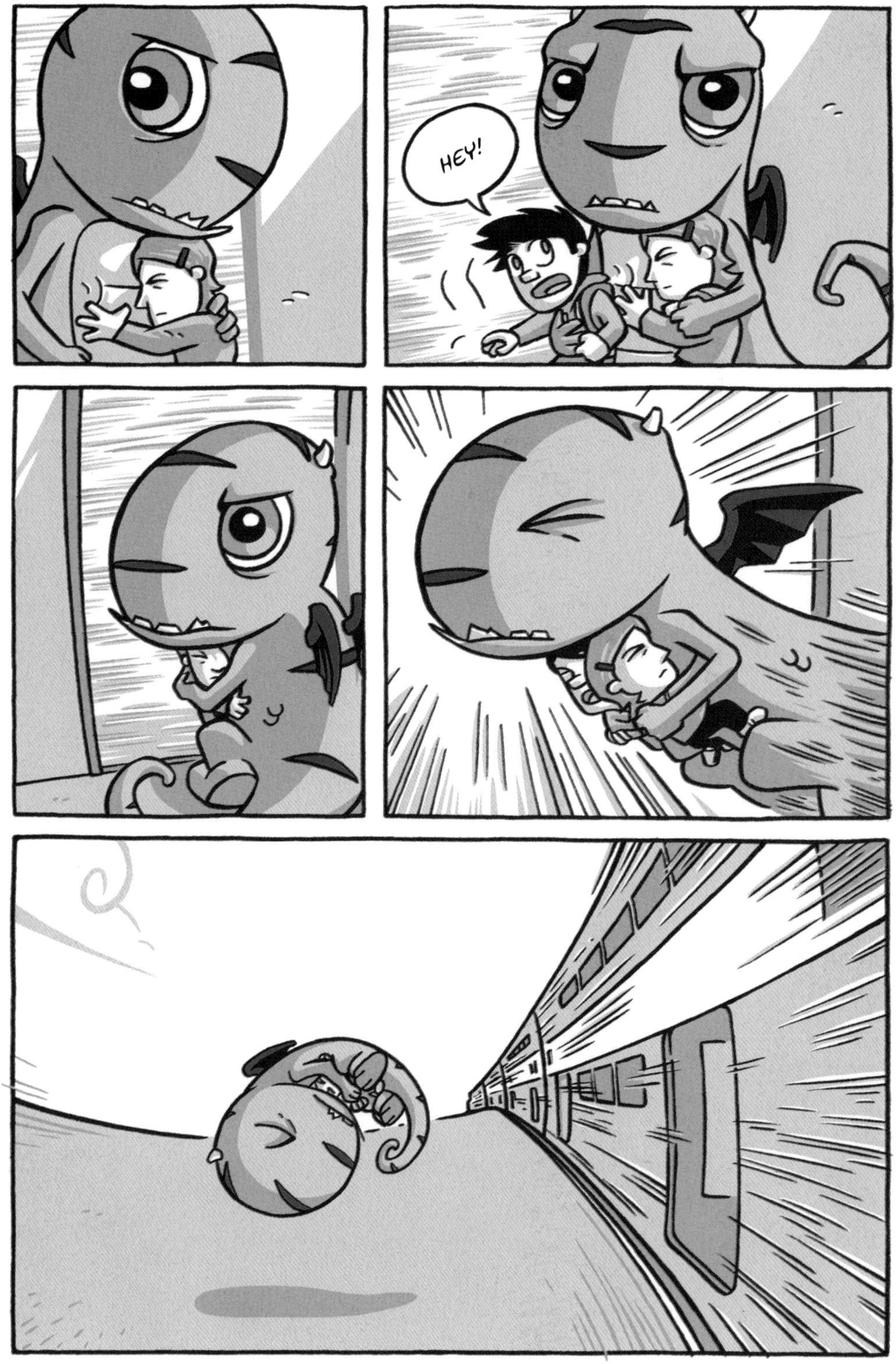
HEY!

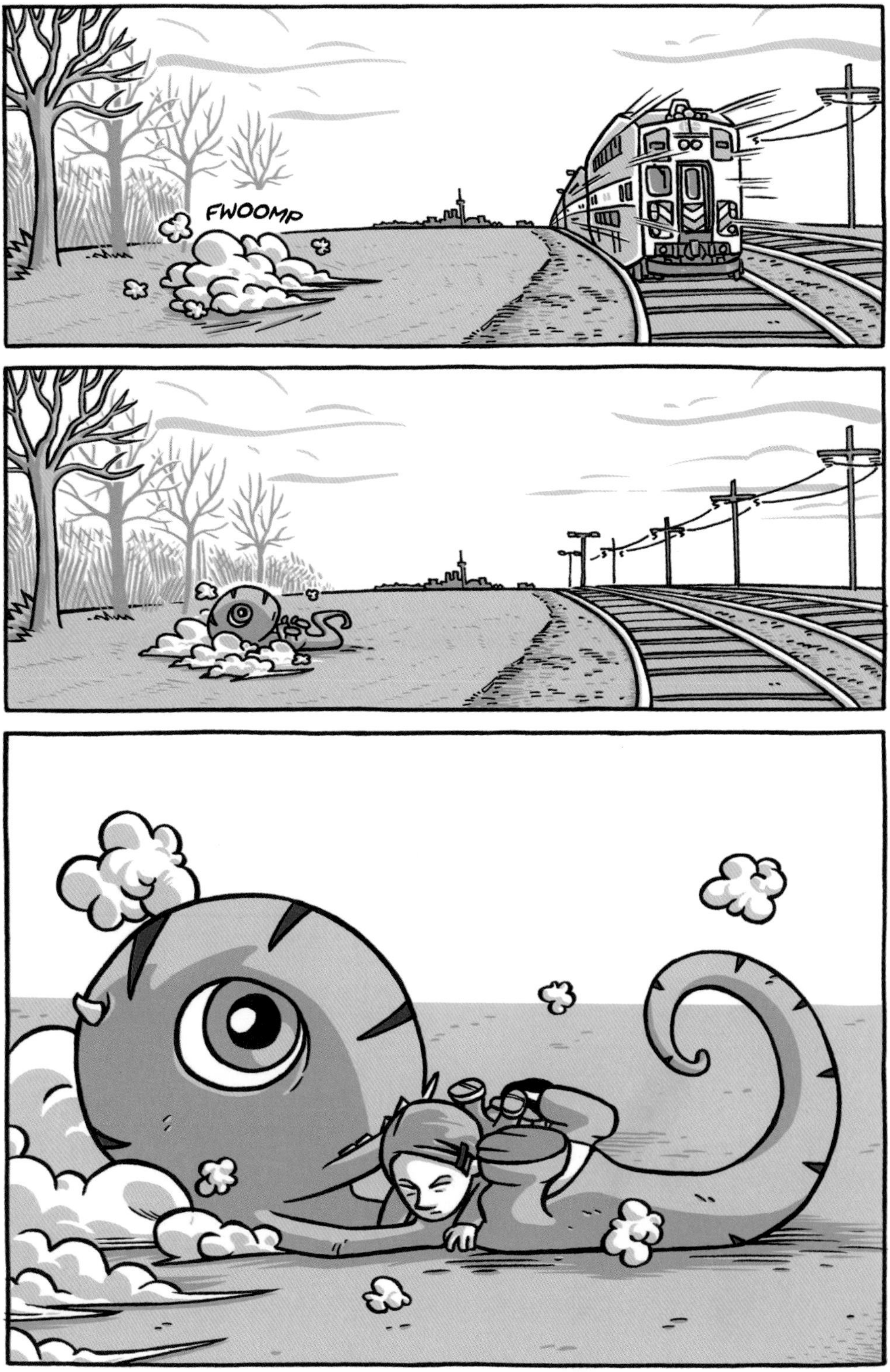
FWOOMP

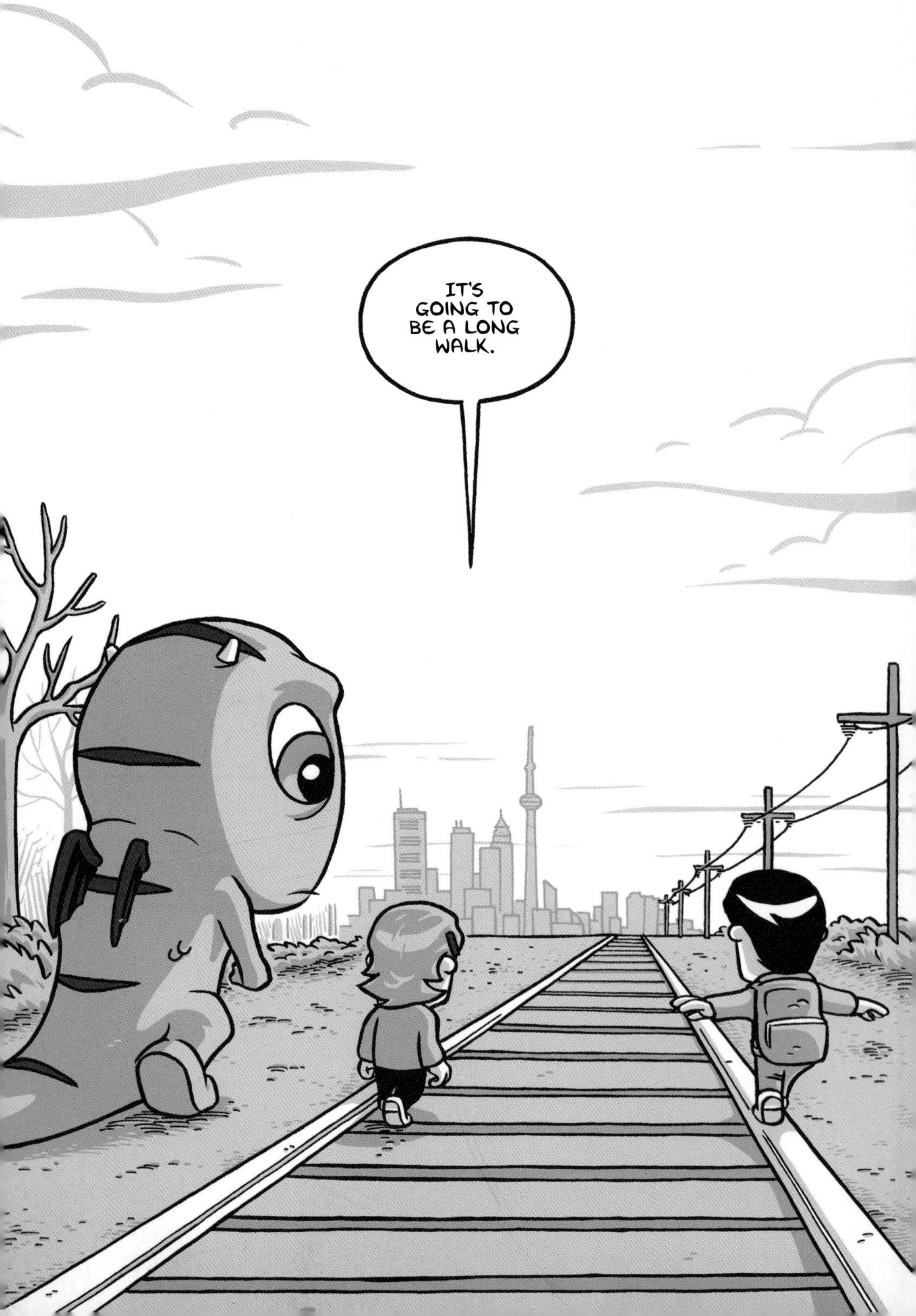
IT'S GOING TO BE A LONG WALK.

TO BE CONTINUED...

ABOUT THE AUTHOR

BORN IN ENGLAND AND RAISED IN HONG KONG, **KEAN SOO**
SETTLED IN CANADA, WHERE HE PLANNED TO EMBARK ON
A CAREER IN ELECTRICAL ENGINEERING. HOWEVER, HE
DISCOVERED THAT HE'D RATHER DRAW COMICS INSTEAD.
KEAN BEGAN POSTING HIS COMICS ON THE INTERNET IN
2002, AND LATER BECAME AN ASSISTANT EDITOR AND
REGULAR CONTRIBUTOR TO THE ALL-AGES FLIGHT
ANTHOLOGIES. HIS ONLINE WORK HAS BEEN NOMINATED
FOR SEVERAL AWARDS, INCLUDING AN EISNER AWARD
NOMINATION FOR *JELLABY*.

KEAN LIKES CARROTS, BUT NOT NEARLY AS MUCH AS HE
LIKES TUNA SANDWICHES, USUALLY WITH LOTS AND LOTS
OF WASABI MAYONNAISE.

PORTRAIT OF THE AUTHOR BY PHIL CRAVEN

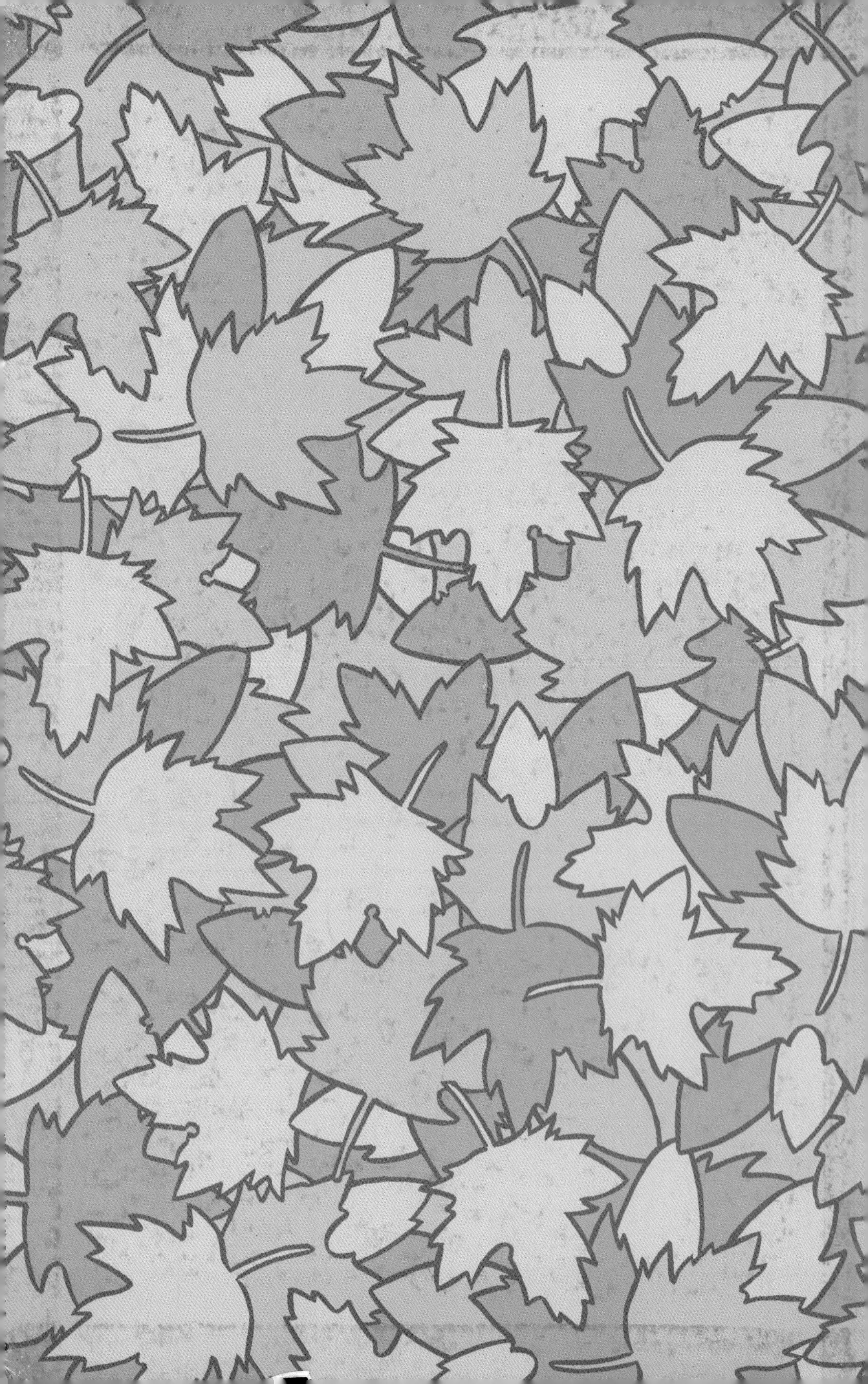